# The Unseen Hand

# The Unseen Hand

## EDWARD MARSTON

Allison & Busby Limited
11 Wardour Mews
London W1F 8AN
*allisonandbusby.com*

First published in Great Britain by Allison & Busby in 2019.

Copyright © 2019 by EDWARD MARSTON

A CIP catalogue record for this book is available from
the British Library.

First Edition

ISBN 978-0-7490-2399-7

Typeset in 12/18 pt Adobe Garamond Pro by
Allison & Busby Ltd.

The paper used for this Allison & Busby publication
has been produced from trees that have been legally sourced
from well-managed and credibly certified forests.

Printed and bound by
CPI Group (UK) Ltd, Croydon, CR0 4YY

# CHAPTER ONE

## Autumn, 1917

Millie Jenks was in agony. After six weeks as a member of the hotel staff, she was still plagued by uncertainty. Desperate to retain her job, she was terrified by the thought that she might make a mistake that led to her dismissal. All that she had to do that morning was to obey an order. What would have been a simple task to any other employee was to Millie a crushing responsibility. It gave her a sleepless night in the cold, tiny, airless bedroom she occupied in the basement. An hour before she was needed, she was dressed and ready, one eye fixed on the clock. When there were still ten minutes to go, she made her way silently up two flights of stairs and stood outside the appropriate door, counting the seconds as they ticked past in her head. In her palm was the master key she'd been given in case the guest couldn't be roused by a sharp knock. She moved it nervously from hand to hand.

At what she felt was the exact time specified, she took a deep breath then rapped on the door. There was no response from inside the room. When a second knock failed to awaken the guest, Millie inserted the master key and opened the door slowly. The bedside lamp was on, creating a pool of light. On the carpet was a sight that made her gasp in surprise. Expecting to wake an elderly lady, she was instead looking down at a much younger one, fully clothed and stretched out on the floor. When she bent down to help the woman up, she saw the tortured expression on her face.

Millie froze in horror.

# CHAPTER TWO

As the police car sped through the streets in the gloom, the detectives sat in the rear seats. London was slowly starting to wake up but Marmion and Keedy were still half-asleep. They were responding to a phone call from Scotland Yard and it had robbed both of them of any breakfast. It put them in a resentful mood.

'Where are we going, Harv?' asked Keedy, sourly.

'The Lotus Hotel.'

'I've never heard of it.'

'Neither have I, Joe.'

'Where the hell is it?'

'It's somewhere in Chelsea.'

'And what are we supposed to find there?'

'Your guess is as good as mine,' said Marmion through an involuntary yawn. 'All I can tell you is that there's been an unexplained death.

According to Chat, the man who raised the alarm was in a real panic.'

'I don't blame him. *I'm* always in a panic when I speak to our beloved superintendent.'

'It seems that the woman who died is a complete stranger. She wasn't a guest at the hotel.'

'Then what was she doing there?'

'That's one of the things we need to find out, Joe.'

Harvey Marmion had mixed feelings about the telephone that Superintendent Chatfield had had installed in the inspector's house. It meant that he could be summoned from his bed at all hours. At the same time, it enabled his wife to contact him at Scotland Yard in an emergency and allowed him – in defiance of the superintendent's orders – to ring her when he was at work. As he yawned again, Marmion decided that, on balance, the telephone was more of a blessing than a nuisance.

'So Chat rang you in person, did he?' asked Keedy.

'Oh, yes. I'd never mistake that voice of his.'

'He spends more time in his office than he does at home. Doesn't he *ever* go to bed?'

'He has four children, Joe, so he must have climbed between the sheets at some point in time.'

Keedy laughed. He was about to make a ribald comment but decided against it. Engaged to Marmion's daughter, he had to be careful when indulging in coarse banter in case his future father-in-law got hold of the wrong idea. As it happened, there was no time to poke fun at the superintendent's private life because, after turning a corner, the car slowed down and pulled up outside the hotel.

They got out of the vehicle to find that they were in a quiet backstreet in one of the more prosperous parts of Chelsea. The Lotus Hotel had a relatively narrow frontage and looked at first glance to be identical to the houses either side of it. Marmion's first impression was that there was something almost apologetic about it, as if it was concealing its real identity. A small brass plate bearing its name was the only indication that it was actually a hotel. Before they could go into the building, someone came out to greet them. He was a tall, slim, excessively well-groomed man in his forties who seemed to glide along.

'Thank goodness you're here at last!' he said with evident relief. 'I'm Rex Chell, the manager. Please come inside.'

He hustled the pair of them into the lobby as if anxious to get them out of sight. Once inside, they realised that the hotel was an optical illusion. It seemed to grow in size before their eyes and open out in all directions as it incorporated adjacent buildings. There was a pervading air of opulence. While Marmion performed the introductions, Keedy was appraising the manager. Poised and well spoken, Chell was quite immaculate. He explained the situation smoothly and succinctly. Marmion took over.

'So it was Miss Jenks who actually made the discovery?'

'Yes, Inspector,' said Chell.

'Where is she now?'

'The girl is in my office, still shaking like a leaf, I daresay.'

'We'll need to take a statement from her in due course – and from the night porter. He was the person who contacted the police.'

'When he'd done that, he got in touch with me.'

'What did you advise?'

'The first thing he had to do,' said Chell, sternly, 'was to pull himself together. Then he was to console Miss Jenks. I got here as quickly as I could to deal with the emergency. Restoring calm was my first priority. We can't possibly have turbulence at the Lotus.'

'You may not be able to avoid it, sir.'

'Nothing must damage our ethos.'

'A Home Office pathologist will be arriving soon,' said Marmion. 'Unless you sneak him in through the back door, *someone* is going to notice him.'

'Can't you just spirit the body away before the guests start to wake up properly?'

'We need to establish the cause of death first, sir.'

'I can tell you that, Inspector. The woman died of natural means.'

'How do you know?'

'I examined her myself.'

'Are you a qualified doctor?' asked Keedy, pointedly.

'I was very thorough, Sergeant. There's not a mark on her.'

'I beg leave to doubt that, sir.'

'Why don't you let us be the judges?' suggested Marmion. 'I suspect that we've had a lot more experience of dealing with dead bodies than you have.'

Chell gave a reluctant nod of agreement, then led them upstairs and along a corridor. There was no danger of their waking other guests because the pile on the carpet was thick. Using a master key, the manager let them into the room, then locked it behind them. Marmion and Keedy had their first look at the woman who'd deprived them of any breakfast that morning. Pale, lean and well dressed, she was still stretched out in the undignified position into which she'd fallen. Only one side of her face was visible. Keedy knelt down to examine her, moving her slightly from time to time.

'You see?' said Chell as if he'd been vindicated. 'No blood, no sign of injury, no indication of anything untoward.'

'I'm afraid that you're wrong,' said Keedy.

'What do you mean?'

'Look at her face.' He turned her over gently so that they could study her properly. Though she'd been an attractive woman, her features were now distorted. 'I've seen expressions like this before.'

'The sergeant used to work in the family undertaking business,' explained Marmion. 'He knows what to look for.'

'My immediate suspicion is that she was killed by some sort of poison. We just need to find out how it was administered.'

Removing her jacket with a care that bordered on tenderness, Keedy exposed a silk blouse. He undid the button on one wrist and peeled back the sleeve. A thin, pale, blue-veined arm came into view, but it had no marks on it. When he peeled back the other sleeve, however, there was clear evidence of a recent injection. Keedy looked up at Chell.

'Well,' he said, 'we've now got some idea of *how* she died. The question is this – are we looking at a case of suicide or of murder?'

# CHAPTER THREE

The pathologist soon arrived and was whisked upstairs by the woman acting as Chell's deputy while he was busy with the detectives. The manager was glad that the man came alone without any uniformed policemen in tow. He still nursed the faint hope that the crisis could somehow be hidden from the guests. Marmion shattered that hope. While the pathologist conducted his examination, the inspector took the manager aside.

'I'm afraid that your ethos is in danger, sir.'

'It's something we pride ourselves on,' said Chell, stiffly.

'You won't be able to do that any more. The Lotus Hotel has become a murder scene.'

'Surely not! The sergeant thought it might be a case of suicide.'

'That was before I had a good look around the room,' said Keedy. 'If the deceased had injected herself, where's the syringe? I can't find one. The only explanation is that the killer took it away.'

Chell was shaken. 'Things like this just don't happen at the Lotus.'

'What was the name of the guest staying here?' asked Marmion.

'Lady Diana Brice-Cadmore.'

'Then why didn't she spend the night in this bed? Clearly, it hasn't been slept in. And your guest would surely have brought luggage, wouldn't she? What happened to it?'

'I don't know.'

'Let's go back to what you told us earlier,' said Marmion. 'Lady Thingamajig had asked to be awakened early so that she could leave the premises at 6 a.m. Is that correct?'

'Yes,' said the other. 'A taxi was booked.'

'What happened to it?'

'Oh, it arrived on time, Inspector. By that stage, I'd got here and taken charge. I told the driver that there'd been a change of plan and that he was no longer needed. When he'd rid himself of every expletive in the English language, he went off in a rage.'

'Who can blame him?' said Keedy.

'What sort of person is the lady who was here?' asked Marmion with a glance at the bed. 'Is she in the habit of reserving a room and not sleeping in it?'

'She's been a model guest, Inspector.'

'Not the kind to make a moonlight flit, then?'

Chell was offended. 'Our guests tend to come from the upper echelons of society,' he said, haughtily. 'Their conduct is always above reproach. Our clientele is exclusively female. They appreciate our high standards.'

Marmion bit back the ironic observation he was about to make. Seeing that the pathologist had finished his preliminary examination, he asked the manager to take Keedy to his office so that the sergeant could question Millie Jenks and the night porter. After a rueful look at the body, Chell led the way out of the room and closed the door softly behind him. Removing his spectacles, the pathologist got to his feet. He was a short, stubby man in his fifties with a puffy face. Over the years, he and Marmion had met at several murder scenes.

'You'll have trouble solving this one, Harvey,' he said.

'None of them is ever easy.'

'The sergeant's guess was right. In all probability, the woman was poisoned. I can't tell you exactly which poison was used but it was a fatal dose. When we've opened her up and had a proper look at her,' he went on, airily, 'we may have to call in a toxicologist.'

'The sooner we have the post-mortem report, the better.'

'These things can't be rushed.'

'Do you have any idea of the time of death?'

'She was killed at some time in the night. Rigor mortis hasn't occurred yet and that can start to manifest itself as early as four hours after death in some cases. Let me have a closer look at her and I might be able to narrow it down a little.'

'When it's been photographed, I'll get the body moved.'

'You've now got the problem of identifying her.'

'We have one useful clue,' said Marmion. 'She's wearing a wedding ring and the other rings on her fingers look as if they cost a pretty penny. That tells me she has a rich and indulgent husband. He'll soon report her missing.'

'It looks as if we're pioneers,' the other remarked. 'The manager said that this hotel caters only for women. That means we're probably the first men privileged to get inside one of these rooms – apart from the killer, that is.'

'How do you know the murder was committed by a man?' asked Marmion. 'Women can use a syringe just as well – even in the upper echelons of society.'

\* \* \*

14

When he was conducted to the office by the manager, Keedy made the acquaintance of Millie Jenks and Leonard Rogan, the night porter. As the newcomers entered, Millie was sobbing into a handkerchief, but she put it away when she saw Chell and sat up straight. Rogan was already on his feet, shaking hands with the sergeant when introduced and showing the same deference towards the manager as his companion. The night porter was a short, balding, straight-backed man in his fifties in a smart uniform. He turned to Chell.

'I've tried to calm her down, sir,' he said, 'but she's too upset.'

'I'm all right now,' claimed Millie, bravely.

'Mrs Gosling is the best person to look after her.'

'Don't presume to tell me my job, Rogan,' said Chell, acidly. 'I'd already made that decision of my own accord. Before I summon Mrs Gosling, I'd prefer to let the sergeant question the girl.'

Rogan was quashed. 'Very well, sir,' he mumbled.

'I'll leave the pair of them to you,' Chell continued, looking at Keedy. 'Guests will begin to stir from their beds fairly soon. They'll become aware of the commotion. I need to be there to reassure them. Don't snivel,' he warned Millie. 'Try to maintain some dignity.'

He swept out and closed the door behind him. Keedy took a quick inventory of the room, noting its generous size, the large desk, the gleaming furniture, the thick carpet and the well-stocked bookshelves. The office belonged to a man who loved order. Nothing was out of place.

He produced his notebook and smiled at Millie.

'If it helps,' he said, gently, 'feel free to use your handkerchief. I know how much of a shock you must have had.'

'Thank you, sir,' she said, pathetically grateful.

'In your own words, tell me what happened. There's no rush. I won't hurry you along. I just want the facts. If you need to stop at any point, I'll be happy to wait until you start again.'

'You're very kind, Sergeant.'

He opened his notebook. 'I'm ready when you are, Miss Jenks.'

It took her some time to compose herself. Then, after clearing her throat, she told her tale. It was garbled for the most part but Keedy was able to pick out the salient details.

'Thank you,' he said. 'This is all very helpful.'

She was still apprehensive. 'I won't get the sack, will I?'

'I shouldn't think so. You've done nothing wrong.'

'The manager made me feel as if I had.'

'You were simply obeying a request, Miss Jenks.'

'My name won't be in the papers, will it?'

'It's highly unlikely,' said Keedy. 'From what I've seen of him, I think that Mr Chell will give reporters a bare minimum of information. He's keen to protect the reputation of the hotel. For our part, we always exercise discretion when dealing with the press.'

'See?' interjected Rogan. 'It's like I told you, Millie. You're in the clear. So am I. We're not at fault.' He grinned helpfully. 'Is it my turn now, Sergeant?'

Keedy nodded. 'My pencil is poised.'

The night porter not only had his story ready, he had clearly been rehearsing it. Summoned by Millie, he'd gone to inspect the body, then contacted the police and the manager. Rogan stressed how quick and resourceful he'd been, pointing out that he'd rung Scotland Yard rather than the local police station because he knew that Chell would hate the idea of uniformed officers arriving at the hotel. Though he was grateful for a coherent recitation of the facts, Keedy felt that there was something missing.

16

'How long are you on duty, as a rule?' he asked.

'It's usually around ten hours,' replied the other.

'How do you manage to stay awake?'

'I *make* myself, Sergeant. Besides, it's not as if I'm entirely alone. I often have to let in guests who come back here late – after midnight, in some cases. Then, of course, we have the kitchen staff. They have to be up at the crack of dawn if anyone wants an early breakfast. Millie and the other girls must be on duty to serve it.'

'That's right,' she said. 'Mrs Gosling expects us to be out of bed by six o'clock. The guests' needs come first.'

'Do you like working here?' asked Keedy.

'I did until today.'

'What about you, Rogan?'

'It's a privilege to work at the Lotus,' he said, loyally. 'There's nowhere quite like it. The guests are always so well behaved. That's not been the case in other hotels where I've worked. I've had to deal with some very nasty situations, I can tell you. Some men get completely out of control when they've had too much to drink.' He lowered his voice. 'Then there are those who think the female members of staff are there for them to take liberties with. We've never had that kind of problem here.'

'And we've never had anyone die at the hotel,' Millie piped up, 'as that poor woman did this morning. What on earth was wrong with her, Sergeant? Did she have some terrible disease?'

After looking from one to the other, Keedy inhaled deeply.

'There's something you both ought to know . . .'

# CHAPTER FOUR

Having her daughter at home for a whole night was a treat for Ellen Marmion. Since she didn't have to go on duty in the Women's Police Force until a later shift, Alice was able to have a long, lazy breakfast with her mother. They had something important to celebrate. After months of prevarication, Joe Keedy had finally agreed on a date for the wedding. It was to be in the following June. Though they'd talked about it at length the previous evening, the women returned to the subject with renewed gusto.

'We'll have to speak to the vicar,' said Ellen.

'There's no rush.'

'The church has to be booked and the banns have to be read.'

'Not for a long time yet.'

'We must do everything properly, Alice.'

'We will, I promise you. Joe and I don't want anything too fancy, by the way. Tell Daddy that we'll be happy with a quiet wedding. We'll have to be more careful with money from now on because we're saving up to buy a house.'

'If all else fails, you can always move in here.'

'No,' said Alice, firmly. 'That wouldn't work at all. We'd get under each other's feet and there'd be no real privacy for any of us. By next June, we'll have found a place of our own.'

'Make sure that it's somewhere close to us.'

'We'll have to take what we can get, Mummy. Our main worry is that the war will still be going on. Joe seems to think it will be finished by spring of next year, but I don't share his optimism.'

'When it started,' recalled Ellen, gloomily, 'we thought that it would be over and done with by Christmas. That was three years ago.'

'I prefer not to think about it. I don't care if German bombs are dropping all round the church. Now that we've finally fixed the date, I intend to get married on that Saturday afternoon, whatever happens.'

'Have you discussed the guest list with Joe?'

'Yes, it will be on the short side.'

'We can't scrimp on everything, Alice. Why don't I get pencil and paper and jot down the obvious names?'

'I'd rather do that nearer the time, Mummy.'

'It won't hurt to start right now.'

'Yes, it will.'

'Why do you say that?'

'It's because one name will be missing off that list.'

Ellen was jolted. While enjoying the prospect of her daughter's wedding, she'd forgotten all about her son. Paul Marmion had been injured at the Battle of the Somme and invalided out of the army. He'd been so disruptive at home that his mother was unable to cope with his shifting moods and bad behaviour. When she least expected it, Paul had run away and made no attempt to contact anyone in the family. An intense search by his father had proved fruitless and they'd begun to think he might no longer be alive. To their relief, they discovered he'd been working as a labourer on a farm in Warwickshire but, when they went to see him, they learnt that Paul had been sacked from his job. Once again, they were completely in the dark.

Alice made an effort to be positive about her wayward brother.

'You never know,' she said. 'He may be back home by then.'

'I doubt that somehow.'

'Things will be different when winter comes. Paul will start to have second thoughts about living hand to mouth. Having a roof over his head will become much more important to him.'

'I don't want him driven back here because of bad weather,' said Ellen, baulking at the idea. 'I'd like him back because he's missing his family.' She pursed her lips. 'That may be too much to ask.'

'Paul's my brother. He *ought* to be there for my wedding.'

'How can he do that if he doesn't even know when it is?'

Alice was deflated. 'That's a fair point.'

'If he had any intention of coming home, he'd have turned up months ago. We have to be realistic, Alice. He's gone for good.'

When he'd assigned the case to Marmion, the superintendent had reminded him that he expected to be kept informed of developments at every stage. Once he'd gathered enough information, therefore, the inspector was driven straight back to Scotland Yard so that he could report to his superior. Seated behind his desk, Claude Chatfield listened with interest to what the detectives had found at the Lotus Hotel. The

20

manager had given Marmion a plan of the property. He now opened it in front of the superintendent.

'How did the murder victim get into the building?' he asked. 'That was my first question. The second one is linked to it: how on earth did Lady Diana Brice-Cadmore, who occupied that room, leave the hotel with her luggage without being seen?'

'How many exits are there?'

'Three, sir – there's one at the front and two at the rear.'

Marmion used a finger to indicate each in turn. Chatfield pondered.

'A hotel employee must be involved,' he said at length.

'That was my feeling.'

'How reliable is that night porter?'

'Sergeant Keedy said that he seemed alert enough when he was questioned, and the manager spoke up for Rogan. Including Mr Chell, there are four male members of staff at the Lotus, but the manager is the only one who has any real contact with the guests. The others are largely invisible. One of the attractions of the hotel to prospective guests is that it's run by and solely for women.'

Chatfield frowned. 'Does that mean it's a haven for suffragettes?'

'It's a place that offers respectability and a degree of luxury. That was how the manager described it. Until today, it also provided a guarantee of safety for its guests.'

'They won't be feeling very safe now.'

'Mr Chell will be working madly to placate them.'

'What's your next step?'

'Lady Brice-Cadmore lives in Berkshire. The house has no telephone, apparently. I'll go by train to Didcot then take a taxi out to the estate. If she's there, I'd like to find out why she made a sudden exit from the hotel. I'm also hoping that she may have some idea of the identity of the woman who was in her room.'

'What about the sergeant?'

'I left him at the Lotus, taking statements from all and sundry. I can't believe that it was so easy for one woman to leave unseen and for a complete stranger to end up dead in her place.'

'I agree. Somebody must have seen *something*.'

'If they did,' said Marmion, confidently, 'then Sergeant Keedy will soon get the truth out of them. He's very thorough.'

Keedy had taken so many notes that his hand was beginning to ache, but he forced himself on, talking to each person – guest or employee – in succession. He always felt uneasy in the presence of wealth and it was very much on show. Accommodation was very expensive and the exquisite jewellery worn by some of the women he interviewed told its own story. In a previous case, he'd visited another London hotel and immediately fallen out with the manager. His first impression of Rex Chell was that the man was cut from the same cloth – proud, arrogant, authoritative and more concerned in protecting his hotel from damaging publicity than in helping to solve a murder. On closer observation, Keedy had to revise his judgement. Chell turned out to be a master of diplomacy, quiet, patient, watchful, sympathetic and able to smooth the most ruffled feathers. Watching him in action was an education. Angry guests who came to hector the manager went away with contented smiles on their face. Those who threatened to leave instantly were somehow persuaded to stay. Chell had undeniable charm.

Bracing himself, Keedy began yet another interview.

'How long have you worked here, Mrs Gosling?' he asked.

'I started at the Lotus when it first opened.'

'When was that?'

'It must be all of five years ago,' she said.

'And where were you before that?'

'I was the housekeeper at the Belfry in Leicester Square.'

'That's a much bigger hotel, isn't it?'

'I prefer to work here, Sergeant.'

'Why is that?'

'Well, there's the manager, for a start. It's a pleasure to work for Mr Chell. He makes you feel appreciated. Also, I have much more of a free hand here. I like that.'

Lena Gosling was a plump, motherly, middle-aged woman with red cheeks and sparkling eyes. Keedy warmed to her at once. He knew that she'd been comforting Millie.

'How is Miss Jenks?'

'She's still badly shaken,' she replied, 'but I've managed to stop her blaming herself for what happened.'

'It wasn't her fault,' said Keedy.

'I kept telling her that.'

'The manager said that you'd taken her under your wing.'

'She needed someone to look after her,' said Mrs Gosling. 'Millie has never been away from home before. The Lotus can be a bit scary to someone like that.'

'What do you know of Lady Brice-Cadmore?'

'She's stayed here once before. She is a very nice woman, though she can be fussy about her food.'

'Was her behaviour in any way erratic?'

She gave a shrug. 'I don't understand.'

'Leaving the hotel without notice was very impulsive of her. Did she seem like the sort of person to do something like that?'

'No, she was far too considerate.'

'Why did she ask Miss Jenks to wake her this morning?'

'Millie had been looking after her room.'

'Yes, but she's the most junior member of staff. Why pick on her when other people would have seemed more reliable – Mr Rogan, for instance. He told me that he's often had to wake guests up early in the morning. Has Miss Jenks ever done that before?'

'No,' she said, thoughtfully. 'She hasn't.'

Keedy sat back in his chair. 'I'm told that you keep this place working properly behind the scenes.'

She laughed. 'That's not true at all.'

'I think you're being modest.'

'I simply do my best.'

'Tell me a little more about yourself, Mrs Gosling.'

'Oh, I'm not important.'

'I think you are.'

Encouraged by his interest, she launched into her life story. It was tinged with sadness. London had a sizeable population of war widows and she had a special reason to understand the plight of those who'd lost their husbands in action. Her own tragedy had occurred during the Boer War when the man she'd recently married was shot dead in a skirmish. Though Lena Gosling had been deprived of the chance to have the children she'd coveted, she didn't descend into self-pity. She simply threw herself wholeheartedly into her work and built up a reputation for reliability and diligence. Over a period of years, she'd earned a series of promotions in various hotels. She had now ended up at the Lotus with responsibility for the housekeeping.

'Girls like Millie Jenks are my family now,' she said, fondly. 'They come here as complete innocents and need someone to look out for them.'

'You obviously do that job well.'

24

'I don't see it as a job, Sergeant. It's a treat.'

'How do you get on with the manager?'

'We get on very well. I have no complaints about Mr Chell and I make sure he has none about me. He's the person who makes this hotel run like clockwork.'

'I can imagine that.'

'And he's such a handsome man. The guests adore him.'

Keedy was quizzical. 'Don't you think it's rather odd?'

'What is?'

'Well, in a hotel where the vast majority of people are female, most men would feel out of place. I certainly would.'

'Mr Chell would be at his ease anywhere. It's a gift.'

It was not one that Keedy possessed. Talking to hotel employees like Lena Gosling, he was completely relaxed. It was a different matter when he'd had to question some of the guests. They came from a world of wealth and entitlement. Keedy would never aspire to such things. In their presence, he was made to feel that he belonged to a lower order of creation and it rankled with him.

Mrs Gosling looked him in the eye and wagged a finger.

'Can I make one thing clear?' she asked.

'Yes, of course.'

'You think a member of staff was responsible, don't you?'

'It's a possibility we have to explore,' he said.

'Then let me save you a lot of wasted time, Sergeant. I know every person who works under this roof and I can vouch for each one of them. None of them would dream of doing anything that would cause trouble to the Lotus. We've bonded together here,' she said, grasping his arm. 'Don't treat us as suspects. It's unfair on us and it will mislead you. We'd die rather than let this hotel down.'

Keedy was taken aback by her passion and forthrightness. He was also glad when she loosened the tight grip on his arm.

'You like it here, don't you?' he said.

'I *love* it, Sergeant. This is my home.'

# CHAPTER FIVE

After responding to the crisis at the hotel, then delivering his report to the superintendent, Marmion was glad to have time to review the situation. Though he was in a full compartment of a train to Didcot, he was able to block out the sound of his fellow travellers and concentrate on the case. Questions proliferated. Who was the murder victim? What was she doing at the hotel and what possible motive had prompted someone to kill her? Where was Lady Diana Brice-Cadmore and why had she left the hotel without any kind of warning? Was there any connection between the two women? Could it be that the missing guest was implicated somehow in the murder? That seemed inconceivable. Rex Chell had described her as a model guest and hotel managers tended to be shrewd judges of character. It was part of their stock-in-trade.

Marmion was baffled. He was confronted by a grotesque

conjuring trick in which a live guest disappeared from the stage in a flash to be replaced by a dead stranger. Such an extraordinary act of deception needed careful planning and an intimate knowledge of the Lotus Hotel. The more he thought about it, the more convinced Marmion became that his starting point had to be Lady Brice-Cadmore. Having ordered a taxi for 6 a.m., she had instead left the hotel by some other means during the night and headed for an unknown destination. Marmion hoped that she'd gone home to the address he'd found in the hotel register, but that was by no means certain. The fact that her luggage had vanished with her suggested that she would have needed help. Did that come from a friend or an accomplice in a murder?

The key element in the investigation was the Lotus Hotel itself. It was comparatively small, highly exclusive and tucked away where it would attract little attention. What was the rationale behind it? Why was it frequented by a particular clientele? Gentlemen's clubs abounded all over London – one had featured in a recent case handled by Marmion and Keedy – but similar establishments for women were much less common. Why had the Lotus come into being? Was it satisfying a need for a privileged sector of the female population? Who exactly stayed there and why did they prefer it over the countless other hotels in the capital?

Marmion accepted that he and Keedy were at a disadvantage because of their gender. While they could subject the Lotus to close scrutiny, there were aspects of its operation they might never uncover. Not for the first time, he wished that Scotland Yard could see the value of having female detectives, able to elicit information out of other women in a way that was beyond their male counterparts. But the Metropolitan Police Force was far too hidebound even to consider the idea. Marmion's daughter, Alice, a prime candidate for promotion to detective status, was not allowed anywhere near investigations into serious crimes. They were a male preserve. The Women's Police Force was kept firmly in its place. Marmion and Keedy would have to do without the insights that only a woman could bring. As they had done for centuries, male values and attitudes would continue to dominate law enforcement.

Marmion racked his brains until the train juddered to a halt in Reading Station. Another question then pushed itself roughly to the front of the queue.

What had Lady Brice-Cadmore been doing in London?

It was a paradox. Alice Marmion arrived at work with wonderful news yet was unable to pass it on. Bursting to share it with a friend, she was held back from doing so by an invisible hand. After being given their orders by the imperious Inspector Gale, she and her beat partner, Iris Goodliffe, set off on their shift. They lapsed into inconsequential chatter. Since Iris was her closest friend in the Women's Police Force, she ought to be told that a date for the wedding had finally been decided, and she would initially share Alice's joy. But her pleasure would be edged with pain because Iris would be reminded how empty her own private life was. Alice was being tactful, knowing that her delight would throw Iris's misery into sharp relief.

Unlike her shapely friend, Iris was a big, chubby, plain young woman, highly conscious of her lack of appeal to the opposite sex. When a man had finally taken an interest in her, the relationship had ended in disaster. Iris had been badly wounded by the experience. As a result, a bubbling extrovert had been turned into a morose and fearful young woman. Out of consideration for her friend's feelings, therefore, Alice decided to hold back her good news. She was not allowed to do it for long. In spite of her many faults, Iris had keen instincts.

'Something's happened, hasn't it?' she said.

'No,' replied Alice, 'nothing in particular.'

'You're positively glowing.'

'I spent the night at home, that's all.'

'Then it must be something to do with your brother. Has Paul been found?' Alice shook her head. 'You only ever go to see your mother when you have a good reason. What was it this time?'

'It was nothing particular.'

'You're a terrible liar, Alice Marmion.'

'No, I'm not.'

Iris snapped her fingers. 'So that's it!' she said, face igniting. 'You've twisted Joe's arm and got him to set a date at last.' Alice couldn't resist beaming. 'I'm right, aren't I?'

'Well . . .'

'Oh, this is so exciting!' said Iris, stopping to embrace her friend. 'When is it? What are you going to wear? How many bridesmaids will you have? You're going to invite *me*, aren't you? Will you and Joe have a proper honeymoon?'

The questions eventually gave way to envy and regret. Happy for her friend, Iris was depressed by her own situation. They walked on in silence for several minutes. Alice could sense that Iris was suffering. Wanting to cheer her friend up, she couldn't think of a way to do it. Iris suddenly broke the silence.

'I never told you what happened between Doug and me, did I?'

'It's none of my business, Iris.'

'I've kept it bottled up all this time.'

'You were hurt,' said Alice. 'That was obvious. The last thing you needed was someone trying to pry.'

'I closed down,' admitted Iris. 'I was so ashamed that I didn't want to talk about it to anyone. Can you understand that?'

'Yes, I can.'

'But I'm wondering if it was a mistake.'

'Only you can decide that.'

'After that last evening with Doug, I was badly bruised. I kept blaming myself for . . . what he did. But the bruises are slowly disappearing now. I'm getting over it.'

'That's good to hear.'

Iris came to a halt. 'Do you mind if I talk about it now?'

Alice could see the mingled fear and embarrassment in her eyes.

'Perhaps you should,' she said.

Superintendent Chatfield had already released a statement to the press and reporters were now baying for detail. He was therefore pleased when Keedy returned from the hotel to pass on the information that he had gathered there. In spite of his reputation for impatience, Chatfield was a good listener, waiting until the sergeant had finished before making any comment.

'You've done well,' he said.

'Thank you, sir,' said Keedy.

'The only things you haven't provided are names of possible suspects.'

'It's too early to do that.'

'A member of staff *has* to have helped.'

'I agree, sir, but that person doesn't necessarily have to be still working at the Lotus. It could be a disgruntled employee who left under a cloud.'

'Good thinking.'

'I had a list of former members of staff from the manager.'

'How many of them are there?'

'Only four,' said Keedy. 'That tells you something about the place. It inspires loyalty. Most of the people who've worked there enjoy it enough to stay. Mrs Gosling is a case in point. She's the mother hen of the hotel. According to her, none of the staff would do anything to cause problems for the Lotus.'

'What did you make of the night porter?'

'Rogan seems to be efficient enough, but I had a feeling that he was holding something back from me. He'd repay a second visit.'

'Make it fairly soon,' advised Chatfield, 'and away from the hotel. You might get more out of him if he's in his own home.'

'That's a good point, sir. When I questioned him, he always spoke as if afraid that the manager was listening as well.'

'Is Mr Chell such a tyrant?'

'He's one of those people far too aware of their power, sir.'

Chatfield's eyes flashed at the perceived criticism of him. Marmion and Keedy didn't hide their view of the superintendent's despotic inclinations. It was a constant irritation for Chatfield. Before he could chide the sergeant, however, he was interrupted by a knock on the door. He looked up as a uniformed officer entered.

'Yes?' he snapped.

'Someone is insisting on seeing you, Superintendent,' said the newcomer. 'It's to do with the murder at the Lotus Hotel.'

'Then he'll have to wait until I'm ready.'

'I'm not waiting for anybody,' said an angry voice.

And a big, handsome, middle-aged woman in a tweed coat, skirt and hat stormed into the room and confronted Chatfield. She adjusted her monocle so that one gimlet eye focused on him.

'I am Griselda Fleetwood,' she declared.

'And what's your interest in the Lotus Hotel?' he asked.

'I own it.'


Living and working in the capital had spoilt Marmion. When he had no access to a police car, he knew that he could always summon a taxi. Assuming that he'd be able to do the same in Didcot, he had a rude awakening. All that the town offered him by way of transport was a horse and trap. Inevitably, it was a slower and less comfortable means of travel, but he had no choice. Clambering up beside the driver, a pimply youth with a mouth permanently agape, he gave directions then put a hand quickly to his hat as a gust of wind threatened to dislodge it. There was an immediate problem. While the driver had heard of Elmstead Manor, he'd never been to the house before and was not quite sure how to get there. The journey was therefore punctuated by occasional stops to ask directions from random people. On the ordnance map that Marmion had consulted beforehand, it had looked fairly close to East Hagbourne, a village within easy driving distance of Didcot, yet in reality Elmstead Manor turned out to be farther than anticipated. Marmion began to despair of ever reaching his destination. His eye then fell on a fingerpost.

'Stop!' he yelled.

'Why?' asked the driver, hauling on the reins.

'We've just passed a sign to the house.'

'I didn't see it, sir.'

'Well, I did. Turn round and go back.'

'Yes, sir.'

'And be quick about it, please.'

'Very good, sir.'

Tugging on the reins, the driver did as he was told. When the trap was eventually pointing in the right direction, they found themselves bouncing and swaying along a rutted track. Autumn leaves rustled on either side of them as they rode through an avenue of trees. Marmion got his first fleeting glimpse of the house through the branches of an old oak. It was a large, rambling, half-timbered Tudor building set in broad acres of parkland. The track soon opened out into a wider drive, giving them a clearer view of the manor. As he studied it, Marmion's hopes of finding Lady Brice-Cadmore there began to fade very quickly. Something warned him to brace himself for disappointment. His journey could be in vain.

The trap pulled up in front of the house and he got down onto the gravel. As Marmion approached the front door, it opened before him and a manservant came out to greet him.

'Can I help you, sir?' he asked.

'Yes,' said Marmion. 'I've come in search of Lady Brice-Cadmore.'

The man was taken aback. 'There must be some mistake.'

'I can assure you that there isn't. I'm Inspector Marmion of Scotland Yard and I'm here in connection with a crime that was committed in the Lotus Hotel in London. Until last night, Lady Brice-Cadmore was a guest there.'

'That's impossible, Inspector.'

'I've seen her signature in the hotel register.'

'I very much doubt that, sir.'

'Isn't her ladyship at home?'

The man's voice lowered to a whisper. 'No, she isn't.'

'Then can you suggest where I might find her?'

'Did you come through East Hagbourne, sir?'

'Yes, we did.'

'Then you passed the parish church of St Andrew,' said the man, solemnly. 'Lady Brice-Cadmore was laid to rest there three years ago.'

# CHAPTER SIX

Keedy and Chatfield took time to acclimatise themselves to their unexpected visitor. When she'd first burst into the room, she dazzled them. There was a potency about her that was almost intimidating. Chatfield offered her a seat with exaggerated politeness as if in the presence of minor royalty. Keedy, meanwhile, was marvelling at her compound of power, determination and good breeding. Neither of them had met anyone quite like Griselda Fleetwood before. Her manner was haughty, her tone peremptory.

'I've just come from the hotel,' she said, 'and was told that an Inspector Marmion was in charge of the case. He is not available, it seems, so I was advised to speak to Superintendent Chatfield.'

'That's me,' he said before indicating Keedy. 'And this is Sergeant Keedy, who is also working on the investigation.'

'The manager mentioned you,' she said, eyeing Keedy with clear disapproval. 'He found your questioning intrusive.'

'That's in the nature of a murder inquiry, madam,' explained Keedy. 'We had to probe deeply in order to build up a detailed picture of how your hotel operates.'

'Mr Chell could have told you that. He didn't see the need for a cross-examination of each one of our guests, and nor do I. When they stay at the Lotus, they rely on us to protect them from any interference. You broke the contract we have with our patrons, Sergeant.'

'With respect, Mrs Fleetwood, it was the killer who did that. Had there been no crime on the premises, Inspector Marmion and I would never have been to the hotel.'

'Don't quibble, young man.'

'My detectives are known for their meticulousness,' said Chatfield, trying to establish his authority, 'and they followed recognised procedure. It has already produced results.'

He went on to describe the steps that had been taken, the evidence gathered and how he'd given the press a description of the murder victim so that an appeal for information could be made to the public. Chatfield felt certain that they would soon have the name of the unknown woman found dead at the hotel. What he couldn't guarantee, he admitted, was a quick solution to the crime because they had, as yet, no definite suspects.

'One of them must be employed at the hotel,' said Keedy.

'I was just about to say that,' added Chatfield, treating him to a glare. 'Inside help was vital to the killer, Mrs Fleetwood.'

'Well, it didn't come from any member of my staff,' she asserted.

'I beg to differ.'

'The people we employ are above reproach.'

'Then perhaps you can suggest who *did* commit this murder.'

'That's exactly why I'm here, Superintendent. Your men are clearly looking in the wrong direction. The Lotus is not like other hotels. It has unique qualities that sets it apart. We cater for ladies of high society who – when they visit London – prefer to stay in a place that offers an essentially feminine atmosphere. There's no political significance in that,' she stressed. 'The Lotus is not a suffragette citadel. Indeed, our guests deplore the activities of those desperate women who caused so much wanton damage in the name of equality.'

'To be fair,' said Keedy, 'the suffragettes have abandoned their campaign for the duration of the war.'

'That's immaterial. They continue to bring shame on our sex.'

'I agree,' said Chatfield, jumping in before Keedy could say anything else. 'But – if you would, please – I'd like you to justify your claim that we're looking in the wrong direction.'

'Your detectives are unaware of our record of success.'

'That's not true,' argued Keedy. 'The manager boasted of it.'

'Yes, but he didn't tell you what the consequences have been. Success always invites envy,' she said, 'and that has so far been confined to sniping at us in the newspapers. When that failed to dent our popularity, our rivals resorted to nastier methods. This latest outrage is the culmination of a sophisticated battle that's being waged against us.'

'What are you telling us, Mrs Fleetwood?' asked Chatfield.

'The murder took place at our hotel for a reason.'

'And what was that reason?'

'Sabotage.'

Alice Marmion was horrified at the story she heard. It took a long time for the full details to emerge because they were on duty and had to deal with a number of minor incidents as they strolled side by side around their beat. There was also the problem of Iris's sense of shame. It meant that her account was halting and apologetic. Alice was roused.

'Stop doing that!' she said, coming to an abrupt halt. 'None of this was your fault, Iris. He must take full responsibility.'

'Without realising it, I must have led him on.'

'That's nonsense.'

'I simply can't believe that Doug would have done that unless I'd given him . . . the wrong signals.'

'Stop taking his part,' said Alice, vehemently. '*You're* the victim, not PC Beckett. When you escaped from his clutches, you should have reported him.'

Iris shuddered. 'Oh, I couldn't do that.'

'Why not?'

'I felt so guilty,' said the other, 'and so stupid. Because Doug was that much older than me, I thought that I was completely safe. I now see that I trusted him far too much.'

'It's not too late to make him pay for what he did.'

'I'm too frightened to do that.'

'Do you want him to get away with it?' asked Alice. 'If you hadn't stopped him, he'd have . . .'

'Don't say that word. I can't believe that Doug would have gone all the way. He's a policeman whose job is to help people.'

'Well, he certainly wasn't trying to help *you* that night.'

Alice was fuming, less at the behaviour of Constable Beckett than at her friend's response to it. During their brief relationship, Iris had enjoyed some very pleasant evenings out with him. It was only when she went to his house that he changed dramatically. The gentle, patient man she knew suddenly revealed a darker side to his character, leaping on her when they sat on the sofa and trying to take off her clothes. Iris had only managed to escape by taking out her hair slide and jabbing it hard into the side of his face. Caught by surprise and howling in pain, he'd been unable to prevent her from pushing him off and rushing out of the house.

'Report him,' urged Alice. 'It's your duty.'

'He could lose his job.'

'He deserves to, Iris. He ought to be behind bars.'

'It would be his word against mine.'

'Any fair-minded judge would believe you.'

'Oh, I just couldn't face it,' wailed Iris. 'I've read about trials for attempted . . . you know. The woman always seems to lose. It would be a nightmare, having my private life raked over in public.'

It was an understandable fear. Alice was also familiar with details of cases of sexual assault, which ended all too often in the acquittal of the man. In the course of trying to defend herself, a woman could lose her reputation altogether, even though she was the innocent party. Albeit hesitant, Iris's account had the ring of truth. Alice accepted it without reservation. A jury of strangers might take a different view and Beckett's years of service as a policeman would count in his favour. Wanting to embrace her friend by way of consolation, Alice knew that a public street was not perhaps the place to do so. She simply gave Iris a sympathetic smile.

'Now I can see why you never talked about it before,' she said.

'I just couldn't, Alice.'

'You went quiet and miserable. That was very unlike you.'

'I know,' said Iris, sadly. 'I'm usually a real chatterbox.'

'Have you seen him since?'

'Yes. I did see him once, days later. I ducked down a side street immediately.'

'Didn't it occur to you to challenge him?'

'I didn't have the courage for that, Alice.'

'Did he try to contact you in any way?' Iris shook her head. 'So he's never tried to apologise?'

'No,' said Iris.

'That tells you all you need to know about the man.'

'He's probably forgotten me already.'

'He could also be too busy looking for someone else to entice into his house. If you make an accusation against him, you might be saving other young women from suffering the same fate.'

'It's not as simple as that,' said Iris, earnestly. 'I went out with Doug willingly, I let him kiss me and hold my hand. I felt relaxed in his company. It's a terrible thing for a woman of my age to admit, Alice, but the truth is that he was my first real boyfriend. I was . . . well, hoping I might finally have found Mr Right.'

Sir Godfrey Brice-Cadmore was a wizened old man in a crumpled suit who kept fingering his goatee beard as if he was in danger of losing it. He and Marmion sat opposite each other in leather armchairs. They were in a low-ceilinged room that was occupied by dozens of stuffed birds, perched inside a series of display cases. Marmion was particularly impressed by the osprey poised to descend on its prey from the top of a glass-fronted cabinet. Sir Godfrey gestured with a skeletal hand.

'I love ornithology,' he said, 'and, by great good fortune, so did my late wife. It's a shared interest that drew us together. We met by chance at the Three Choirs Festival in Gloucester. A magical evening in every way! It was at the premiere of *Scenes from Shelley's Prometheus Unbound*. The composer, Hubert Parry, also conducted. That was in 1880. What an extraordinary coincidence!'

'I don't follow, Sir Godfrey.'

'Well, the law of averages suggests that you might actually meet someone with *one* similar passion but to find someone with two was asking far too much. Yet it's exactly what happened to Diana and me. Each of us adored birds and music with equal veneration. Have you ever been to the Three Choirs Festival, Inspector?'

'My job leaves me little time for leisure, I'm afraid.'

'What a pity! Gloucester, Worcester and Hereford each have a cathedral that's the perfect venue for choral music. It hangs in the air and stirs the soul. As for my future wife,' he went on, 'I couldn't take my eyes off her. She reminded me of an illustration I once saw of Diana the Huntress.' He chortled to himself, then saw Marmion's blank face. 'Evidently, you're not a man with a classical education and, even if you were, you wouldn't come to Elmstead Manor to talk about it. Forgive me boring you with my maudlin reminiscences.'

'I wasn't in the least bored, Sir Godfrey.'

'You've had a wasted journey, I fear.'

'I think it's been rather fruitful.'

'Really?'

'What you've told me has been interesting. You and your wife deliberately chose to live a fairly isolated life that allowed you to pursue your own interests. Everything you needed was here. You said that you couldn't remember the last time when either of you ventured anywhere near London.'

'We hated the place, Inspector. And as it happened, rural seclusion is a safer choice at this moment in time. London is being bombed in daylight now as well as at night. The Germans are highly unlikely to divert their planes to Elmstead Manor.' He raised a palm. 'But I interrupt you. I apologise.'

'Somebody posing as your wife stayed at a hotel in London.'

'Yes, and it's a confounded cheek!'

'It was a calculation, Sir Godfrey. The woman involved could count on the fact that no other guests would know the real Lady Brice-Cadmore and be aware that she'd passed away.'

'In other words . . .'

'It was a safe disguise,' said Marmion, 'but it proves one thing.'

'And what's that?'

'The false Lady Brice-Cadmore knew the real one, or was at least aware that she lived out here and rarely mixed in society.'

Sir Godfrey was appalled. 'Are you saying that this person might have been a friend of ours?'

'No friend would behave the way that she did.'

'Then who is she?'

'Someone who might have met you both at some stage and knew the kind of lives you led. If it's not too much trouble, Sir Godfrey, there is a favour I'd like to ask of you.'

'I'll do anything that will help to snare this vile creature pretending to be my late wife.'

'Well,' said Marmion. 'If I may, I'd like to borrow a photograph of Lady Brice-Cadmore.'

'You can have one gladly.'

Hauling himself out of his chair, Sir Godfrey walked across to a desk and pulled open a drawer. After taking out a photograph album, he began to leaf through it slowly. Marmion waited patiently. He could see how moved the other man was by the sight of his wife in happier times. It was minutes before Sir Godfrey was able to make a decision. Extracting a photograph, he handed it to his visitor.

'This is how I'll always remember her,' he said. 'Diana had such a radiant smile. The camera caught it perfectly.'

43

Marmion studied the photograph. Taken in a garden, it showed a slim, striking, dignified woman smiling serenely at the camera. A pair of binoculars dangled from her neck on a leather strap.

'We were about to go birdwatching,' explained Sir Godfrey. 'We had a couple of hides built in the woods years ago. Doesn't she look beautiful? And she seems to be brimming with good health. You'd never have guessed that she had only a few months to live.'

'This is very interesting,' said Marmion.

'Why?'

'Mr Chell, the hotel manager, gave me a detailed description of the bogus Lady Brice-Cadmore. It could easily fit your wife.'

'That's monstrous,' said Sir Godfrey. 'Not content with stealing my wife's name, this woman is trying to impersonate her. She must be caught as soon as possible, Inspector.'

'She will be, Sir Godfrey.'

'Diana has the right to rest in peace.'

'And you have the right to mourn her without having her identity stolen.' Marmion got to his feet. 'Thank you for your help, Sir Godfrey. This photograph will make our task much easier. I'm sorry to have brought such disturbing news. Next time, I hope, I'll have happier tidings to pass on to you.'

# CHAPTER SEVEN

Griselda Fleetwood astounded them. She was not only a highly intelligent woman, she had undoubted business acumen. Married to a wealthy financier, she also had independent means that allowed her to follow her own inclinations. Having had the urge to open an exclusive hotel, she waited for years until the right premises became available, using the intervening time to study the way that establishments of a similar size operated. As she talked about the success of her venture, Keedy took notes. Chatfield threw in the odd question, but they were listening to what was essentially a monologue.

'The most vital decision I had to make,' she told them, 'was to choose the name for the hotel. I rejected dozens of possibilities before I settled on "lotus". Are either of you familiar with Buddhism?'

'No,' admitted Chatfield.

'The same goes for me,' said Keedy.

'In Buddhism,' she explained, 'the lotus has always been associated with purity, spiritual awakening and faithfulness. I regard those as feminine virtues rather than male attributes. The flower is considered pure because of its ability to emerge from murky waters every morning yet be perfectly clean. It's miraculous.'

'I never thought of it that way,' said Chatfield.

'That's because you have a closed mind, Superintendent.'

He sat up instantly. 'I refute that, Mrs Fleetwood. I'm known for my ability to adjust to any situation.'

'My point, exactly,' she said. 'You can only react to events. You can never think ahead and show true initiative. Like most men, you have a blinkered approach to life.'

As the superintendent blustered, Keedy had to conceal his grin.

'Steady on, madam,' said Chatfield, affronted.

'I was merely stating a fact.'

'Let's go back to your original claim that what happened last night at the Lotus Hotel was the work of a rival.'

'It's not a claim,' she insisted. 'It's the only possible conclusion.'

'We must agree to differ on that point.'

'You don't know the full story of what's been going on.'

'That's true, Mrs Fleetwood. What you've told us has given us valuable insights. So far, you've named the owners of three hotels.'

'Four, sir,' corrected Keedy. 'You're forgetting the Unicorn.'

'Very well, then,' said Chatfield, irascibly. 'It was *four* hotels. How well do you know these establishments, Mrs Fleetwood?'

'I know them intimately.'

'Have you ever stayed at any of them?'

'I stayed at all four,' she replied, 'because they are identical in size and status to the Lotus. Before I committed myself to what was, after all, a major capital investment, I did my homework very thoroughly.'

'That was very wise of you, Mrs Fleetwood,' said Keedy.

'The success of the Lotus is not entirely due to my commercial skills, of course. Catastrophic as it's been in many ways, the outbreak of war was an unlikely bonus. It brought people flooding into the capital. London has always been a dangerous place for a woman to visit alone,' she went on, 'but that's even more the case now. We have foreigners with dubious moral standards roaming our streets, not to mention soldiers – British and American – who seem to treat the capital as if it's there to provide them with opportunities for excessive drinking and debauchery.'

'You hardly need to tell us that,' said Chatfield, peevishly. 'It's the reason we police the city as tightly as we can. Unhappily, our resources have been badly weakened. We lost thousands of officers to the army.'

'There,' she said, pointing an accusatory finger at him. 'That's another example of your blinkered view. You only see the problem from *your* point of view, Superintendent. Put yourself in the position of a woman wishing to stay in London. It's a frightening prospect. That's why a hotel like the Lotus has such an appeal.'

'Only for those who can afford such high prices,' said Keedy.

'That's beside the point.'

'When you visit London yourself,' asked Chatfield, 'do you always stay at your own hotel?'

'Of course,' she said, disdainfully. 'Even if I come to town with my husband, I stay at the Lotus while he reserves a room at his club. Several of my married acquaintances do the same. They part with their spouses for a night or more so that they can have peace of mind at the Lotus.'

Keedy was on the point of saying that peace of mind would be in short supply at the hotel for a while, but he had second thoughts. Griselda

47

Fleetwood was in a truculent mood. He didn't wish to incur her hostility.

'Who would stand to gain most from your predicament?' he asked, looking up from his notebook.

'Fraser Buchanan.'

'And why is that?'

'There are two reasons. Firstly, he owns the Unicorn which, like the Lotus, is favoured by guests from high society.'

'It has a good name, then.'

'It was unrivalled until I came on the scene.'

'Did Mr Buchanan resent the competition?'

'He resented the fact that it came from a woman.'

'You said that there were two reasons why you picked out Mr Buchanan,' said Chatfield. 'What's the second one, Mrs Fleetwood?'

'That's personal,' she snapped.

And the conversation came to a dead halt.

Ellen Marmion was proud of the fact that her husband was a detective inspector in the Metropolitan Police Force. While his rank brought privileges, it also committed him to long hours working on major crimes. There were days when she hardly ever saw him until he tumbled into bed beside her in the small hours. One way of keeping herself occupied had been to dedicate herself to war work, but Ellen was still left with acres of free time to fill. When her domestic chores were finished, therefore, she'd become an avid reader of library books. Romantic novels had been her staple choice at first because they offered a pleasant escape from the realities of living on the Home Front in an increasingly destructive war. She had now tried to widen the range of her reading and had found John Buchan's *The Thirty-Nine Steps* utterly engrossing.

On her way to the library to exchange the book, Ellen bumped into one of the women in her sewing circle. They exchanged greetings.

'No need to guess where you're going,' said Rene Bridger, looking at the book in Ellen's basket. 'What are you taking back?'

'It's a wonderful story – *The Thirty-Nine Steps.*'

'I know. I've read it. Did you fall in love with Richard Hannay? I did. He made me feel young again.'

'I just couldn't put the book down,' confessed Ellen. 'In a strange way, it sort of . . . cheered me up.'

'Well, I can't say that of the last one I read,' said the other, glumly. 'To be honest, it frightened me and made me worry for the future.'

'Why is that, Rene?'

'I'll tell you.'

She took a step closer to Ellen as if about to impart confidential information. Rene Bridger was a short, fleshy woman in her fifties with frizzy red hair poking out from under her hat. Like Ellen, she'd sent a son off to war and feared for his chances of survival. Paul Marmion had returned, albeit in a damaged condition. Alec Bridger was buried under French soil. Her personal tragedy had made his mother more apprehensive than ever.

'We're going to lose this war,' she whispered.

'I don't believe that. We're going to win. We must.'

'You have to face facts, Ellen. They're already here, you see.'

'Who are?'

'The Germans, of course – that's why the book upset me so much. It told the truth.'

'What was it called?'

'*The Invasion of 1910.* It made my flesh creep.'

'Is it a novel?'

'Yes.'

'Then it's simply a story that someone's made up. You're not supposed to take it seriously, Rene.'

'I couldn't help it. Read it yourself,' said her friend. 'It may be just a story, but it sounds horribly real to me.'

Ellen's curiosity was aroused. 'Who wrote it?'

'He's got a foreign name and I'm not sure how to pronounce it. But that doesn't matter. He knows what he's talking about, believe me. We've already been invaded by a silent enemy.'

Once her anger had subsided, Alice was filled with remorse. She felt that she'd let her friend down. Iris had been suffering for months yet Alice had been unable to relieve her pain. From Iris's retreat into a kind of bruised silence, she should have realised that something serious had happened. Now that she'd finally been able to talk about it, Iris seemed to relax slightly. Alice, by contrast, was tense and rueful. She sought to make amends for her failure.

'Would you like *me* to speak to him?' she volunteered.

'No!' cried Iris in alarm. 'Please don't do that.'

'Someone ought to tackle him.'

'I've already told you. I just want to forget it.'

'But that's not easy to do. You've been brooding on it for months already. It's not going to go away, Iris.'

'It's got better over time. Besides, I don't want anyone fighting my battles for me. I'm old enough to do that for myself. What I needed was some sympathy, that's all. You gave it to me.'

'I want to do more than that.'

'You've done enough, Alice. In fact—'

She broke off as they came around a corner and saw two young boys fighting. One was on his back on the pavement while the other

50

was straddling him. Both were punching each other hard. Iris moved in quickly to lift one boy off while Alice helped the other up from the ground. The two of them were tousled and panting for breath. When they continued to issue threats to each other, Iris took over, silencing them with a dire warning, then telling them how ashamed they should be. By the time she'd finished admonishing them, both hung their heads in disgrace. Iris sent them off in opposite directions.

'You see?' she said. 'I can act decisively when I need to.'

'Dealing with a couple of young boys is one thing, Iris. When it's a fully grown adult like Doug Beckett, it's a different matter. You were in real danger with him.'

'I don't need reminding, Alice.'

'What will you do if he does cross your path?'

'I'll ignore him.'

'I couldn't do that. I'd have to confront him.'

'Yes,' said Iris, woefully, 'but you wouldn't have let yourself get into the position that I did. You're much more experienced at dealing with men. I'm hopeless. The awful truth is that I was so grateful that someone actually liked me that I was completely off guard.'

'I fancy that you'll be more careful in future,' said Alice.

'Oh, yes!' resolved her friend. 'From now on, I won't even *look* at a man.'


Murder on the premises had shaken the Lotus Hotel to its foundations. The manager had quelled the worst fears of the guests but even he couldn't dispel the general air of uneasiness. Chell was grateful that the body of the victim had been discreetly removed by the police. He could now try to restore a degree of normality. When Marmion returned to the hotel that afternoon, the manager took him into his office before any of the guests could see him.

'Did you *have* to rush me in here like that?' asked Marmion. 'At most murder scenes, people find the sight of a Scotland Yard detective rather comforting. It shows that the crime is being dealt with.'

'I'd rather it was dealt with behind closed doors,' said Chell. 'Have there been any developments?'

'Yes, sir, there's been a rather surprising one.'

He told Chell about the discovery that Lady Brice-Cadmore had died three years earlier and that the person staying at the hotel under that name was therefore an impostor. The manager was astonished. Marmion described his visit to Elmstead Manor and his conversation with the widowed husband. He then took out the photograph and handed it over. Chell's eyebrows twitched. After staring at the photograph for some time, he looked up.

'This is uncanny,' he said.

'Why?'

'In some ways, she looks like the guest who has been passing herself off as Lady Brice-Cadmore. She's younger than her – there's no question about that – but the likeness is clear.' He gave the photograph back to Marmion. 'Our guest could be her older sister.'

'Lady Brice-Cadmore had no sisters.'

'Then who was the woman staying here?'

'It's a question I've been asking myself, sir. In stealing someone else's identity, she was committing a crime and it's therefore logical to assume that she may have been involved in the murder of your uninvited guest. But,' said Marmion, 'I keep thinking about that taxi she ordered.'

'It wasn't needed.'

'She obviously thought it would be. Had she been an accessory to a murder, then means of transport would surely have been laid on for her

52

by someone else so that she could melt away into the night. But that didn't happen, did it? The taxi turned up here on time.'

'I'm not sure that I follow your reasoning, Inspector.'

'When she requested it, the guest known as Lady Brice-Cadmore fully expected to leave the hotel at 6 a.m. I believe that someone arranged an earlier departure for her.'

'It must have been her accomplice.'

'That was my initial response. I've grown to distrust it.'

'But the woman was fraudulent. You've proved that.'

'Fraud and murder are very different crimes, sir.'

'I still think she has blood on her hands.'

'So why was that taxi ordered?'

'It must have been a mistake.'

'From what you've told me about her, it sounds as if she was a very self-possessed woman. Posing as someone else requires a lot of confidence. You enjoyed having her as your guest.'

'We did,' confessed Chell.

'Did she mingle with the other guests?'

'No, she kept herself to herself.'

'She was obviously taking no risks,' said Marmion. 'How did she come to stay at this particular hotel?'

'It was recommended by a friend, apparently.'

'Did she mention the name of that friend?'

'No, Inspector,' replied Chell, 'and, in hindsight, that may be significant. Frankly, I'm shocked at myself for letting someone pull the wool over my eyes. As far as I'm aware, that's never happened to me before and I resent it. I'm not easily deceived.'

'You can't be blamed, sir. Evidently, she was very convincing.'

'I took her at face value. It was a grave mistake.'

'So where was that taxi going to take her?'

'Is that relevant?'

'It could be. Did the taxi driver say where he was supposed to take the false Lady Brice-Cadmore?'

'He was booked to go to Euston Station.'

'Then that was certainly her intended destination,' Marmion concluded. 'A woman as composed and well organised as the one you describe would not do anything on impulse. She planned to leave here at six o'clock this morning but was prevented from doing so. We know that her bed was not slept in. I fancy that she was forced to leave during the night.'

'This is all very hypothetical,' complained Chell. 'You don't have any idea of the identities of our guest or of the woman found dead in her room. That's why Mrs Fleetwood was so furious.'

'Who is Mrs Fleetwood?'

'She's the owner of this hotel. When I sent her a telegram earlier on, she responded immediately. After coming here to establish the facts, she went off to Scotland Yard in search of answers. Mrs Fleetwood is a woman of great determination, Inspector,' he warned. 'She won't rest until the murder has been solved and the ugly stain on this hotel has been well and truly removed.'

# CHAPTER EIGHT

Joe Keedy was still reeling from his encounter with Griselda Fleetwood. By sheer force of personality, she'd startled both himself and Chatfield. It was only when she tried to issue orders that the superintendent had had to remind her that he would make any operational decisions relating to the investigation. Chatfield agreed that her main business rival did merit a visit, but he was not prepared to accept her assertion that Fraser Buchanan had to be regarded as a prime suspect. With Griselda's imprecations still ringing in his ears, Keedy had been dispatched to interview Buchanan. On his way to the man's home, he reflected on the sense of purpose that had driven Griselda Fleetwood to open the Lotus Hotel and he was bound to admire the way she'd prospered in a highly competitive market. Keedy had met her in a pugnacious mood. When she rubbed shoulders with the minor aristocracy who favoured her hotel, he suspected her tone would be far more reverential.

Keedy found himself thinking about her husband, wondering how he coped with his wife's temper and her compulsion to dominate. It was a Herculean task that most men would shun. Alice had occasional bursts of anger, but they paled beside the pulsating rage of Griselda Fleetwood. When they were married, Keedy reflected, he wouldn't dream of spending a night away from his wife if it could possibly be avoided. Mr Fleetwood, by contrast, probably yearned for escape. In every way, his wife would be a daunting bedfellow.

When he reached the house in Regent's Park, he had no idea what to expect. Griselda had described her rival in the most unflattering terms, leaving Keedy with the idea that he'd be confronted by a cold, ruthless, guileful ogre without even a scintilla of humanity. What he actually found when admitted to the Buchanan residence was a tall, genial, middle-aged man with an open face, fringed by side whiskers and lit up by a disarming smile. In spite of his ancestry, Fraser Buchanan had no hint of a Scottish accent. After pumping Keedy's hand, he indicated the sofa. The two men sat opposite each other in what was a large and tastefully decorated lounge.

'I've been expecting someone to come,' said Buchanan, cheerily. 'When there's a spot of bother at the Lotus, I always get the blame.'

'It's much more serious than a spot of bother, sir.'

'Did Griselda give you my home address?'

'Yes, sir, she did. It's only fair to warn you that Mrs Fleetwood is not exactly an admirer of yours.' Buchanan laughed heartily. 'We're involved in a murder investigation, sir. I'm sorry you find that a cause for amusement.'

'I wasn't laughing at what is clearly a heinous crime, Sergeant. It was Griselda's reaction to it that tickled me. The idea of weighing the evidence carefully before making an allegation would never occur to her. She immediately points an accusing finger at me. If it wasn't so absurdly comical, I'd feel both hurt and insulted.'

'How did you come to know about the murder?'

'News travels fast.'

'Could you be more explicit?'

'My own hotel, the Unicorn, is a mere two streets away from the Lotus. If anyone so much as flushes a toilet at Griselda's dainty little refuge for titled ladies, I get to hear about it.'

'What have you been told in this instance?'

'I know that a murder took place during the night and that the police have no idea who the victim might be. That's common knowledge by now, Sergeant.'

'May I ask where you were last night, Mr Buchanan?'

'You can certainly ask,' replied the other, smoothly, 'but I don't feel obliged to tell you anything about my private life. Suffice it to say that I was not kidnapping a guest at the Lotus and leaving a dead body in exchange. That's simply not my style.'

'And what *is* your style?'

'Stay at the Unicorn and you'll find out.'

'I can't afford that luxury, sir.'

'That's a pity. You'd see how a hotel *should* be run.'

Keedy was irritated by the man's complacent grin. Buchanan made no effort to disguise his delight at the misfortune of a rival hotel. He was unashamedly gloating. Though Keedy could understand why Griselda Fleetwood loathed him so much, however, he didn't get the feeling that the man was involved, directly or indirectly, in the fate that had befallen the Lotus. Buchanan was far too cocksure, basking in his innocence. Seeing no reason to stay, Keedy rose to his feet.

'I'm sorry to have disturbed you, sir,' he said.

'You have your job to do, Sergeant. I suppose there's no point in sending regards and commiserations to Griselda, is there? Believe it or not,' Buchanan went on, 'I'm genuinely sorry that she's in such a dire situation. It's bound to affect business at the Lotus.'

'Mrs Fleetwood is bracing herself for that.'

'She has this strange conviction that I resent her setting herself as a hotelier simply because she's a woman. That's arrant nonsense. What I resent is the fact that she's a dabbler, a rank amateur who is only playing at being a hotel proprietor instead of learning the trade properly.' Sudden anger brought Buchanan to his feet. 'As well as the Unicorn, I own the Roath Court in Piccadilly, not to mention hotels in Bath, Manchester and Edinburgh. Security is paramount in all of them. Unlike Griselda, I'd never employ women to do jobs that only men can handle. Every hotel of mine has former police officers on duty twenty-four hours a day. That's why I'd never be in the kind of unholy mess that she is now in. Griselda Fleetwood has only herself to blame.' His mood changed instantly and he beamed at Keedy. 'It was good to meet you, Sergeant. You've no need to come here again . . .'

Ellen Marmion had been struck by what her friend, Rene Bridger, had told her. When she went into the library, therefore, Ellen immediately began to search for a novel called *The Invasion of 1910*. It was on a shelf of recently returned books. The author was William Le Queux but, like her friend, Ellen had no idea how to pronounce the surname. She simply went to the desk and had the book stamped. On the walk home, she was in two minds, not knowing if she should actually read it or if it might be more sensible to exchange it at once for a romantic novel. The latter would be in no danger of upsetting her. At the same time, it was unlikely to throw new light on the wartime situation.

*The Invasion of 1910* had been so realistic that it had unsettled Rene Bridger at a deep level. Ellen decided that it might teach her something she ought to know. To that end, she fought off the urge to take it back to the library and carried it swiftly home. Once inside the house, she put down her basket, took out the book and sat at the kitchen table to read it. When she opened the first page, however, something dropped out and fluttered to the ground. Ellen bent down to pick it up.

After his discussion with the manager at the stricken hotel, Marmion went straight back to Scotland Yard. He found the superintendent seated at his desk with his head in his hands. When the inspector entered the room after knocking, Chatfield took time to realise that he had a visitor. Sitting upright, he looked at Marmion as if he was a complete stranger.

'Are you all right, sir?' asked the inspector, worriedly.

'Yes, yes, of course I am.'

'You look rather peaky, that's all.'

'I feel fine,' rasped Chatfield, 'so you can stop staring at me like that.' He adjusted his tie. 'How did you get on?'

'It was an afternoon of surprises, sir.'

'Did you get to meet Lady Brice-Cadmore?'

'I was too late to do that,' said Marmion. 'She died three years ago.'

'*Died?*'

'She's buried in the local churchyard. I took the trouble to read the inscription on her gravestone. The mason had chiselled a pair of doves into the marble. Lady Brice-Cadmore adored birds, it seems. And so did her husband.'

Marmion went on to describe his visit in detail and described how aggrieved Sir Godfrey had been when he learnt that someone was pretending to be his wife. Having delivered his account of the trip to Berkshire, Marmion told the superintendent about his second visit to the Lotus Hotel. When mention was made of the hotel's owner, Chatfield let out a groan of despair.

'Mrs Fleetwood sounds like an exceptional woman,' said Marmion.

'She was far too exceptional for me,' confessed the other.

'You've met her, I believe.'

'It was like having an army of occupation in my office.'

'Mr Chell spoke of her with the utmost respect.'

'I have sympathy for the man,' said Chatfield. 'Having to work for someone like that is a punishment I wouldn't wish on my worst enemies. She must operate a reign of terror at the hotel.'

'That's not the case at all, sir. The manager was full of praise for her. He said that she was both efficient and approachable.'

'Well, *I* wouldn't care to approach her, I can tell you that.'

Chatfield gave him an edited version of her visit to Scotland Yard to claim that a rival hotelier had been behind the murder and the disappearance of a guest.

'I sent the sergeant to interview the man,' he explained. 'According to Mrs Fleetwood, he should be clapped in irons and thrown into a cell. She actually tried to insist on being present at the arrest.'

'An arrest is unlikely, sir.'

'I'm sure it is, Inspector. She and Mr Buchanan have been engaged in a feud of some kind, but I simply don't believe most of what she said about him.'

'Sergeant Keedy will find out if he's a credible suspect or not.'

'He will *always* be a credible suspect to Mrs Fleetwood. She did give us the names of three other hoteliers but, in her estimation, this fellow, Buchanan, is the real villain.'

Heaving a sigh, Chatfield sat back in his chair and ran an absent-minded hand through his hair, disturbing his centre parting as he did so. He went off into a reverie. After waiting patiently for a short while, Marmion prodded him out of it with a question.

'Is there any word from the laboratory, sir?'

Chatfield shook himself awake. 'What's that, Inspector?'

'I was asking about the post-mortem.'

'That won't be completed until late this evening, I'm afraid, but one thing is now beyond doubt. She was definitely killed by poison and it wouldn't have been a gentle death.'

'Let's hope that someone identifies her very soon.'

'We can't rely on that happening, Inspector.'

'She's a married woman, sir. A husband will be missing her.'

'Not necessarily,' said Chatfield. 'There's a war on, remember. Most men of his age will be in uniform. That means he may not even be alive. And if he *is* alive, he may not be in this country.'

'What makes you think that, sir?'

'When the pathologist removed her clothing, he saw that it was made in Paris. It looks as if the deceased – her husband as well, perhaps – might be French.'

Having confided the details of her failed romance at last, Iris Goodliffe was a different person. The haunted look on her face had disappeared and much of her old ebullience had gradually returned. She was able to laugh for the first time in months. Alice was at once relieved and concerned, glad that her friend had finally told her the truth but troubled that Iris had not turned to her immediately after her frightening experience. As they continued their patrol, it was Iris's turn to ask questions.

'Why did Joe finally agree to a date for the wedding?' she asked. 'Did you give him an ultimatum?'

'No,' replied Alice. 'I've tried that before and it doesn't work.'

'So he came round to the idea of his own free will, is that it?'

'Not exactly – a lot of persuasion was needed.'

'Why was he dragging his heels? When two people love each other as much as you both do, they should be desperate to be together.'

'Joe wants us to find a house first.'

'That shouldn't be difficult.'

'We both have jobs we like, Iris. And the sort of house we have in mind won't be cheap. We'd like to live in a nice area and that costs money. Then there's the problem of furnishing it, of course. We've both started saving madly.'

'At least you know when you'll walk down the aisle now.'

'Yes, it makes such a difference.'

'It's such a pity that your brother won't be there.'

'We don't know that for sure.'

'I thought you'd given up hope of ever seeing him again.'

'Situations can change.'

'But he's made no attempt to get in touch with the family.'

'It won't stop us looking for Paul,' said Alice, stoutly. 'We'll never give up. My father has circulated a description of him to every police force in the country.'

'Then why has nobody ever caught sight of him?'

'Paul is not the only missing person, Iris. There are untold numbers of them, most of whom don't wish to be found. Then there are deserters from the army. They've got even more reason to go to ground.'

'Yes – they'll face a death sentence.'

Before she could make a comment, Alice was distracted by the sight of two uniformed officers turning into the street thirty yards or more ahead of them. Almost immediately, the policemen came to a halt, then went quickly back around the corner.

'Did you see who that was?' asked Alice.

'No, I didn't.'

'Unless my eyes deceived me, it was PC Beckett.'

Iris was alarmed. 'Are you *sure*?'

'Yes, I am, and you should be pleased.'

'Why?'

'*He* was the one who dodged out of the way, Iris. You've no need to be afraid of him any more. Doug Beckett is too scared to face you.'

Once she'd started to read the book, Ellen Marmion couldn't stop. The details of the supposed invasion of England were so convincing that they took on the solidity of established fact. She was shocked at the audacious way that the German army had planned its attack on Britain and taken it completely by surprise. Ellen had no difficulty in believing the horror stories she'd heard of the bestial way in which enemy soldiers had treated their captives. The thought that they could and, in the novel, already had invaded England made her tremble all over. She soon came to see why her friend had been so terrified by the book.

Ellen eventually forced herself to put it aside so that she could make a restorative cup of tea. Because her son had fought in the war, she read the newspaper every day to chart its progress, wincing every time she saw the latest details of British casualties. Conflict was no longer something that only happened on foreign soil. Now that German bombers were carrying out daylight raids, it was part of daily life in London. She remembered how frightened she'd been when her husband and Joe Keedy had gone to France to arrest two British soldiers and bring them back to England to face justice. Fortunately, the two detectives had returned unharmed but, if Le Queux's novel was to be believed, they'd come back to a country that was already in the grip of German agents.

When she felt strong enough to read on, Ellen first picked up the handbill that had fallen out of the book. It listed a series of lectures to be given by a man named Quentin Dacey, described as an academic, author, translator and renowned public speaker. The title of his lectures was *The Unseen Hand* and the brief description of their contents showed that his views were very similar to those of William Le Queux. He claimed to understand the German mentality and to have access to secret documents that justified his bold allegations against enemy infiltration. Though she didn't understand what they meant, Ellen was duly impressed by the abbreviated qualifications after Dacey's name. The photograph of him showed a once-handsome, balding, poised man of middle years with an aura of distinction about him. His eyes burnt with conviction.

Ellen was entranced. She looked down at the dates of his lectures and noted their venues. *The Invasion of 1910* had had a real impact on her. Quentin Dacey might be able to explain how true its unnerving claims really were. Her eyes had been opened.

Ellen wanted to know more.

# CHAPTER NINE

After learning of the crisis at the hotel, Rex Chell had quickly adapted to the emergency. There was no whiff of panic about him. He was calm, controlled and resourceful. With oil needed to pour on troubled waters, he seemed to have an inexhaustible supply of it. His example helped to steady the nerves of the staff and, in her own way, Lena Gosling did the same. She rallied her charges. Anyone entering the lobby would have seen hotel employees going quietly about their usual business. To the naked eye, nothing was amiss.

Griselda Fleetwood was less adept at concealing her emotions. When she entered the Lotus, she was still throbbing with indignation. The manager escorted her swiftly into his office.

'I've already had the locks on the relevant doors changed,' he said. 'Someone must have had a key to one of our three exits. Well, it won't be any use to them now.'

'We must tighten security in every way.'

'Everything is in hand, Mrs Fleetwood.'

'What of the guests?' she asked. 'Have any of them left?'

'That was inevitable, I'm afraid. I managed to soothe most of them at first, but a few had second thoughts and checked out. It was the sight of detectives flitting about that upset them. Talking of which, Inspector Marmion popped in here again. He brought some disturbing news.'

'We've already had enough of that.'

'I suspect that there's more to come,' he warned.

'Why?'

Chell told her about Marmion's visit to the former home of Lady Brice-Cadmore. When she heard that a guest had been brazenly impersonating a dead woman, she was flabbergasted. She simply couldn't believe that anyone would dare to practise such deceit at the Lotus.

'It's so *uncivilised*,' she said, wrinkling her nose in disgust.

'I suppose that one has to admire the barefaced audacity of it.'

'Don't ask me for admiration. I despise the creature.'

'The odd thing is that she resembled the real Lady Brice-Cadmore.'

'How do you know that?'

'The inspector borrowed a photograph of her from her husband.'

'That was enterprising of him. I commend his initiative.' She rolled her eyes. 'I can't speak so well of his colleagues. They were floundering.'

'What happened at Scotland Yard?'

Taking a deep breath, she launched into an attack on Chatfield and Keedy for refusing to take her accusations seriously. Their ignorance of the hotel trade, and the dog-eat-dog culture at the heart of it, meant that their investigation was bound to be flawed. It was only by cracking the whip over them that she'd achieved a concession.

'They finally agreed to confront Mr Buchanan.'

'His name was bound to come to mind,' he said, choosing his words with care, 'because we know that he's been casting covetous glances at the Lotus ever since it opened. But there are easier ways to put pressure on us than by stooping to murder.'

'Oh, he wouldn't do the deed himself,' she said, contemptuously. 'He'd hire some thug. I just know that he's involved somehow.'

'We don't as yet have any evidence of that.'

She tensed. 'Are you disagreeing with me?'

'Not at all, Mrs Fleetwood,' he said, hastily.

'I spent years planning this hotel. Nobody is going to steal it.'

He ventured a smile. 'I sincerely hope not. It's a joy to work here and to provide unparalleled service to our guests. As it happens,' he continued, 'I may have stumbled on something that supports your theory about Mr Buchanan.'

'Go on.'

'Well, we've always been able to rely on the loyalty of our staff. There's a constant change of personnel in other hotels but not at the Lotus. That's because every single applicant was carefully scrutinised before any offer of employment was made. I underwent the process myself,' he recalled with a smile. 'It was the most rigorous interview I'd ever faced.'

'You passed with flying colours,' she reminded him.

'Only four members of staff have left this hotel. One of them was clearly unable to stand the pace. Two left in order to get married and had to forfeit their jobs as a result.'

'I want no married women here. It complicates matters.'

'I agree, Mrs Fleetwood. That brings me to Maitland.'

'Who was he?'

'Maitland was – or so I thought – a promising young man. When the war started, he tried to enlist but was refused on medical grounds. He was more intelligent than the average porter and worked hard when he first came to us. Then the trouble started.'

'Trouble?' She was peevish. 'Why wasn't I told about it?'

'There was no need to bother you, Mrs Fleetwood. I dealt with the situation promptly and dismissed Maitland.'

'What had he done?'

'He'd been pestering one of the waitresses.'

'Did she encourage his attentions?'

'Quite the opposite,' he said. 'She was very distressed. When Mrs Gosling alerted me, I sacked Maitland on the spot.'

She frowned. 'I can't see how any of this supports my theory about Mr Buchanan's culpability.'

'Sergeant Keedy asked if any former employees left here with a grudge. I told him that none had done so. I've had second thoughts.'

'Do they concern this young man, Maitland?'

'Yes, Mrs Fleetwood. I did a little detective work of my own. The first thing I did was to recruit Mrs Gosling. She's worked in the business for most of her life and has an encyclopaedic knowledge of who is at which hotel and what position they hold.'

'Did she remember Maitland?'

'Very well.'

'Where is he is now?'

'He's working at the Roath Court Hotel,' said Chell, 'and that could be significant. Maitland has been there since he left here. In short, Mr Buchanan is employing someone who holds a grudge against us and who knows every inch of this hotel.'

Griselda smiled grimly. 'We've got him.'

* * *

68

The first thing that Keedy did when he left Buchanan's house was to buy a copy of the *Evening Standard*. On the drive back to Scotland Yard, he flicked through it. As it had done since the first shots were fired, war dominated the news. There was extensive coverage of the Battle of Passchendaele, which had now become a virtual stalemate. Losses were high on both sides and gains were minimal, often measured in mere hundreds of yards of muddy terrain. Passchendaele – the third battle of Ypres – had come to symbolise the futility of armed conflict. It had now been going on for two months and those who peered cautiously out of their bunkers could see no end in sight.

On one of the inside pages, Keedy found a brief mention of events at the Lotus Hotel. A single paragraph had been inserted at the last moment before the newspaper was printed. The citizens of London would have to wait until the following morning before a longer account of the crime, and a description of the murder victim, were available in various newspapers. Keedy turned the pages until he came to the one that really interested him. He was soon working his way through a long list of advertisements. Taking out the pencil from his notebook, he used it to encircle a couple that interested him.

When he got back to Scotland Yard, he first reported to Chatfield and was amazed by what he was told. As soon as he'd finished with the superintendent, he rushed off to Marmion's office. The inspector was collating all the information they'd so far gathered.

'Ah,' he said, breaking off, 'I was hoping you'd come back soon.'

'Chat has just told me about Lady Brice-Cadmore being dead.'

'I can confirm that, Joe. I stood beside her grave.'

'Somebody *stole* her identity?'

'Unfortunately, she was in no position to protest. Her husband, however, is and he'll be doing so very soon. Sir Godfrey is going to leave his rural retreat for once and come to London. When I first met him,' recalled Marmion, 'he struck me as a mild-mannered old gent, living out his final years in the comfort of his manor house. By the time I'd left, he was starting to breathe fire through his nostrils.'

'Mrs Fleetwood did that,' said Keedy. 'The only way to appease her was to agree to confront the man she's named as the prime suspect.'

'Chat told me about Buchanan. How did you get on with him?'

'It was a waste of time and a bad tactical move.'

'Why?'

'We showed our hand too soon, Harv. I think that Buchanan *could* be a possible suspect, I suppose, but we should have done covert investigation about him before making a direct challenge. To be honest,' admitted Keedy, 'I left his house with egg on my face.'

'What about the other hoteliers mentioned by Mrs Fleetwood?'

'I persuaded Chat that we should leave them alone until we've deployed officers to make discreet enquiries about them. For once, Chat agreed with me.'

'That's a triumph, Joe.'

'The only trouble is that he'll claim it was *his* idea.'

'Ah, well,' said Marmion with a sigh, 'we're used to him doing that. He steals our good ideas then blames us for mistakes that *he* made. But tell me about Fraser Buchanan. What's he like?'

'He's one of those rich, smug, two-faced businessmen who pretend to be your best friend to catch you off balance. To be fair, he clearly knows his trade and thinks that Mrs Fleetwood is a raw newcomer who simply doesn't belong in it. Buchanan has a greasy charm,' said Keedy, 'but he's as hard as nails underneath.'

'Someone should hire a boxing ring and put the two of them in it.'

Keedy laughed. 'I'd pay money to see that fight.'

'Who would you bet on – Mrs Fleetwood or Buchanan?'

'Buchanan – he'd resort to dirty tricks.'

'Is that what he's done at the Lotus?'

Keedy shrugged. 'I wouldn't rule it out,' he said. 'But what's this latest information about the murder victim? Chat says she's French.'

'She was wearing French clothing, it seems, but that doesn't mean she *is* French.'

'No, I suppose not. Her husband wouldn't be the first Englishman to bring back underwear from Paris for his wife.'

'If she *has* a husband, that is.'

'She was wearing a wedding ring, Harv. We both saw it.'

'That means nothing.'

'I don't follow.'

'When I popped in to see how the post-mortem was going on, they were able to give me some more detail. In addition to the poison that killed her, she had a considerable amount of alcohol in her blood. And there's one other discovery.'

'What is it?'

'The woman found dead at the Lotus was a virgin. Whether British or French,' said Marmion, 'there are very few wives like that.'

When she first joined the Women's Police Force, she'd found the idea of spending so much time on her beat quite daunting, but Alice Marmion had soon learnt to cope with being on her feet so long. It was only when she and Iris finished their shift that she felt a touch of fatigue in her legs.

'I'm exhausted,' said Iris, blowing hard. 'You're so much fitter than me, Alice.'

'We both need a sit-down.'

'In my case, it's a lie-down in a hot bath that I need. My feet are like balls of lead.'

'The feeling will soon wear off.'

'We need more resting places in the course of our beat.'

Having signed off, they adjourned to the canteen for a cup of tea. Being able to flop down on a chair was a bonus for both of them. Iris bent down to rub her calves while Alice undid some buttons of her uniform. After a first sip of her tea, Iris sighed.

'I should have been more honest with myself,' she admitted. 'The simple truth is that I'm big, fat and ugly. I should have realised that no man would take a serious interest in me.'

'That's nonsense,' said Alice, hotly. 'You were unlucky to attract the wrong man, that's all.'

'I don't believe that I attracted anybody, Alice.'

'Yes, you did.'

'Doug only pretended to like me. I've got a horrible feeling that he was egged on by his friends. They probably bet him that he'd never get me to . . .' She grimaced. 'He came very close to winning that bet.'

'It was nothing to do with a bet,' insisted Alice. 'PC Beckett has his faults, but he'd never sink that low. I saw the way that he reacted when he caught sight of you. The guilt on his face was obvious.'

'And so it should be.'

'He knows what he did was unforgivable.'

'All I ask is that he keeps out of my way.'

On the verge of a reply, Alice noticed that Inspector Gale was coming towards her. She stiffened instantly. Relations between the two women had always been tense and Alice felt that she was being deliberately picked on by her superior. Because she was such a disciplinarian, Thelma Gale had earned the nickname of Gale Force. Alice had felt its

72

impact many times. On this occasion, however, the inspector was more subdued. She was carrying an envelope.

'This came for you by hand,' she said, giving it to Alice. 'You might remind Sergeant Keedy that we are not a post office. I have a major police operation to run here. He knows the time of your shift. Please ask him to contact you when you are both off duty.'

'Alice *is* off duty now,' Iris interjected.

'Keep out of this, Constable.'

'It's a fair point.'

'I won't tolerate insolence,' warned the other, causing Iris to wilt under her fierce glare. 'Hold your tongue.'

'Thank you, Inspector,' said Alice, keen to save her friend from further reproach. 'It won't happen again.'

'I should hope not.' Her voice softened. 'There's no news of your brother, I take it.'

'No, there isn't.'

'How is your mother coping with the situation?'

'It's . . . causing a lot of stress.'

'That's understandable.'

'If only Paul would tell us where he is and how he's managing.'

'He must have his reasons for not doing so.'

'I'm sure that he does, Inspector.'

'Right,' said the other, 'I'll get on and leave you to read your letter. Don't forget to warn Sergeant Keedy. Oh, and do up those buttons on your uniform. You know my rules.'

Alice obeyed then watched the other woman walk away. As soon as the inspector disappeared from sight, Alice tore open the letter and read it. Her face fell.

'Bad news?' asked Iris.

'Yes,' said Alice. 'Because we haven't seen each other for a fortnight, Joe promised to take me out for a meal this evening. It's had to be cancelled because he's just been assigned to another murder investigation.'

'Oh dear! What rotten luck!'

'I was so desperate to see him.'

'Look at it from another point of view, Alice. It shows how highly thought of he is at Scotland Yard. Joe and your father always get to handle the most important cases. It's a compliment, really.'

'I want to be with the man I love.'

'Then bring forward the wedding. You'll see him every night.'

'Not if he's working on a complex investigation,' said Alice, dejectedly. 'When there's a crisis, he and Daddy seem to be on duty around the clock. They've spent nights at Scotland Yard before now.'

Iris was realistic. 'That's not going to change, is it?'

'No, I'm afraid it isn't.'

'Then you'll just have to make the most of it.'

'I suppose I will,' said Alice, folding the letter. 'I'll have to do what Mummy does.'

'And what's that?'

'Take up knitting and borrow lots of books from the library.'

Ellen Marmion had read an endless number of romantic novels. While they'd given her pleasure of varying degrees, none had stayed in her memory. She couldn't even remember the authors of most of them. William Le Queux was different. His name was etched into her mind for eternity. He'd not only provided her with a thrilling narrative, he'd educated her about the war. She discovered that it was not fought entirely by armed soldiers. German spies and British traitors had played their part unseen. They were still doing it. What Ellen had always thought of as an impregnable country was riddled with enemies.

All of a sudden, she felt under threat. Putting the book aside, she ran to the front door and pushed the two bolts into place. She then checked the back door and every window in the house. Even then there was no sense of safety. Out in the darkness, someone might have the house under surveillance. From now on, she vowed, she had to be suspicious of everyone.

When she returned to the living room, she saw the book on the arm of her chair. There were still several chapters to go. It took minutes before she could muster the courage to pick it up again. *The Invasion of 1910* had frightened her so much that she hesitated to read on. At the same time, she wanted to know the full truth about the German menace. Was the country *really* destined to lose the war? Did the book offer truth or fantasy? Whichever it was, she told herself that she must find out.

With her heart pounding, Ellen started another chapter.

# CHAPTER TEN

In any murder investigation, it was the evidence gathered in the initial twenty-four hours that was vital. At the end of their first long, intensive, exhausting day, Marmion and Keedy were worried. They felt as if they had little to show for their efforts. They were left with far too many unanswered questions and almost no potential suspects. No matter how much they speculated, neither of them could suggest a convincing motive for the murder of one woman – who had not even been a guest at the hotel – and the mysterious disappearance of another, who'd been staying there under a false name. As they reviewed the case in Marmion's office, they were frankly bewildered.

When they reached the head-scratching stage, they lapsed into a sullen silence. Minutes passed before Marmion sat up abruptly and looked across at his companion.

'A penny for them, Joe.'

'I'm not sure my thoughts are worth that much,' said Keedy. 'To be honest, I wasn't thinking about the case. I was worrying about Alice.'

'Why?'

'I'd promised to take her out for a meal this evening.'

'Disappointing the woman you love is part of being a policeman, I'm afraid. We have no control over our lives. I've had to let Ellen down hundreds of times.'

'I hated having to break the bad news to Alice.'

'You'll soon come through the guilty phase and she, in turn, will learn to accept that your life together will be . . . well, let's call it "irregular". Oddly enough,' Marmion went on, 'I was thinking about my daughter as well. It was in connection with this investigation.'

'But Alice has nothing to do with it.'

'Yes, and that's a pity.'

'Pity?'

'We're dealing with a case involving two women in a hotel with an entirely female clientele. One was murdered there and the other vanished into thin air after using a third woman's name as an alias. On top of all that, the Lotus is actually owned by a woman.'

'Don't remind me.'

'Yes, I know you found Mrs Fleetwood a bit overwhelming, but do you take my point?'

'To be honest, Harv, I don't.'

'We're male detectives trying to get into the minds of women. In other words, we're severely handicapped. What we need are the insights that only another woman can bring.'

Keedy gaped. 'You're surely not suggesting that we ask Alice to join us?' he said. 'Chat would go berserk at the very idea, and so would the commissioner.'

'I'm not saying that we co-opt Alice. She's had no training as a detective but she – or someone like her – could be an asset in a case with so many females involved. As you may have noticed,' he added with a smile, 'my daughter is an intelligent young woman. When the brains were divided between her and Paul, she got more than her fair share. Our son has his own virtues, mind you, but he can't compete with Alice.'

Keedy shook his head. 'Women will never become detectives.'

'I disagree.'

'Think of the danger involved.'

'Allan Pinkerton took that into account, yet he still employed women agents. With their help, he built up the largest private detective agency in the world. During the American Civil War, his female operatives were very effective as spies for the secret service.'

'What's that got to do with the Lotus Hotel?'

'It shows that, given the chance, women can do our job just as well as we can.'

'But they won't *get* that chance.'

'Then there's only one option left.'

'Is there?'

'Yes – in order to crack this case, we must learn to think the way that a woman would. Why, for instance,' asked Marmion, 'did so many of them choose to stay at a place like the Lotus Hotel?'

'Perhaps they're all enchanted by the manager.'

'I'm serious, Joe. We need to find out the answer.'

Details of the murder crept onto the front pages of most of the morning newspapers, albeit occupying much less space than the latest bulletin from the war. Reaction was immediate. When she called at the hotel that morning, Griselda Fleetwood heard the bad tidings in the privacy of the manager's office. Rex Chell was apologetic.

'Two guests who'd each booked in to stay for a week have already left,' he said, 'and we've had three telegrams cancelling reservations.'

'Don't they realise it's perfectly safe here now?'

'It's a natural response, Mrs Fleetwood. We can't really blame them.'

'I can,' she said, angrily. 'It's so disloyal of them. I've a good mind to cross the deserters off our list.'

'That would be a big mistake,' he argued. 'It's only by wooing them back that we'll get the stigma removed from the Lotus.'

'There's no hope of doing that until the murder is solved.'

'We simply have to remain calm under fire.'

'Don't tell me to remain calm,' she growled, 'because I'm seething. We both know who's behind all this. The police promised to confront him but I'm not sure if they actually did so. I intended to go to Scotland Yard first thing, but my husband felt that he should go instead. In some ways, he can be more persuasive than me.'

'I'm glad to hear that Mr Fleetwood is helping us.'

'It's a crisis, man. We need all hands to the pumps.'

'Did you mention Maitland?'

'Of course, I did,' she retorted. 'I want the police to have every scrap of evidence we can find. Thanks to you, we've found a clear link between Maitland and Fraser Buchanan. My husband will pass on that information.'

'It may just be a coincidence, of course.'

'I don't believe in coincidences.'

'And Maitland is hardly the type to murder someone.'

'He knows the Lotus well and could advise the killer how to get in here at night. He's tied up in this somehow.'

Chell was beginning to harbour doubts but it was no time to voice them. When she was in such a hostile mood, it was better to agree with her. She picked up the newspaper on the desk and scowled.

'Look at that headline,' she said, jabbing a finger at it. 'HOTEL IN CHAOS. What kind of an advertisement is that for us? Before the day is out, I'll be speaking to the editor about it.'

'Don't antagonise the press, Mrs Fleetwood.'

'They deserve it.'

'Journalists always have more ink,' he warned.

'I'm simply demanding the right of reply,' she said, discarding the newspaper. 'Misleading headlines can cause us real and lasting damage.' She remembered something. 'You said that two of our guests checked out. Who were they?'

'Mrs Prior-Pitt was the first to go.'

'What was the name of the other?'

'Lady Carvington,' he replied.

'That's deplorable!' she cried. 'I play bridge with Phyllis Carvington. I hoped I could rely on her.'

'I daresay that Lady Carvington will return in due course, when things settle down. But there is some good news,' he went on, trying to cheer her up. 'After one horrendous night at the hotel, we had a very quiet and restful one.'

'How do you know?'

'I took the trouble of spending the night here.'

She was impressed. 'That was very good of you, Mr Chell.'

'I did it for two reasons. One was to reassure the guests and the other was to see exactly what goes on here after midnight. It enabled me to check on the night porter, for instance.'

'Did he do his job properly?'

'I couldn't fault Rogan. He was vigilant.'

'It's a shame he wasn't more vigilant on the previous night.'

'He has to be careful, Mrs Fleetwood,' he explained, 'and exercise due discretion. The last thing our guests want is a man padding endlessly around the corridors. As a rule, he does a circuit of the hotel every three hours. Last night, I made him do the rounds every hour.'

'Was there anything to report?'

'Nothing at all – it was eerily silent.'

She pulled a face. 'That's because so many guests have fled.'

Before she could bewail their misfortune again, there was a knock on the door and it opened to allow Millie Jenks to enter with a huge bouquet of flowers. She curtsied before handing them over.

'These came for you, Mrs Fleetwood.'

'They're lovely!' said the other, inspecting them before inhaling their scent. 'At least *someone* is offering me sympathy.' When she read the card, her voice became a snarl of rage. 'The flowers are from *him*! Buchanan is rubbing salt into the wound that he inflicted on me in the first place.' She thrust the bouquet back into Millie's arms. 'Take them out of my sight, girl, and throw them in the dustbin.'

Experience had taught Ellen Marmion that there were times when her husband didn't want to indulge in idle chatter. His mind was elsewhere, struggling to make sense of the latest investigation. Marmion was polite and even attentive for fleeting moments, but she could see that he was in no mood to discuss the latest book she'd been reading. Though it had had a profound effect on her, he would dismiss it out of hand as an irrelevance and chide her for taking its message so seriously. Ellen, therefore, had to keep her troubling thoughts to herself.

Sections of the book had been so distressing that she had skipped whole paragraphs. By the same token, there were passages so startling that she read them again and again. A slow reader, she'd spent most of the day with *The Invasion of 1910* and had still not reached the halfway point. That was mainly because she needed frequent stops to make herself a cup of tea and to reflect on what the author was claiming. As soon as her husband left the house that morning, she was drawn back inescapably to the doom-laden novel.

When she broke off after another harrowing chapter, Ellen looked at the handbill she was using as a bookmark. Quentin Dacey's face intrigued her. Above all else, he looked like a man who could be trusted. William Le Queux had chosen to send his message in a work of fiction. Dacey, by contrast, preached the same sermon but he did so from a public platform. In doing that, he would have to offer evidence in support of his claims. He could be questioned. Ellen noticed that the next time he was due to speak was on the following day in central London. She was at once tempted and timorous, eager to hear more about German penetration of Britain yet apprehensive about what she might find out.

With the handbill in place, she closed the book and set it aside. Then she went into the hall and looked at herself in the mirror. Two men had set out to open the eyes of the British public. Did Ellen have the courage to listen to them or would it be more sensible to return the book to the library with the handbill still in it?

She stood there dithering.

Orders from the superintendent had to be obeyed but Chatfield's advice was a different matter. It could, theoretically, be ignored and that was often Marmion's way of dealing with it. Keedy, however, had liked the suggestion that he should interview the night porter at his home rather than at his place of work. It was wise counsel. Caught unawares, Rogan might not be quite so well defended. There was another advantage for Keedy. He'd be able to ask him questions that he could never have put to the man in front of Chell and Millie Jenks.

The house was in the seedier part of Paddington, a small, end-of-terrace dwelling in need of repair. Keedy noticed the perished brickwork and the missing slates. Leonard Rogan clearly moved between two disparate worlds. By day, he lived in a working-class community with all the deprivation that that implied; by night, he was under the same roof as titled ladies who'd left their country mansions to spend leisure time in the capital. In the course of twenty-four hours, the night porter moved between squalor and luxury.

Keedy saw a crack in one of the dust-covered glass panels on the front door. He used the knocker, then stood back. Voices could be heard from inside, then footsteps scurried along the passageway. The door was opened by a short, stooping, scrawny woman in a pinafore and a turban. At the sight of a well-dressed man on her doorstep, she almost cowered. While Keedy was raising his hat and introducing himself, Rogan came into view wearing a vest above a pair of pyjama trousers. He was startled to see the detective.

'I'll handle this, Win,' he said, dismissing his wife with a flick of the hand. She vanished immediately. Rogan narrowed his lids. 'What are you doing here, Sergeant?'

'I wanted another chat with you, sir.'

'You could have come to the hotel.'

'That's exactly what I did – to get your home address.'

'The place is in a bit of a state,' said Rogan, embarrassed. 'My wife hasn't had time to clean it yet.'

'I'm not here to inspect the property. I just need to ask a few questions. If you'd rather talk out here in the street, that's fine with me.'

'No, no, you'd better come in.'

He stood back so that Keedy could go into the house, then pointed to the living room. Rogan excused himself and went off to put something else on. His visitor found himself standing in the middle of a cluttered room with the lingering smell of fried food. A mottled three-piece suite competed for space with a dining table, four chairs, a smaller table covered in old newspapers and an empty coal scuttle. Faded with time, the wallpaper had a floral pattern. The only thing on display was a framed sampler with HOME SWEET HOME sewn neatly into it.

There was a loud bang on the front door and Mrs Rogan reacted immediately, darting out of the kitchen to open the door. When he glanced into the passageway, Keedy saw her helping an old man into the house. Supporting himself on two walking sticks, he struggled towards the kitchen. Aware that Keedy was watching, Rogan's wife offered an explanation.

'It's my father-in-law. He lives with us.'

Aided by her, the old man hobbled out of view.

When Rogan reappeared, he was wearing an old dressing gown and had put some slippers on his bare feet. He seemed to have recovered from the earlier shock of seeing Keedy and even managed a smile.

'Sit down,' he said.

Keedy lowered himself onto a chair but Rogan stayed on his feet.

'What did you want to ask me, Sergeant?'

'Well, first of all, I wondered if you had any trouble last night?'

'None at all,' replied the other. 'It was as quiet as a tomb. We didn't hear a peep from the guests.'

'*We?*'

'The manager stayed the night.'

'That was kind of him.'

'He felt that it was his duty.'

'Mr Chell is an interesting man. How did he come to get the job in the first place?'

'It was the same way that I did,' said Rogan. 'We were both spotted by Mrs Fleetwood. Before she opened the Lotus, she went scouting for staff. She picked me up at the Vanbrugh and was impressed by Mr Chell when she saw him working as deputy manager at the Savoy.'

'What sort of man is he?'

'You've met him.'

'Yes, but I only saw what was on the surface.'

'Mr Chell is the best hotel manager I've ever worked with.'

'I'm not talking about his fitness for his job,' said Keedy. 'What's he like as a person? Is he friendly, caring, kind to his staff, or is he bossy, demanding and overbearing? How would you describe his character?'

'He's . . . good to us,' said Rogan without any real conviction. 'And he's always honest.'

'Do you like him?'

'It's not my place to like or dislike him, Sergeant.'

'Is he married?'

'People like Mr Chell don't get married.'

'Yet he obviously likes women.'

'He prefers his job,' said Rogan, perching on the arm of the sofa. 'Nothing gets in the way of that.'

Keedy took out his notepad and flicked through the pages until he came to the ones he wanted. They contained details of Rogan's original statement. When he took Rogan through it line by line, the night porter made a few changes, growing peevish when Keedy asked him why he hadn't mentioned the new facts at the time of the interview.

'I was shaken up, Sergeant,' he said. 'Wouldn't *you* have been in the circumstances? I was as accurate as I could be.'

'You've just made some important corrections. Why was that?'

'Certain things came back to me.'

'And are there any more "certain things" you forgot to tell when we spoke yesterday morning?'

Rogan bridled. 'Why are you hounding me?' he asked. '*I* didn't kill that woman. I'd never set eyes on her before. Shouldn't you be out trying to find the killer instead of bothering me?'

'No,' said Keedy. 'Without realising it, you may have information that could lead us to the killer. I'm just trying to tease it out.'

'I've told you all I know – I swear it.'

Keedy studied him carefully. He looked hunted and resentful. Without his uniform, he'd lost his protective shell and didn't seem at all like the helpful hotel employee interviewed the previous day. Keedy had clearly scared him and wondered why. He tried a new tack.

'How do you get on with Mrs Fleetwood?'

'I see very little of her.'

'She struck me as the sort of woman who keeps a beady eye on everybody she employs. Correct?' Rogan nodded. 'What do you think of her as a hotel owner?'

'I'm glad to work for Mrs Fleetwood.'

'Don't you find her domineering?'

'No, I don't.'

'She's very formidable.'

'You have to be in the hotel trade.'

'What's her husband like?' asked Keedy. 'He's an unusual man if he can cope with someone like Mrs Fleetwood.'

Rogan smirked. 'Mr Fleetwood can cope with anyone,' he said. 'If you think his wife is a handful, you should meet him. He wears the trousers in that marriage, I can tell you.'

When he heard that Harold Fleetwood had called on him, Chatfield quailed slightly. Disturbing memories of the visit of Fleetwood's wife flooded back. Before he asked for his visitor to be shown into his office, the superintendent sent for Marmion, feeling the need for moral support. In the event, both men were pleasantly surprised by the newcomer. He was a big, broad-shouldered man in his sixties, impeccably dressed and well groomed. He oozed prosperity. While his wife had been loud and demanding, Fleetwood was subdued and respectful. When he shook hands with each of them in turn, he looked deep into their eyes. Marmion felt that the financier was weighing him in the balance.

'I believe that my wife came to see you yesterday,' said Fleetwood. 'Not unnaturally, she was in a state of high excitement. That probably made her more truculent than she needed to be. I apologise on her behalf.'

'Mrs Fleetwood was entitled to know how the investigation was going,' said Chatfield. 'Unfortunately, she derided our efforts. What she perceived as our lack of progress irked her. She urged us to arrest a man named Fraser Buchanan.'

'Did you question him?'

'I sent someone to interview him, sir. Sergeant Keedy found no grounds whatsoever for making an arrest.'

'Buchanan is a tricky customer.'

'Are you also claiming that he was party to the murder?' asked Marmion.

'Not at all,' replied Fleetwood. 'He may be completely innocent, though I daresay it's not beyond the bounds of possibility that he *might* have been involved somehow.'

'Why do you say that, sir?'

'I know him only too well, Inspector. As it happens, Mr Chell, the manager of the Lotus, has come up with a piece of information that may be relevant.'

'What is it?' asked Chatfield.

'A young man named Ian Maitland used to be employed at the Lotus. For reasons I won't go into now, Chell was forced to sack the man. Maitland had a streak of malice in him, apparently. To put it another way, he has an axe to grind.'

'Is there any connection between this man and Mr Buchanan?'

'Maitland works as a porter at the Roath Court Hotel.'

'So?'

'It's owned by Fraser Buchanan.'

'Is he likely to associate with a mere porter?'

'He'd make use of anyone who served his purpose. Maitland worked at the Lotus when it first opened. He knows every nook and cranny of the building.'

'I see . . .'

'Thank you for telling us, Mr Fleetwood,' said Marmion. 'It's something we need to look into, if only to eliminate this man.'

'That's fair enough,' said the other. 'I see that there was an appeal for help in the newspapers this morning, along with descriptions both of the murder victim and of the missing guest. Has anyone come forward as a result?'

'Not yet, sir.'

'Then perhaps the British public needs a little encouragement. My wife and I would like to offer a substantial reward to anyone who can identify the dead woman and tell us the whereabouts of the one who vanished from the hotel.'

'That would certainly help,' agreed Chatfield.

'And it will definitely provoke a response,' added Marmion, 'even though most of it will be useless to us. The promise of money always brings in a lot of false claims. Hopefully, it will also elicit the details we desperately need.'

Marmion went on to give him a summary of the evidence they'd so far gathered. He told Fleetwood that full details of the post-mortem would only be released at the inquest. All he was prepared to say was that the victim had been poisoned. How the woman came to be in the hotel, he didn't know but they were exploring a number of theories. Fleetwood was disappointed to be told so little about the investigation.

'I was hoping to take good news back to my wife.'

'We are working around the clock,' said Chatfield. 'Nobody could do more than that, sir.'

'We want results.'

'A case like this can only be solved by the slow, steady, patient accumulation of evidence. Following in my footsteps, Inspector Marmion has become a master of that process.'

'So when might we expect some good news?' said Fleetwood, arching an eyebrow. 'Next week? Next month? Next *year*?'

'There's no need for sarcasm, Mr Fleetwood.'

'For you and the inspector,' said the visitor, injecting steel into his voice for the first time, 'this is simply one more murder investigation. It's much more than that to me. It's an operation to rescue my wife's dream of running the best hotel in London.' He got to his feet and rose to his full height. 'Bear that in mind, gentlemen.'

'We don't need prompting, sir,' said Marmion. 'We're as anxious to solve this crime as you and Mrs Fleetwood are.'

'Our position is simple. We demand results, the sooner the better. As for that reward I mentioned,' he went on, pointedly, 'I'll discuss the amount with the commissioner. Sir Edward and I are old friends, incidentally. We happen to be members of the same club.'

Turning on his heel, he swept out of the office and left the door wide open. Chatfield exchanged a glance with Marmion. They could see trouble ahead.

# CHAPTER ELEVEN

Sir Godfrey Brice-Cadmore had been so infuriated by the news that someone had been posing as his late wife that he was determined to do what he could to catch the impostor. The moment that Marmion had left Elmstead Manor, therefore, the older man had emptied drawers and burrowed into cupboards in order to find every photograph album or souvenir of his beloved wife. He also began a careful search through his diaries for the last five years. Somewhere in the mass of precious memories he gathered was, he believed, a clue as to the identity of the confidence trickster, the woman who'd not only stolen her name but who also contrived to look like Lady Brice-Cadmore.

By the following morning, his fury had still not subsided. He felt the need to see Marmion again and pass on what he felt were legitimate suspicions of certain individuals. To that end, he was driven to Swindon and bought a first-class ticket to Paddington. On the journey there, he reviewed the history of his courtship and marriage, taking solace from the fact that theirs had been a happy union based on similar tastes and a readiness by both parties to compromise. Whenever he heard favourite pieces of music or saw particular species of birds, he was reminded of special moments shared with his wife. Those moments had to be protected from interlopers. He owed it to his wife to do everything in his power to find the person who'd dared to impersonate her.

Sir Godfrey wanted revenge.

No sooner had Keedy returned to Scotland Yard than he was sent off on another errand. Marmion asked him to go to the Roath Court Hotel in search of one of its porters. Keedy was more careful this time. Having been embarrassed at his meeting with Fraser Buchanan, he didn't wish to repeat the experience at one of the man's hotels. Discreet research was in order rather than a direct confrontation. To that end, he went to the Roath Court and found it much larger and altogether busier than the Lotus. The plush lobby was a hive of activity. Guests were arriving or leaving, and porters were working at full stretch to carry luggage in and out of the building. Keedy chose an armchair from which to watch.

All that he knew about Ian Maitland was what Fleetwood had said during his visit to Scotland Yard. The porter was a young man. Scant though the information was, it turned out to be enough because only one of the porters was in his twenties. The rest were clearly older. Maitland turned out to be a smart, eager, good-looking individual with a sharp eye for a guest in need of assistance. He also had a willing smile. Keedy watched him handle heavy suitcases with ease. Maitland gave every indication of enjoying his work and earned himself regular tips for his pleasant manner and efficiency.

There was, however, another side to his character. When he thought that nobody was looking, Maitland would sidle up to one of his fellow porters and make a comment out of the side of his mouth. It was a technique Keedy had often seen being used by prisoners who were able to communicate to each other without appearing to do so. In Maitland's case, his remarks always produced a snigger from his friends. The helpful young porter evidently had a vulgar streak.

Keedy bided his time until he saw Maitland standing alone by the lift. Getting up, he drifted across to him.

'What's the food like in this hotel?' he asked.

'I'm told that it's excellent, sir.'

'Don't you know from experience?'

Maitland grinned. 'I can't afford to eat here on my wage.'

'It must be galling for you, watching all these wealthy people come and go. In your position, I'd be envious of them.'

'I simply do what I'm paid to do, sir,' said Maitland, evenly. 'Are you staying here?'

'No, but a friend of mine is. He's arriving this afternoon. I wanted to do a little research before he actually arrives.'

'The Roath Court is one of the finest hotels in London.'

'That's what it says in the advertisements.'

'It's true, sir.'

'Have you always worked here?'

'No,' replied the other, 'I started off, at the age of fourteen, doing odd jobs at the Regent Palace. When my friends joined the army years later, I tried to go with them but I got turned down because I'm almost blind in one eye. So I stayed at the Regent Palace until I got a promotion to a smaller hotel in Chelsea.'

'Which one?'

'You won't have heard of it, sir. The Lotus is exclusively for women – rich, well-bred ladies who are used to high standards. I got bored there after a while and applied for a job here. There's a lot more going on at the Roath Court.'

'My friend will be glad about that.'

'We'll look after him,' said Maitland with a confident smile.

His gaze was then diverted by an elderly man who'd just entered the lobby with a bulky suitcase. Maitland went quickly off to help him. Keedy left the hotel quietly. He'd learnt enough.

There was a discernible difference in Iris Goodliffe. In manner and appearance, she was much more alert and inclined to laugh at anything she thought remotely amusing. Alice Marmion was pleased to see the change in her friend and glad that she'd been largely responsible for it. Having bared her soul to Alice, Iris had felt a sense of release. The irony was that, while one woman felt liberated from her obsession with an unpleasant experience in her private life, the other had become more and more entangled with it. Iris had been the victim of a frightening sexual assault. In Alice's opinion, simple justice dictated that Douglas Beckett should be punished in some way. When she raised the subject yet again, it was waved away by her beat partner.

'I don't want to hear Doug's name ever again,' she said.

'He molested you, Iris.'

'You hardly need to tell me that. I'd rather put it behind me and concentrate on happier things – your wedding, for instance.'

'That's not until next year.'

'You can never start planning early enough.' She nudged her companion. 'Are you going to invite Gale Force?'

Alice gave a hollow laugh. 'What do you think?'

'She'd love to come, I'm sure.'

'It's my wedding, not my funeral.'

Iris let out a cackle of joy, something she hadn't done for a long time. People looked in their direction, wondering what had produced such a high, sustained, piercing noise. The two policewomen carried on walking. Iris became serious.

'I hope that he *is* able to come,' she said.

'Who?'

'Your brother, of course. According to you, he used to like Joe a lot and a family ought to be together at a time like that.'

'We're not really sure if Paul is still part of our family,' said Alice, softly. 'He's turned his back on us.'

'He loves you too much to do that.'

'I wish that were true.'

'He'll surely get in touch with you at Christmas.'

'Will he?'

'Paul is your *brother*.'

'*We* know that – he doesn't.'

'Oh, I feel so sorry for you, Alice.'

'There's no need,' said the other, brightening. 'In marrying Joe, I'll get what I want more than anything in the world. Paul is the one to feel sorry for. He's got no money, no purpose and no future to speak of. He's drifting through life like a tramp.'

'I always used to think that tramps led an adventurous life. They shuffle off all responsibilities and have the freedom of the open road.'

'Open roads are subject to rain, sleet and snow. I don't see any adventure in that. Paul's life must be a daily struggle.'

'He'll survive,' Iris predicted. 'He's like you. He's got inner strength. And didn't you tell me once that he was good-looking?'

'Well, yes, I suppose that he is.'

'Then he won't be alone for long, will he? Handsome young men are few and far between. Most of them went off to war. Paul will have his pick of girlfriends.'

Alice winced. What she hadn't told her friend was that Paul had been sacked from his job on a farm in Warwickshire because he'd got involved with the farmer's daughter. Her parents were angry that an itinerant worker like Paul had dared to take an interest in the girl when he had nothing whatsoever to offer her.

'My brother's had bad experiences with girlfriends,' she confessed. 'In any case, what woman would want to share the kind of life that he leads? He's on his own, Iris, and it will stay that way.'

Harvey Marmion was not surprised to see Sir Godfrey Brice-Cadmore but he was worried about his condition. To reach the detective's office, the old man had climbed two flights of stairs and they'd taken their toll on him. He was breathing heavily and looked frail. Marmion helped him into a chair and asked if he would like a cup of tea. Sir Godfrey waved the offer away. What had taxed his strength, he claimed, was the large leather satchel he'd brought with him. When he'd got his breath back, he put it on his lap and took out some diaries and photograph albums. He stacked them on the desk.

'We don't have time for reminiscences,' warned Marmion.

'I've brought you evidence, Inspector.' He tapped the pile in front of him. 'Somewhere in here may be the woman that you want.'

'How do you know?'

'Well, it stands to reason that she must be someone who actually met my wife. How else could she take such trouble to look like her?'

'That's true, Sir Godfrey.'

'It prompted me to search the family archives. I found two women who do have more than a fleeting resemblance to my wife and an entry in my diary that refers to one of them.'

'What date was that entry?'

'It was four years ago.'

'That was before Lady Brice-Cadmore died.'

'I know. Fate can be so cruel. In the year before her death, my wife had never looked so beautiful. She was blooming. It seemed impossible that she'd pass away in the following January.'

'Had there been no warning signs?'

'None at all, I fear. That's what made it so hard to bear.'

'You have my profound sympathy,' said Marmion.

'Thank you, Inspector.'

'Now then, what exactly have you brought me?'

'I've brought you something that I hope may be of use to you,' said Sir Godfrey, opening an album and flicking through the pages with a trembling hand. 'Here we are,' he added, stopping at a photograph of a group of people standing in front of some trees and wearing outdoor clothing. He turned the album around so that Marmion could see it. 'My wife is beside me in the centre.'

'I recognise her from that photograph you kindly lent me.'

'Now look at the woman on the extreme left.'

Marmion did as he was told. 'You're right,' he said. 'There is a resemblance to Lady Brice-Cadmore. This lady is the same height, weight and roughly the same age. What's her name?'

'Cecily Prentice. She was only an acquaintance, really. My wife took pity on her when Cecily suffered a tragedy. That's how she came to be on that birdwatching expedition with us, you see. We felt sorry for her. After that, she faded out of our lives.'

'You mentioned a tragedy.'

'Yes,' said the other, grimacing. 'It was a bad business in every way. Her husband was, as far as we knew, a decent, dependable man who indulged his wife in every way. What none of us realised was that he was a compulsive gambler. Year after year, the cards fell in his favour but, eventually, his luck ran out.'

'What happened?'

'He was suddenly up to his neck in debt and in a state of panic. He didn't know which way to turn. Unable to cope with the disgrace, Nigel Prentice shot himself. His family were left virtually penniless.'

'It was kind of your wife to come to the widow's aid.'

'That was the sort of woman she was, always ready to help those in need. In fact,' recalled Sir Godfrey, 'if I remember aright, the coat that Cecily Prentice is wearing in the photograph once belonged to my dear wife. I can give you an exact date of that birdwatching expedition because I recorded it in my diary. We saw the most extraordinary range of species.'

After leafing through a diary, he found the correct page and held it out to the inspector. Marmion made a note of the date before looking back at the woman in the photograph. He estimated that she was roughly the same age as Lady Brice-Cadmore and, having studied her gravestone, he knew that the latter had been fifty-six when she died. Sir Godfrey was substantially older than his wife.

'Do you have an address for Mrs Prentice?' he asked.

'No, Inspector, she disappeared from the area and from our lives. There were rumours that she moved to more modest accommodation in Leicestershire, but I can't confirm that.'

'We'll find her,' said Marmion.

He did, however, have reservations about doing so. If the Prentice family had fallen on hard times, the woman would hardly be able to afford to stay at the Lotus Hotel. Besides, why would she steal the identity of someone who'd been so generous towards her? Marmion had the uneasy feeling that, in pursuing Cecily Prentice, he'd be going into a blind alley. He turned his attention to the second suspect. When Sir Godfrey found the other photograph, Marmion saw that it was taken at some kind of function and that a dozen or more people were standing in a line at the bottom of a sweeping staircase. After spotting that Sir Godfrey and his wife were in the centre, Marmion ran his eye slowly over the others. Of the six women, none struck him as being in any way like Lady Brice-Cadmore.

'Who am I supposed to look at?' he asked.

'It's the lady next to me,' replied the old man. 'My wife was on one side, as you can see, and this complete stranger was on the other. Never set eyes on her before or since. We were at the Hunt Ball. Even hermits like us used to go to that,' he explained. 'If people had friends staying with them over Christmas, they'd bring them along on the principle of the more, the merrier. That's how this lady came to be there, I daresay.' He looked at Marmion. 'Are you a hunting man?'

'It's in the nature of my profession, Sir Godfrey.'

'Is it?'

'I don't keep a pack of hounds, but I do have a number of detectives I can deploy to pick up a scent.'

'Ah, I see,' said the other, chortling. 'I catch your drift, Inspector.'

Marmion studied the mystery woman beside Sir Godfrey in the photograph. Now that he concentrated his gaze on her, he could see that there was a likeness to the wife. What had stopped Marmion from noticing it at first was the fact that the woman was somewhat older than Lady Brice-Cadmore – ten years, at least. In fact, she was far closer in age to Sir Godfrey than to his wife.

99

'How could I identity this lady?' he asked.

'I'm blowed if I can tell you, Inspector. My wife might have remembered the name – Diana was our memory bank – but I haven't a clue who any of those people were, ourselves excepted.'

'There must be a way to trace her, surely?'

'She was somebody's guest at that ball.'

'Then whoever organised it might tell us who she was.'

'It's possible, Inspector.' The old man sat back with a sigh. 'Oh, I do wish my memory wasn't starting to crumble. It's strange, you know. I can remember every Three Choirs Festival I ever attended and can even tell you what I heard there. Yet I can't remember the names of any of the people who organised the ball for the Old Berkshire Hunt. Isn't that ridiculous?'

'How long ago was this photograph taken?'

'It must be almost four years.'

'Do you recall who the Master of the Hunt is?'

'I'm afraid not. We weren't really part of the hunting set. We just bought the tickets and went along. Wine flowed freely at such events, so they tended to pass in a blur.'

'When you went through your albums,' said Marmion, pointing a finger at the photograph, 'this lady stood out for some reason.'

'Yes, she did.'

'What was that reason, Sir Godfrey?'

'That's the trouble,' replied the other, shrugging his shoulders. 'I can't remember.'

Griselda Fleetwood called on her husband in his office in the city. She was far too restless to accept his offer of refreshment and, while he stayed seated behind the desk, prowled around the room like a tiger in a cage. He was fearful.

'I don't like it, Harold.'

'Everything will be all right, my love.'

'Well, it doesn't *feel* like it. The future of the Lotus is under threat. Guests have been checking out before they were due to leave. One of them – would you believe? – was Phyllis Carvington.'

'But she was the person who gave you the idea of opening a hotel in the first place. Don't you remember? Lady Carvington said that there was nowhere in London tailored specifically for people like her – in other words, for haughty, old, female snobs.'

'Haughty, old, female, *moneyed* snobs,' she corrected.

'Yes, they do have one virtue.'

'My first instinct was to ban her from the Lotus, but Mr Chell advised against it. That man has been a godsend,' she went on. 'Not only did he spend the night there, he refused a large amount of money to leak the names of our customers to a journalist.'

'Thank goodness for that!'

'If we lose our reputation for discretion, we're dead and buried.'

'What's the mood like among the staff?'

'It's sombre, Harold.'

'That will only change when the police actually find out what went on there. I've done my best to light a fire under them,' he said, airily. 'When I told them that Sir Edward Henry is a good friend of mine, the superintendent realised he was dealing with someone of consequence. The commissioner will keep him and Marmion on their toes.'

'I'm more concerned with keeping the Lotus on its feet,' she said, stopping in front of his desk. 'I wouldn't admit this to anyone but you, Harold – the hotel is tottering.'

'We'll prop it up between us, my love.'

'Not if the Phyllis Carvingtons of this world turn against us.'

'That ugly old turtle will come back, I guarantee.'

'Meanwhile, Buchanan is rubbing his hands with glee. Do you know what he had the nerve to do?'

'No – what was it?'

'He sent me a bouquet of flowers as a gesture of sympathy.'

He was outraged. 'I hope you sent them straight back.'

'I had them thrown out.'

'That man is despicable.'

'It was clear proof to me that he's behind this whole business.'

'Unfortunately, it's not the kind of proof that would stand up in court, so don't rise to the bait. I've warned you before against making intemperate accusations. Buchanan wouldn't hesitate to sue you for slander.'

'He's been dying to bring us down.'

'But he's not the only one. Bear that in mind. Other hoteliers would love to see you fail. I'll make sure it won't happen.'

'Is that a promise?'

'You have my word on it, Griselda.' Getting to his feet, he came around the desk and embraced her. When they pulled away, Fleetwood grinned. 'I've been saving up some good news for a time when it's most needed,' he told her. 'This may be it.'

'What's happened?'

'Nothing as yet, but I've caught wind of a rumour.'

'Go on.'

'My name may be put forward for inclusion in the New Year's Honours List,' he said, fingers in the lapels of his coat. 'We may be going up in the world, my love. It might even be a knighthood. People in the realm of finance will have to call me Sir Harold and there'll be a hotel in Chelsea owned and run by a certain Lady Fleetwood.'

She hugged him impulsively. 'That's wonderful!' she cried. 'Why didn't you tell me when you first heard?'

'I was keeping it as a surprise. Just think of it, Griselda. You will be able to mix more easily with all those titled ladies of yours and there's another bonus.'

'Is there?'

'Yes – it will be one in the eye for Fraser Buchanan.'

Buchanan allowed himself the pleasure of reading the newspaper coverage of events at the Lotus Hotel once again. Having bought every morning paper, he was delighted to see that they all carried the story. It was bound to have an adverse effect on bookings. Who would wish to stay at a hotel where a murder had occurred? He was still chuckling to himself when he heard the toot of a car horn in the road outside. Gathering up his briefcase, he went into the hall, plucked his hat off its peg and left the house. He climbed into the rear of the vehicle and sat back.

'Is it the usual, sir?' asked the taxi driver.

'Yes, please – the Roath Court Hotel.'

'Did you find him, Joe?' asked Marmion.

'I picked him out because he was the youngest porter there,' said Keedy. 'My guess is that Maitland is also the brightest of them.'

'Why do you think that?'

'He's bright, quick off the mark and tireless. Also, he clearly has a way with female guests. They seem to love him.'

'His charm didn't work on a member of the female staff at the Lotus. That's why Mr Chell got rid of him.'

'Maitland told a different story, Harv.'

'Really?'

'Yes, he reckons that he got bored at the Lotus and left of his own volition. The Roath Court is much bigger. They obviously pay him more.'

'And what does he have to do for the money?'

'I had the feeling that he'd do anything he was told.'

They were in Marmion's office, now vacated by Sir Godfrey Brice-Cadmore. Having first reported to the superintendent, Keedy had come to see the inspector. He gave him a brief description of what happened at the Roath Court along with his appraisal of Maitland. He then turned to his visit to Leonard Rogan's home.

'Chat was right,' he conceded. 'Going to his home, I saw a very different side to the night porter. He wasn't quite so cocky there.'

'Where does he live?'

'It's in a Paddington slum. He hated being caught in a vest and pyjama trousers, but I expect that's what he wears most of the time he's there. He went on the defensive immediately.'

'Did you learn anything new?'

'Yes, I discovered that Chell used to be deputy manager at the Savoy.' Marmion blinked in surprise. 'Mrs Fleetwood would have needed to offer him a lot of money to make him give up a job like that. The Savoy attracts the elite.'

'That's what the Lotus is aspiring to do, Joe.'

Keedy told him in detail what had happened when he met Rogan and how the man's original account of the night of the murder had had to be modified slightly. It had made him suspicious of the man. Marmion listened patiently until the sergeant finished.

'Describe him in one word, Joe.'

'Shifty.'

'What about Maitland?'

'Calculating.'

'Are they birds of a feather?'

'They could be,' said Keedy. 'Both of them need money, especially Rogan. He's got a wife and a disabled father to support. Their son has left home. He's got a stall in Brewer Street Market.'

'Well, they obviously know each other because they worked side by side at the Lotus until Maitland was booted out for pestering one of the maids. Are they still in touch, I wonder?'

'It wouldn't surprise me.'

'Find me a link between them,' said Marmion. 'If we can establish that, we might start to get somewhere at last.'


It was late afternoon before Maitland came off duty. After changing out of his uniform, he left the hotel and walked off through a maze of streets. When the porter finally reached the Red Lion, someone was waiting for him at a table in the corner. He scowled at Maitland.

'What kept you?' asked Rogan.

# CHAPTER TWELVE

When she got to the sewing circle that afternoon, Ellen was pleased to see that Rene Bridger was there. Making gloves, socks and scarves for British soldiers was also a social event, a time when the women could exchange gossip, console each other and form friendships. Though she'd never been close to Rene Bridger, she was anxious to speak to her now. As soon as the group started to disperse, Ellen followed the other woman out into the street.

'I've been reading that book you mentioned,' she said.

'It scared me rigid.'

'I can see why. It all sounds so *real*.'

'That's why it depressed me, Ellen.'

'I found a handbill inside the book.'

'It was there when I borrowed it from the library, so I left it there.'

'Did you read what that man, Quentin Dacey, said?'

'I was too frightened.'

'He claims he knows where many of the German spies are hiding. I'm thinking of going to hear him speak tomorrow.'

'Then you're a braver woman than me.'

'Don't you want to know the truth, Rene?'

'German soldiers killed my son,' said the other, bitterly. 'That's enough truth for me. In a sense they also killed *your* son.'

'Paul is still alive.'

'Yes, but he's not the lad you sent off to war, is he? Whatever happened to him over there, it changed him. Why else did he run away from home?'

'He had his reasons,' said Ellen, upset by the other woman's blunt question. 'Paul will come back one day. He just needs to . . . sort himself out, that's all.' She spoke with more certainty than she felt. 'As for that talk by Quentin Dacey, you're not interested in coming, then?'

'I don't believe what he has to say.'

'But he's an educated man – and he once lived in Germany.'

'If they had so many spies over here, we'd have heard of it from the police by now. Well, your husband would surely have told you.'

'He doesn't deal with that kind of thing, Rene. It's left to the secret service. Harvey only works on serious crimes.'

'Have you told him about that book?'

'No, I haven't had the chance.'

'When I showed it to *my* husband, he said it was rubbish and refused even to look at it. But, then, Bert isn't a reading man. What about your husband?'

'He never has time to read anything but police reports.'

'Are you really going to this talk tomorrow?'

'Yes, I am.'

'Will you tell your husband about it?'

It was a question with which Ellen had been grappling and she still didn't know the answer. After a few seconds, she heard herself making a decision.

'No, Rene,' she said, firmly, 'I'm going to say nothing about it to Harvey. He's far too busy.'

Clashes with the superintendent were not unusual and Marmion lost most of them because Chatfield could always pull rank on him, forcing the inspector to back down. This time, however, Marmion was determined to win the argument.

'I'm sorry, sir,' he said, 'but I disagree with you. What Sir Godfrey told me must be considered as crucial evidence.'

'Paying the slightest attention to it is a waste of time.'

'Why?'

'Because we can't solve a complex crime like this on the basis of the ramblings of a confused old man,' said Chatfield. 'You've admitted that his mind wanders and that his memory is unsound.'

'It's true,' conceded Marmion. 'Sir Godfrey spends most of the time in the past with his birdwatching and his visits to the Three Choirs Festival. They remind him of his late wife.'

'Then let's leave him to wallow in the past. My only concern is the present, where I have to attend a press conference very soon.' He tapped the two photographs in front of him. 'And when I do, I am not going to mention either of these women because they are wholly irrelevant to the investigation.'

'I dispute that, sir.'

'My decision is final.'

To reinforce that decision, Chatfield picked up the two photographs and handed them back to Marmion with polite contempt. They'd been left by Sir Godfrey Brice-Cadmore in the hope that they might advance the investigation. Of the two, only one really interested Marmion and that was the woman who'd attended a hunt ball where she'd not only been photographed with Sir Godfrey and his wife, she'd looked as if she was very pleased to be standing next to him. Everyone else was beaming at the camera but her attention seemed to be fixed on the old man.

'Have we had any response from the appeal?' asked Chatfield.

'Suggestions are starting to trickle in, sir. Sergeant Keedy is handling them at the moment. When the public become aware of the size of the reward, the trickle will become a tidal wave.'

'It needs to be carefully filtered.'

'That's why I put the sergeant in charge. He has a nose for fraudsters.'

'They should all be prosecuted for wasting police time.'

'They will be, sir,' said Marmion. 'What do you propose to say at the press conference?'

'I'll release a few more details about the post-mortem but nothing too significant. There are certain things I'd like to keep from them for the time being. I'll tell them about the reward money, of course. We need the public to know just how much is on offer.' He stood up behind his desk. 'What's your next step, Inspector?'

'I want to pay another visit to the Lotus Hotel, sir. I feel that there's still a lot more to learn there.'

'Keep clear of Mrs Fleetwood.'

'After what I've heard of her, I'm keen to meet the lady.'

'She'll try to tell you how to do your job.'

'Oh, I'm used to someone doing that,' said Marmion, getting in a sly dig at his superior. 'Mrs Fleetwood may criticise us, but she has the sense to let her manager run the hotel. Mr Chell is the person I'm really going to see this afternoon. He's a key figure in this investigation.'

\* \* \*

Even in his rare moments off duty, Rex Chell never relaxed. Still wearing morning dress, he was the personification of elegance. Lena Gosling was alone with him in his office, enjoying a cup of tea and a biscuit. Because he trusted her implicitly, she was the one person in whom he felt able to confide freely.

'There's a black cloud hanging over the Lotus,' he said. 'Unless we can get rid of it, we'll be put out of business.'

'Is it that bad?'

'Guests have been cancelling their bookings all day.'

'Some of them are still loyal, surely?'

'We can't survive for long on a handful of patrons, Mrs Gosling. And it's not just our guests who feel uneasy. Our staff must be on edge as well.'

'They are, Mr Chell. There's no doubt about that.'

'How is Miss Jenks?'

'She's still very shaky. I've caught her in tears more than once,' said Lena, 'and she won't start to recover until the murder is solved. Millie told me that she's having nightmares.'

'We're all in the middle of one of those,' said Chell, ruefully. 'However, we must carry on as if nothing had happened. Brave faces are the order of the day.'

'You've set an example to us all, sir. We were all so impressed that you spent last night under this roof.'

'I just wanted to make sure that we had no more trouble.'

'Leonard told me you'd make a good night porter.'

'That's very kind of him,' said Chell, icily, 'but you can tell Rogan that I have higher aspirations.' He crossed to the wall and pointed at the framed ground plan of the hotel. 'I thought that we were completely secure.'

'So did I, sir.'

'The killer got hold of a key somehow.'

'Well, he didn't get it from any of us,' she said, taking umbrage. 'I hope that's not what you're telling me.'

'None of us is above suspicion, Mrs Gosling.'

'If any member of staff betrayed us, I'd *know*.'

'Then someone must have reconnoitred the place,' he decided. 'One of our guests stayed here for the sole purpose of working out the geography of the Lotus and getting some idea of the night porter's routine. Yes,' he went on, seeing the look of disbelief on her face, 'it's hard to accept that any of those respectable ladies who stay here would take part in a crime, but one of them did.'

'I don't believe it. We all know what Mrs Fleetwood set out to do when she opened this hotel – it was to attract the cream of society.'

'And that's exactly what she did.'

'Then why are you saying that one of the guests helped the killer?'

'How else could an intruder find his way around the Lotus at night when the lights were turned off?'

She was stunned. 'I never thought of that.'

'There's something I haven't told you, Mrs Gosling, but I know that you can keep it to yourself. We don't want the staff gossiping about it.' He lowered his voice. 'The guest who disappeared from the room where the murder victim was found signed in as Lady Brice-Cadmore.'

'I remember her well.'

'What we didn't know at the time was that she was an impostor. According to the inspector, the real Lady Brice-Cadmore died years ago. Her name was stolen.' Mrs Gosling's eyes bulged. 'Do you still think that all our patrons belong to the cream of society?'

\* \* \*

When they came to the end of their shift, the two friends found Inspector Gale waiting for them. She wanted a full report of their time on duty and she checked their notebooks carefully to make sure that all incidents were neatly recorded. Giving a grunt of approval, she moved away.

'Why doesn't she ever praise us?' complained Iris Goodliffe.

'She just did,' said Alice.

'I didn't hear her.'

'That grunt is Gale Force's idea of praising us. I think she was annoyed that, for once, she couldn't find fault with what we did. That was an achievement for us, Iris.'

'I'd still like an occasional pat on the back.'

'Well, you won't get it from her. That's asking far too much.'

Now that they were off duty, they went off to the canteen for some refreshments. On the way there, Alice saw another policewoman coming towards them. She recognised Jennifer Jerrold, a lanky young woman with a long stride. Ordinarily, Jennifer would have stopped to exchange a few words, but she didn't even look at them this time. Head down, she ignored the greetings from the two women and walked straight past.

'What's wrong with Jenny?' asked Alice.

'Haven't you heard the rumour?'

'No, I haven't.'

'A little bird told me that she was going to resign.'

'Why? She's very good at her job.'

'Maybe she's fed up with being ordered around by Gale Force.'

'We're all fed up with that, Iris, but it doesn't make us want to get out. We perform a vital service. Jenny was as keen as the rest of us to join the Women's Police Force.'

'I know.'

'She was off ill last month,' said Alice. 'I wonder if it's to do with that? She's a nice woman but she never looks all that healthy.'

'Neither do I,' said Iris.

'That's ridiculous. Your father owns a couple of pharmacies. Whenever you have the slightest thing wrong with you, he'll prescribe tablets for you and hand them over.'

'I take far too many pills.'

'They obviously do the trick. Going back to Jenny, where did she find the courage to tell Gale Force?'

'Maybe she hasn't actually done it yet,' said Iris. 'I'd have to be drunk before I'd dare tell the inspector that I was leaving. She'd do everything she could to stop me.'

'Let's hope that Jenny has second thoughts. I like her.'

'She didn't seem to like *us* when she went past just now. Something's obviously upset her.'

'I wonder what it is. Anyway, whose turn is it to buy the tea?'

'It's yours, Alice.'

'I thought it was yours.'

'Last one there pays,' said Iris before hurrying off.

Alice didn't chase her. She was too busy looking after Jennifer Jerrold and wondering why someone who joined with such enthusiasm was eager to leave a job that she'd always enjoyed.

The first claims came in the form of letters and Keedy dealt with them very quickly. Most of them were written in an illiterate scrawl that discounted them immediately. One man insisted that the dead woman was Joan of Arc and that the missing guest was Queen Victoria. Other hoax claims went into the wastepaper basket after them. It was an hour before someone turned up in person. David Benfield was a skinny man in his forties, wearing what had once been a smart suit but was now badly creased and frayed at the sleeves. Shown into the office, he gave his name then started with a demand.

'I want to know how much I'll get.'

'You'll get a night in the cells if you adopt that tone with me,' warned Keedy. 'As it happens, there will be a substantial reward for information that leads to the arrest and conviction of the killer, but I very much doubt if you'll be in a position to get it.'

'Yes, I will,' said Benfield, indignantly. 'I *saw* him.'

'Who are you talking about?'

'The man you're after.'

'Can you give me a name and a detailed description of him?'

'Not really – but I watched him break into that hotel.'

'Where were you at the time?'

'I was walking home through Chelsea after midnight.'

'Where do you live?'

'Actually,' admitted the other, 'I live in Walthamstow, but I'd . . . been to see friends. As I was passing the hotel, I saw this figure forcing open a window at the back. In fact—'

'That's enough,' snapped Keedy, cutting him short.

'But I haven't finished yet, Sergeant.'

'Oh, yes, you have. You're lying through your teeth. Nobody broke into the Lotus Hotel or tampered with a window at the rear. I examined the building myself and found no sign of forced entry.'

'I saw him clearly.'

'How did you manage that? The place was in darkness at midnight. Now get out of here,' said Keedy, rising from his chair, 'or I'll kick you all the way back home to Walthamstow.'

'I'm a witness. You ought to treat me with respect.'

Keedy had heard enough. Grabbing hold of the man by the collar, he lifted him up and rushed him out through the door before propelling him towards the stairs. Benfield accepted defeat and slinked off.

Keedy resumed his seat and made a note of his visitor's name. It would not be the first time that someone turned up with an absurd story. For the moment, however, he was alone in an office that had a telephone. The temptation was strong and Keedy eventually yielded to it. After stepping out into the corridor to make sure that nobody was about, he went back inside and closed the door. Then he took out his wallet and extracted the piece of paper he'd torn out of the *Evening Standard* the previous day. Lifting the receiver, he dialled the number printed on the scrap of paper. When he eventually got through, a voice came on the line.

'Yes?'

'It's about that job you advertised,' said Keedy.

'What about it?'

'How much does it pay?'

The Lotus Hotel felt empty when Marmion got there. There was hardly anyone about and the place had an almost hollow feeling. Having had his curiosity about the woman aroused, he was disappointed that the owner was not there but pleased to see the manager. Chell invited him into the office and the two of them sat down.

'I've been thinking, Inspector,' said the manager.

'That's always a wise habit to cultivate, sir.'

'My belief is that one of our patrons was part of a conspiracy. Instead of staying here as a bona fide guest, she was simply getting to know the layout of the hotel in order to help the killer.'

'We'd already realised that.'

'I'd like to tell you that the name of that guest was Lady Brice-Cadmore but, in fact, she was a confidence trickster. In reality, she was also an accessory to the murder. Do you follow my reasoning?'

'Yes, sir, I've been down that same path myself until I found a major obstruction across it.'

'Obstruction?' echoed the other.

'Yes, Mr Chell. I mentioned it to you before – the taxi.'

'It must have been ordered by mistake.'

'I don't believe that lady made mistakes, sir. She booked that taxi in good faith because she intended to leave here at 6 a.m. that morning. She'd asked Miss Jenks to wake her up in time. According to Sergeant Keedy, Miss Jenks got to the room and saw a sign dangling from the doorknob that said, "Please Do Not Disturb".'

'It had been hanging there for most of the previous day.'

'Answer me this, sir,' said Marmion. 'If you were an accessory to a murder, would you arrange for someone to come to the room where it took place? In our experience, most killers do their best to delay the discovery of their victim because they want maximum time to make their escape. The post-mortem report estimates that the time of death was somewhere between two o'clock and five o'clock. That being the case, Miss Jenks could conceivably have entered that room when the fatal dose was being injected into the victim.' He gave an enquiring smile. 'Do you still think your guest was an accessory?'

'No,' said Chell, apologetically. 'I hadn't thought it through the way that you have. Thank you for correcting me.'

'Just because she disappeared, it's natural to think that the woman was in league with the killer. At the start, I entertained the idea that she might actually *be* the killer, but I couldn't explain away the taxi.'

'What really did happen, Inspector?'

'We can only guess, sir. A public appeal has been launched for help to identify the murder victim and the missing guest. You may be aware that Mrs Fleetwood's husband is offering a large reward for significant information. That may conceivably bring in the names we desperately need. Meanwhile,' said Marmion, 'we had a visit from Sir Godfrey Brice-Cadmore. He's been ransacking his archives.'

'Has he turned up anything useful?'

'I hope so. He feels, as we do, that the person who posed as his wife must be someone who actually met her at some point and who made an effort to look like her.'

'That makes sense.'

'After trawling through his diaries and photograph albums, he came up with two possibilities. I have them here,' said Marmion, taking the photographs from his pocket. 'Please take a long, hard look before you decide if one of these ladies stayed here under a false name.'

Marmion first handed over the photograph of Cecily Prentice. The manager shook his head vigorously and said that she was far too young. He was then given the photograph of the woman at the Hunt Ball and it intrigued him. Since there were so many faces crowded into a small photograph, he took time to pick out the woman Marmion wanted him to see. Chell was thorough. Unwilling to make too hasty a decision, he took out a magnifying glass from his desk drawer and scrutinised the woman. Minutes went by before he looked up.

'That's her, Inspector.'

'Are you certain of it?'

'I'm absolutely certain,' said Chell. 'She was a little older than she is here, but I'd swear that she stayed at the Lotus as Lady Brice-Cadmore.'

* * *

117

As soon as Ellen finished reading the book, she had the urge to take it back to the library. While getting rid of something that had disturbed her, she knew that she could not forget its central message so easily. The theme of *The Invasion of 1910* would be ever-present in her mind from now on. The librarian was glad to see the book being returned.

'Thank you, Mrs Marmion,' she said. 'We had someone asking for this title earlier on. Did you enjoy it?'

'No, I didn't. To be honest, it shook me up, but I couldn't stop reading it somehow.'

'Other people have said that. It's one of the most borrowed books in the library. We have five copies of it and they're always being borrowed by someone.'

'I'll find something a little more comforting,' said Ellen.

She drifted away to the section where romantic novels were on display, browsing quietly. When she'd worked her way to the end of the bookcase, she saw something she hadn't spotted before. Among the posters on the noticeboard was a larger version of the handbill she'd found in the copy of William Le Queux's book. Ellen went across to study the photograph of Quentin Dacey, staring into the dark, hypnotic eyes until she felt unable to look away. Did he really know something that the authorities didn't? Was the press deliberately suppressing details of German espionage, as he'd claimed? Were the British people being kept in the dark out of fear of mass panic if they knew the truth?

The only way to find out was to hear Dacey speak.

His visit to the Lotus Hotel had produced what Marmion considered to be a breakthrough. If Chell was to be believed, the woman who'd once attended a ball organised by the Old Berkshire Hunt had stayed at the hotel under the guise of someone else's name. It should be possible to find out what her real name was. Marmion's starting point had to be Sir Godfrey. Since the old man was very tired and jangled by the turn of events, he'd decided to stay the night at his club. When he'd left Scotland Yard, he was obviously not in the best of health and Marmion had had to help him down the stairs. He was troubled by the fact that Sir Godfrey had been struggling to stay upright.

The club was in Albemarle Street and Marmion was driven there in a police car. When he entered the building, he was met by a steward who looked him up and down.

'This is a private club, sir,' he said with a courtesy edged with firmness. 'Non-members are not permitted.'

'I'm the exception to the rule,' said Marmion, taking out his warrant card to show to him. 'As you can see, I'm a detective inspector from Scotland Yard.'

The steward was hurt. 'We've never had trouble from the police.'

'I'm only here to see one of your members.'

'What might his name be, sir?'

'Sir Godfrey Brice-Cadmore.'

'That's correct. Sir Godfrey is one of our country members.'

'I'd like to speak to him, please.'

'Then you've come too late, Inspector.'

Marmion was anxious. 'He's gone back home?'

'No, sir,' said the other, solemnly. 'He was in no condition to travel. The stairs here are very steep. When I took Sir Godfrey up to his room, he was puffing and panting on every step. Before we reached the top, he suddenly collapsed.'

'Is he still alive?' asked Marmion in alarm.

'I hope so, sir. He's had some kind of seizure.'

'Where is he?'

'They took him to hospital. If you wish to speak to him, I suggest that you get over there immediately or you may be too late.'

# CHAPTER THIRTEEN

Sir Edward Henry rarely got involved in individual cases. As commissioner of the Metropolitan Police, his role was largely administrative, making sure that the organisation ran smoothly and effectively even though it had limited manpower. Some critics dismissed him unfairly as a mere figurehead but, in fact, he was a fierce defender of the police, taking on the government and the press on its behalf and arguing his case robustly. When the tall, dignified figure of Sir Edward came into his office, Chatfield knew exactly why he was there.

'You've come about Mr Fleetwood,' he said, resignedly.

'Strictly speaking,' said the other, 'I'm here on behalf of *Mrs* Fleetwood. She, after all, is the owner of the Lotus Hotel. How is the investigation going?'

'We've made slow but definite progress, Sir Edward.'

'That wasn't what Harold Fleetwood told me.'

'He has a rather unrealistic view of police procedure. He's a man who seems to believe in instant arrests and summary justice.'

'When someone has become a millionaire on the strength of his business acumen,' chided Sir Edward, 'his views need to be shown some respect. That's why I commend his offer of reward money in connection with this murder.'

'I second that. I was delighted to hear of his generosity.'

'The money is not given freely, Superintendent. Fleetwood expects prompt action in return for it.'

'The reward is bound to generate a response from the public.'

'It's a pity we have to rely on it. I know we're still at the early stage but I'd hoped that we'd have accumulated enough evidence to have at least some idea of who the killer is and what happened to the guest who occupied the room in which a total stranger was found dead. It's almost,' said Sir Edward, fingering his moustache, 'as if somebody is playing with you.'

Chatfield was stung. 'Then he or she has chosen a very dangerous game,' he warned.

'Marmion usually cuts through to the very heart of any mystery. Why hasn't he done so in this case?'

'Give us time, Sir Edward. We are all working flat out.'

'Keep me posted about any developments.'

'I will.'

'Oh dear!' said the other, glancing at the watch he'd just taken from his waistcoat pocket. 'I'll be late for my meeting with the Home Secretary. It's all Dacey's fault.'

'Are you referring to Quentin Dacey, by any chance?'

'Yes, he's just had another go at me.'

'The man is a crackpot, in my view.'

'Unfortunately, he's a crackpot with an increasing number of followers at his back.'

'What is he after this time?'

'It's the same thing as usual. He believes that we're overrun by German spies and that some of them are determined to kill him. He demanded police protection.'

'What did you tell him, Sir Edward?'

'I pointed out that we had finite resources and that their first duty was to ensure the safety of the citizens of London. Technically, he's not one of them because he was actually born in Belgium, though his parents were both British, of course. Besides,' he went on, 'I can't offer him twenty-four-hour protection. That would mean two officers guarding him in eight-hour shifts. We need those six men for more important duties.' He moved to the door. 'Don't forget what I said, will you? Keep me up to date with the investigation. I need to be able to offer Fleetwood some concrete proof that we're making headway.'

He walked out and left Chatfield squirming.


Alice Marmion enjoyed her time in the canteen, chatting to her fellow policewomen and staving off the moment when she'd go home to an empty flat. It was not simply her inability to see Keedy that irked her. There was also the fact that he was once again engaged in an exciting investigation while her experience of police work consisted of pounding the streets of her beat and dealing with minor incidents. What she did was necessary, but it would never lift her spirits and make her blood race.

She was just about to leave the building when she saw someone ahead of her. It was Jennifer Jerrold, who was on her way home. Alice instantly stopped thinking about her own troubles and increased her speed. Catching up with the other woman, she fell in beside her. There was an exchange of greetings and gossip. After a while, Alice became more serious.

'Is everything all right, Jenny?' she asked.

'Yes, of course,' said the other.

'You went past me earlier on without even looking at me.'

'Sorry – I didn't mean to be rude.'

'Iris tells me you're thinking of resigning.'

'It's true, Alice. I don't think I'm cut out for policing.'

'But you're one of the only people Gale Force actually praises. The rest of us get the sharp edge of her tongue.'

'I'm sorry about that.'

'So what's the *real* reason you want to leave?'

'It's to do with my parents,' said Jennifer with a wan smile. 'They think the work is too dangerous for me. My father doesn't like some of the things I've seen on the late shift. And he's afraid of all those drunken soldiers we're bound to meet.'

'You always have a policeman with you, Jenny.'

'I still see prostitutes every day and hear foul language. That really upsets my parents. They're very religious and worried about me. They're afraid I'll be corrupted.'

'You're actually trying to keep the streets of London clean for decent people. Don't they realise that?'

'It's not their fault, Alice. They were brought up with certain beliefs and it's made them narrow-minded. Left to them, I'd be kept indoors all day long.'

'You'd hate that.'

'I know.'

'Besides, you're over twenty-one now. You can make up your own mind, not have it made up for you.'

'As long as I live at home, my parents make all the decisions.'

'That's why *I* moved out, Jenny. I love Mummy and Daddy but I wanted some freedom of movement, so I rented a flat. I can come and go whenever I please now.'

'You're so much braver than I am.'

'I very much doubt that.'

'Oh,' said Jennifer, looking up as a vehicle turned into the street, 'there's my bus. I must go, Alice.'

'Can't you catch a later one?'

'My parents will be expecting me. Nice to talk to you . . .'

She ran off and left her friend standing there. Alice watched until the bus stopped, took passengers on board then drove off. She was puzzled. Something about their conversation troubled her and she didn't know what it was.

As a result of her visit to her husband, Griselda Fleetwood returned to her hotel in a more positive mood. She asked to be shown the room where the murder had been committed. The manager unlocked it for her then stood beside her as she viewed it. She sucked her teeth.

'We can't possibly use this room again,' she said. 'After what happened in here, nobody would want to come anywhere near it.'

'That doesn't mean we write it off,' insisted Chell. 'We simply turn it into a storeroom. We'll get some use out of it then.'

'Won't the staff object?'

'Mrs Gosling and I will talk to them. If they want to continue working here, they'll have to do as they're told. We can't let a perfectly good space like this go to waste.'

'That's a hotel manager speaking,' said Griselda. 'I agree wholeheartedly.'

125

'We'll have to wait until the police have concluded their inquiry, Mrs Fleetwood. When it's over and done with, I'll have the furniture taken out and the carpet lifted. This would be ideal as a laundry room.'

'Did you ever have this kind of problem at the Savoy?'

'We never had a murder – thank heaven – but we had the occasional crisis. The worst was too indelicate to mention.'

'Don't hold back on my account,' she said with a laugh. 'I'm not a shrinking violet. Tell me all.'

'Well,' he said, 'it was when a royal equerry got hopelessly drunk, blundered into a suite in the belief that he was in a bathroom and relieved himself over a foreign dignitary who was fast asleep.' She laughed again. 'I had the misfortune to be on duty that night and had to defuse what might have become an international incident.'

'You were born to manage a hotel, Mr Chell.'

'I can't say that it was ever my ambition. When I fell into it by accident, however, I felt supremely at home.'

'That's why we're so glad to have you here. I hope your attitude towards the Lotus hasn't been soured by what happened in this room.'

'I can put your mind at rest on that score, Mrs Fleetwood.'

'Good man.' She became brisk. 'Have the police been back?'

'The inspector was here not long before you arrived.'

'Did he have any news?'

'He brought a photograph that he'd been given by Sir Godfrey Brice-Cadmore. After close examination, I was able to identify one of the people in the photo.'

'Who was it?'

'The lady who actually booked this room,' he said, 'under the name of Sir Godfrey's wife.'

* * *

Marmion's heart missed a beat when he first set eyes on Sir Godfrey. Propped up in a hospital bed, the old man looked as if he was close to death. His face was white, his eyes watery and his cheeks hollow. Every ounce of energy seemed to have been drained out of him. If he hadn't heard the faint sound of breathing, the inspector would have thought he was gazing at a corpse. The doctor had told him that Sir Godfrey was very weak and might not even recognise him. A nurse stood beside the bed, ready to intervene if the patient had a relapse.

'How is he?' asked Marmion.

'We're keeping him alive, Inspector,' she said.

'The doctor said that he's had a stroke.'

'We're afraid that it's more serious than that.'

'Is he able to talk?'

'Yes . . .' croaked the old man.

'Ah,' said Marmion, leaning in closer, 'you can hear me, then.'

'Someone . . . needs to be told . . .'

'It's being taken care of, Sir Godfrey. I gave the doctor your address and telephone number. Back in Elmstead Manor, they'll soon be aware of what happened to you.'

'Am I . . . going to die?'

'We hope not.'

'Don't worry about me,' said the patient, managing a pale smile. 'I'm not afraid of death . . . I'm ready for it.'

'Don't say that. We need you.'

'Why?'

'We may have discovered her identity.'

'Who are you talking about?'

'It was all thanks to one of your photographs.'

Sir Godfrey frowned. 'What photographs?'

'You brought them to Scotland Yard.'

'Did I? Why on earth should I do that?'

'Don't you remember?'

'No, I don't.'

'But you know who I am, don't you?'

The old man peered at him. 'I'm afraid that I don't.'

'I'm Inspector Marmion.'

'Never heard of you . . .'

He began to dribble and twitch violently. The nurse moved in to hold him gently by the shoulders. When he eventually settled down, she used a cloth to wipe around his mouth.

'I'm sorry, Inspector,' she said. 'You're wasting your time.'

'Does he remember *anything*?'

'No, sir, he's in a world of his own.'

Fraser Buchanan spent a long time with the manager of the Roath Court Hotel, going through the month's accounts with him and discussing how the healthy profits could be increased even more. They were interrupted by the ringing of the telephone. Buchanan snatched it up and was told by the receptionist that Harold Fleetwood was asking to see him. After telling the manager that he needed the use of his office, Buchanan went off to meet his visitor. Fleetwood was standing in the middle of the lobby, looking around with a mixture of interest and disapproval.

'Judging by the look on your face,' said Buchanan, approaching, 'the Roath Court is not to your taste.'

'It has its virtues,' said Fleetwood, 'but they're mostly hidden beneath what I consider to be unimaginative decoration.'

'That's very harsh, Mr Fleetwood.'

'I speak as I find.'

Buchanan didn't offer his hand because he knew that the other man would refuse to shake it. They had met before and maintained a steely antagonism towards each other. Buchanan made a sweeping gesture with his arm and led the way out of the lobby. They were soon alone together in the office, standing face-to-face.

'I've been expecting your wife,' said Buchanan with a sly grin, 'but she sent you to chastise me instead.'

'Griselda doesn't even know that I'm here.'

'Then why did you come – to challenge me to a duel?'

'Duels take place between gentlemen and you will never meet the qualifications to become one. In sending that bouquet to my wife, you showed what an unprincipled little rat you are.'

'It was a sign of sympathy from a fellow hotelier.'

'No,' said Fleetwood, 'it was an example of revelling in the misfortune of someone you hate because she stole guests from you.'

'Some of those guests will be coming back to me, I fancy.'

'That was your intention, wasn't it?'

'Ah, I see. You're here to accuse me of being behind the unfortunate events at the Lotus. It's not enough for Mrs Fleetwood to set the police onto me. She's now unleashed her husband.'

'I'm here in place of my wife. Griselda was keen to tackle you herself, but I managed to persuade her to keep her powder dry. She may need it when this case is finally over and those involved – directly or indirectly – are behind bars.'

'Which one am I – direct or indirect?'

'We both know the answer to that, Buchanan.'

'Are you saying that you have evidence that I was implicated? If that's the case,' said Buchanan with a teasing smile, 'I'll call the manager in so that I have a witness to your absurd claim.'

'That won't be necessary.'

'Ah, we're backing down now, are we?'

'I simply came to tell you that the game is up.'

'What game?'

'I've been to Scotland Yard and spoken to the commissioner, who happens to be a friend of mine. I stressed the importance of looking very closely at you as an obvious suspect. You're driven by sheer envy,' he continued. 'Because my wife has put the Unicorn Hotel in the shade, you wanted to bring her crashing down.'

'That's simply not true.'

'You were her sworn enemy from the start.'

'Then why did she turn to me for advice?' Fleetwood was plainly startled. 'Oh, I see. She obviously forgot to mention that. Years ago, when her dream of opening a hotel was still in its infancy, she had the sense to consult a number of us who'd been in the business for all of our working lives.' He spread his arms. 'I was happy to oblige.'

'I don't believe it. She knows the sort of person you are.'

'Yes, I'm a highly successful hotelier.'

'And you resented her plans from the start.'

'If that's what she told you, it was very naughty of Griselda.'

'Don't you dare call her that!' roared Fleetwood.

'There was a time when I was given the right to do so,' said Buchanan, nonchalantly. Walking to the door, he opened it wide. 'Good day, Mr Fleetwood. It was good of you to call but I'm not the person you need to talk to – it's your wife.'

On the spur of the moment, Alice Marmion changed her mind. Instead of going home to a cold and lonely flat, she decided to call on her mother instead. Guaranteed a cordial welcome, she caught the bus that took her to the family home. When she opened the front door, Ellen's surprise was matched by her elation.

'Alice!'

'Hello, Mummy.'

'Oh, this is such a treat. Come on in.'

After a warm hug, they went into the living room. Alice was pleased to see a fire flickering in the grate and giving off enough heat to make it noticeable. They sat beside each other on the sofa. When she'd explained why she'd decided to visit her mother, Alice had a question.

'You took a long time to answer the door, Mummy.'

'Yes, I know.'

'Why was that?'

'I didn't realise it was you.'

'Were you expecting someone else?'

'No,' said Ellen, 'but I've learnt to be very careful, that's all.'

'Careful?'

'I'm frightened, Alice.'

'But you're perfectly safe here.'

'Am I?'

Ellen looked so haunted that her daughter was worried. She wanted to know why such a brave and level-headed woman as her mother was now so nervous and hesitant. Alice grasped her mother's hands.

'What's the problem, Mummy?'

'It's not really a problem . . .'

'It must be if you're scared to open the front door. Nobody will hurt you. Compared to many districts in London, this is a very safe one. You're in no danger.'

'I am, Alice. We all are.'

Once she'd started, out it all came. She told her daughter about the novel by William Le Queux and how it had made such a deep impression on her. Because she could see how fraught her mother was, Alice was very patient but increasingly worried. She'd never seen Ellen in such a state. When she heard that Quentin Dacey was giving a lecture on the following day, her advice was brusque.

'Don't go, Mummy.'

'I feel that I have to. I must know the truth.'

'And what makes you think it will come from Mr Dacey?'

'He's done research. He knows how many German spies there are.'

'They were all rounded up at the start of the war.'

'That's not true.'

'Talk to Daddy,' urged Alice. 'Better still, listen to Joe. He went to the Isle of Man. That's where German civilians living in this country are interned. They were imprisoned in huge numbers. If there were any spies, they're behind barbed wire in one of the camps Joe told me about.'

'You don't understand. That novel explained it all. You don't have to be a German to be a German spy. They've been recruiting people from other countries as well – many of them from Britain.'

'Mummy—'

'They're so clever, Alice,' said her mother, 'and so cunning. They were planning this war for years. It's the government's fault. The signs were there but they didn't take them seriously. Germany was ready for war, but we were caught cold.'

'I don't know the author of that novel,' admitted Alice, 'and I've never heard of this man, Dacey, but I know their type. They enjoy scaring people with horror stories. Ignore the two of them. It's the only way to have peace of mind.'

'But they were so convincing.'

'People like that always are. They know how to work on your mind. When I last saw you,' recalled Alice, 'you were in such a relaxed and happy mood. All of a sudden, you're terrified of opening the front door and you probably jump whenever a floorboard creaks. That's no way to live. Do you really want to go on like this?'

'No, I don't.'

'Then forget all about this lecture tomorrow.'

'Maybe I will.'

'Mrs Bridger had the right idea. She refused to go.'

'That's true.'

'Promise me that you'll shake off these anxieties and try to live a normal life again. I'm sure that Daddy said the same thing to you.'

'He didn't get the chance.'

Alice was shocked. 'Do you mean that you haven't told him?'

'He's never here long enough.'

'If *you* don't speak to him, then I will.'

'No, you won't,' said Ellen, sitting up. 'It's my job to do that. And you've given me the advice I needed. I'm so grateful for that. I won't borrow any more books like that from the library and I certainly won't go to hear that lecture on *The Unseen Hand*.'

As he knew from experience, detective work could so easily become a series of false dawns. Just when he thought he'd garnered decisive evidence, Marmion had seen it exposed as nothing of the kind. It had taught him to be extremely cautious. Nevertheless, he felt a surge of excitement as he left the Lotus Hotel. Its manager had identified someone in a photograph as the missing person at the heart of the case. It could be a huge bonus. Set against the good news was the fact that Sir Godfrey Brice-Cadmore could be of no further help to him. Marmion had been saddened by the sight of him in his hospital bed and suspected that the profound shock of learning that his late wife's name had been used by someone else might have contributed to his collapse.

Back at Scotland Yard, he went straight to the superintendent's office. Claude Chatfield fired a warning shot across his bows.

'If you've brought bad news,' he said, 'I don't want to hear it. I had the commissioner in here earlier, demanding a sign of progress in this case. As he threatened, Mr Fleetwood has been complaining about us.'

'That's his prerogative, sir.'

'So what's your decision? Are you staying or going?'

'I'll stay if I may,' said Marmion, closing the door behind him, 'because I believe that my visit to Mr Chell may have marked a turning point in this investigation.'

Chatfield groaned. 'We could certainly do with one.'

Marmion was succinct. He told him how the hotel manager had taken a long time studying one of the photographs before identifying the woman who'd stayed with them under a false name. Having set the relevant photo down on the desk, he pointed to the lady in question. In doing so, he'd hoped to bring a smile to the superintendent's face, but Marmion instead saw the other man's scowl darken. Chatfield was pessimistic.

'The hotel manager was mistaken,' he decided.

'He gave me his word, sir.'

'How could he identify a woman he could hardly see? It might be different if she was looking directly at the camera but she's turning away. All that's visible is the side of her face.'

'Would you recognise your wife if that's all you saw of her?'

'Yes, of course.'

'It would be the same with my wife, sir. Mr Chell, you must

remember, got to know the self-appointed Lady Brice-Cadmore on her previous visit to the hotel. He has an excellent memory.'

'You told me earlier that he was a good judge of character.'

'I stand by that.'

'Then why was he so easily fooled by this woman?' asked the other. 'He allowed a criminal to stay at the hotel.'

'We don't know that she's exactly a criminal, sir.'

'She's hiding behind someone else's name, Inspector.'

'Granted, but we can't be sure that she's doing it for criminal purposes. You're assuming that she's party to the murder when she might well be another victim of the person who committed it.'

'Then where is she?'

'I've no idea,' said Marmion, 'but I believe that the photograph might somehow lead us to her. If we know her real name, it will be much easier to trace her.'

'But how the devil will you find out her name?'

'She attended a ball held by the Old Berkshire Hunt. That means she was taken there as a guest by someone who might well be in this same photo. Our starting point will be the Master of the Hunt. He'll know who organised that event and who might well have a record of those who were there.'

'I suppose so,' said Chatfield, grudgingly. 'Sir Godfrey should be able to point you in the right direction.'

Marmion shook his head. He explained that the old man was no longer able to remember anything that might be of use to them. They would have to manage without him.

'I have two requests, sir,' he declared.

'What are they?'

'I'll need to take Sergeant Keedy with me. My guess is that we may be involved in a long and tortuous search. It will be easier if we can divide the work between us.'

'But you put Keedy in charge of dealing with the information that came in from the public.'

'Someone else can do that, sir.'

'I'm not happy about this,' said Chatfield. 'You're asking me to send my two best detectives off on what could be a wild goose chase.'

'The Old Berkshire Hunt prefers to chase foxes, sir.'

'Don't be flippant.'

'Then there's the second request I mentioned.'

Chatfield grimaced. 'Why am I feeling the need to brace myself?'

'It's a simple question of need. A train might get us to Berkshire, but it won't be able to take us here, there and everywhere. We must have the use of a police car.'

'I can't sanction that unless it's for a very important reason.'

'We want to solve a murder and a possible abduction, sir,' said Marmion, seriously. 'Can you think of a more important reason than that?'

# CHAPTER FOURTEEN

Alice Marmion had brought a breath of fresh air into the house. She not only provided company for her mother, she'd relieved her of a burden she'd been carrying since she'd started reading *The Invasion of 1910*. Suddenly, none of its ominous predictions seemed to matter. Their hold on Ellen had been broken. Over a cup of tea in the kitchen, she expressed her gratitude.

'I'm so glad that you came to my rescue, Alice. I could think of nothing else.' She stirred her tea. 'Will you stay the night?'

'No, Mummy, I'd better get back in due course.'

'Have you had any more thoughts about the wedding?'

'Yes,' said Alice. 'I made the mistake of confiding in Iris and she keeps coming up with new ideas for it – expensive ones.'

'Your father won't like that.'

'It's not fair that the father of the bride always has to foot the bill.'

'That's traditional.'

'It doesn't mean that it's right.'

'Someone told me once that it was like paying a dowry, which is what they used to do in the old days.'

'I always thought that was a terrible thing to be forced to do. It's as if the father is paying someone to take a daughter off his hands because he can't wait to get rid of her.'

'That's not the case here,' argued Ellen. 'Nobody is trying to get rid of you, Alice. If the decision was left to me, you and Joe would move in here and not have to worry about buying a place of your own.'

'We want to be independent.'

'Wait until your first child comes along. You'll need to depend on us then. Have you talked about having a family?'

'There's plenty of time to do that when we're married.'

'Joe is quite a bit older than you, remember.'

'I know. I tease him about it sometimes.'

'You need to be fit and healthy if you have children.'

'He's one of the fittest and healthiest people I've ever met. Joe plays football whenever he has the chance and hasn't been near a doctor for years. Just before war broke out, he won the police half-marathon.'

'Your father used to love running at that age.'

'What stopped him carrying on?'

'You and Paul arrived.'

It was bound to happen. Though they'd each resolved to keep off the subject of Paul, he was bound to intrude into the conversation sooner or later. A wedding meant a gathering of the family and it was more than possible that one of its principal members would not even be there. Rather than talk about her brother again, Alice created a diversion.

'Iris came up with the most ridiculous idea.'

'Did she?'

'Yes, she said that we should take advantage of the fact that Uncle Raymond holds an important position in the Salvation Army. That means he has a brass band at his disposal.'

'It is *not* coming to the wedding,' protested Ellen.

'Uncle Raymond and Auntie Lily will be very welcome,' said Alice, 'but the band can stay away. I refuse point-blank to come down the aisle to the strains of "Onward Christian Soldiers"!'

Keedy and Marmion had been friends as well as colleagues. Because of the former's reputation as a ladies' man, there'd been some awkward moments between them when he took an interest in the inspector's daughter. Marmion kept asking himself how long it would last before Alice was discarded like her predecessors. Once the relationship had blossomed into a firm commitment, Keedy could feel the tension between him and Marmion gradually easing away. It was a source of great relief.

As the two men were driven out of London in the early evening, Marmion began to talk about the investigation. Keedy's mind, however, was elsewhere. He was in a quandary. Wanting to keep a secret, he was conscious of the fact that he was sitting beside his future father-in-law. In hiding something from Marmion, he was not only being unfair, it might lead to a serious breach between them at a later stage. If the older man eventually discovered the truth, he would be furious. For that reason, Keedy elected to be honest with him. After waiting until his companion lapsed into silence, he spoke up.

'There's something I've been meaning to tell you, Harv . . .'

'Then this is the perfect time. We've all of fifty miles or more to drive. What is it?'

'Before you got married, did you have to save up?'

'Of course – it's a time when you really need money.'

'Yet you didn't move into your own house.'

'We couldn't afford to, Joe.'

'I want to make sure that Alice and I can.'

'Then I admire your courage.'

'That's because you know the pay scales in the Metropolitan Police Force. They're not very generous. We get no allowance for the dangers we face on a daily basis. There is some payment for overtime, I know, but even that is rather niggardly.'

Marmion turned to him. 'What's got into you, Joe?'

'I've had to face facts. I need to earn more.'

'And how to you propose to do that?'

'I've been looking for another job.'

'You want to *leave* Scotland Yard?' asked a horrified Marmion.

'No, of course not,' said the other. 'I love the work and I like the people I do it with – even Chat, believe it or not. But if we want the sort of house we're after, it will be more than Alice and I can manage. Don't look so frightened,' he went on as Marmion tensed. 'I'm not going to ask you for a loan. I've always prided myself on paying my way, however much effort it takes.'

'What's this other job you mentioned?'

'It'd be work as a nightwatchman in a factory.'

'You can't do a night shift, Joe. It would kill you.'

'It's only for six hours and the pay is quite reasonable.'

'Forget it. Apart from anything else, you know that it's forbidden to take on work outside the police. If you're caught – and you would be, sooner or later – you'd be kicked out.'

'I know,' confessed Keedy, 'but I'm still tempted somehow.'

'Work more overtime, then,' said Marmion, 'but make sure you leave yourself enough hours of the day to have a good sleep. You're only human, Joe.'

'There is another way to do it.'

'Do what?'

'Get some more money out of my present job.'

Marmion grinned. 'You're going to replace Chat as superintendent, are you?'

'I'm not joking, Harv.'

'Then what are you going to do? March up to the commissioner, hold out a bowl like Oliver Twist and say, "Please, Sir Edward, can I have some more?" You'd be wasting your breath.'

'I would be if I was doing it on my own.'

'You've no choice.'

'Yes, there is. I could be part of a union. Size makes all the difference. Unity is strength. If we all campaigned on behalf of a wage rise,' said Keedy, earnestly, 'they'd *have* to listen to us.'

Griselda Fleetwood had retired to her private suite at the Lotus Hotel. Heartened by the fact that the commissioner was taking a personal interest in the murder committed on her premises, she was thrilled by the possibility that her husband might be awarded a knighthood. It would be a just recognition of his philanthropy and her title would earn her the respect she coveted. Owning the hotel gave her the opportunity to rub shoulders with the aristocracy. With luck, she might soon become part of it. Standing at the window, she looked out at the streets of London as the first shadows began to fall across the buildings. She was still gazing down when she saw her husband's chauffeur-driven car pull up at the kerb outside. His unexpected arrival delighted her.

'Come and join me, Sir Harold,' she purred.

Less than a minute later, she was opening the door to let him in. Expecting an embrace and a kiss, she was disappointed when he walked past her with a grim expression on his face. Whisking off his hat, he placed it on a side table.

'Is anything wrong, Harold?' she asked.

'Sit down, please.'

'You don't look at all well.'

'SIT DOWN!' he yelled, the force of his command making her lower herself instantly to the armchair behind her. He sat on the sofa opposite. 'I've been to see Buchanan.'

'I thought you said we should keep away from him.'

'I said that *you* should, Griselda, but it seems I was too late.'

She was flustered. 'What on earth do you mean?'

'Is it true that you consulted him about how to run a hotel?'

'No, it isn't.'

'But you did take advice from some people.'

'There were other hoteliers, yes. They were happy to give me free advice. The one person I kept clear of was Buchanan.'

'Why was that?'

'Something about the man made my skin crawl.'

'He has a different tale to tell.'

'Then he's lying.'

'According to Buchanan, you gave him permission to use your Christian name. He taunted me with the fact. You could only have done that if you were alone in his company at some point.' Fleetwood's eyes were glowing with anger now. 'Is that what happened?'

'I never went anywhere near the man.'

'Then why is he claiming that you did?'

'He just wanted to hurt you, Harold. If you went to confront him, he'd have been resentful. Buchanan simply struck out at you.'

'It wasn't done on impulse, I promise you. He's far too cool a customer to lash out at me. He bided his time then slipped the knife between my ribs with a grin.'

'What's going on?' she asked, worriedly. 'And what's all this nonsense about a knife between the ribs? As far as Buchanan is concerned, I've got nothing with which to reproach myself. I ought to be angry that you took him so seriously,' she continued, moving to the sofa to sit beside him with a hand on his arm. 'I'm your wife, Harold, and I've always been thrilled to be so. Are you going to believe a duplicitous rogue like Fraser Buchanan over *me*?'

'*Something* happened between you,' he said, glowering.

'I've only ever met the man twice and it was always when we were surrounded by other people. He's not interested in me, Harold. I'm a happily married woman with a wonderful family. Buchanan is a bachelor with a roving eye,' she told him. 'Everyone knows that. Why look twice at a middle-aged woman like me when there are so many single ones available, half my age and twice as beautiful.'

'They can't compare with you, Griselda,' he said, gallantly.

'Then let's hear no more about that evil man – all right?'

There was a long pause. 'All right,' he said at length.

'Promise me you won't ever see him again.'

'I felt as if I wanted to punch him on the nose.'

She laughed. 'And there was you, warning me to watch my language with Buchanan. All *I* was after was a chance to call him a few rude names. *You* came close to assaulting him!'

Shaking off his anger, he joined in the laughter.

* * *

143

Two streets away, a taxi pulled up outside the Unicorn Hotel. After getting out of the vehicle, Fraser Buchanan paid the driver then went up the steps to the entrance. As soon as he entered the lobby, the staff on duty there immediately stood up straight and gave him a dutiful smile. He went across to the reception desk and spoke to the duty manager.

'Have you had any new bookings today?' he asked.

'Yes, Mr Buchanan.'

'How many?'

'Six in all, sir,' said the man.

'Did any of the guests come straight from the Lotus?'

'Yes, sir – there were two of them. In view of what's happened, they said they felt very uncomfortable there.'

With a broad smile on his face, Buchanan went off to the manager's office to discuss a way to give the newcomers special privileges so that the Unicorn was their first choice in the future.

When they'd set out, Marmion had hoped that the journey would give them time to sift carefully through all the details of the murder. Out of the blue, however, he was confronted with the fact that Keedy had been looking for another job so that he could supplement his wage. Since he'd surely have discussed the idea with Alice, it meant that both of them had been – as Marmion now saw it – plotting behind his back. Wounded by what was, in essence, a minor conspiracy, he was hurt even more by Keedy's reference to union action. What had started out as the John Syme League in 1912 had expanded in two years into the National Union of Police and Prison Officers. Marmion regarded it as anathema.

'Have you actually joined NUPPO?' he demanded.

'I've been thinking about it, Harv – especially after those reports about the French army.'

'What the hell have they got to do with it?'

'They got together and fought for their rights.'

Marmion was baffled. 'You've lost me, Joe.'

'Don't you remember? Conditions were so bad in the trenches that French soldiers had a series of mutinies. They're a people who're used to taking on authority, as you know. That's what they did with the French Revolution and they tried something similar with the army.'

'The soldiers didn't try to *overthrow* the government,' Marmion contended. 'They simply drew attention to the fact that they were expected to fight in what they claimed were inhuman conditions.'

'The point is that they won their argument. Instead of putting the mutineers up against a wall and calling for a firing squad, they had the sense to realise that the soldiers had a valid complaint. As a result, they made the improvements that were being demanded.'

'That's not how I see it.'

'Use your eyes. The generals yielded to concerted pressure. There's a lesson in that for us.'

'Yes – don't join the French army.'

'If we all stick together, we can achieve anything.'

Struggling to contain his irritation, Marmion took a deep breath.

'Have you forgotten the regulations to which you subscribed when you first joined the police?' he asked. 'Being part of a union is strictly forbidden.'

'And we both know why, don't we? It was to stop us speaking up for ourselves. We simply have to do what we're told for the money they decide to pay us. It's not right,' affirmed Keedy. 'That's why John Syme fought to establish a union that could speak on our behalf.'

145

'Syme is a madman.'

'He talks a lot of sense, in my opinion.'

'He's been to prison two or three times.'

'It's only because he had the courage to tell the truth.'

'You obviously don't know the full story,' said Marmion. 'As it happens, I once worked with Syme. I was a constable at Gerald Road Station in Pimlico when he was an inspector there. Syme was a wild Scottish Presbyterian with a belief that he was *always* right. Dealing with someone like that is a real trial.'

'He sounds like Chat – only with a kilt and a funny accent.'

'Oh, he was far worse than the superintendent. Chat knows the importance of keeping on the right side of the commissioner. John Syme couldn't do that. When he was transferred to another station,' said Marmion, 'he protested to Sir Edward. He was then suspended while his complaint was investigated. The Disciplinary Board recommended that he was reduced to station sergeant.'

'That was cruel. No wonder he turned to the Home Secretary,' said Keedy. 'The *Police Review* supported Syme and there was quite a lot of sympathy for him. When he appealed to Churchill, the Home Secretary considered the case and offered him reinstatement – though not as an inspector.'

'And what did that idiot do?'

'He refused the offer on principle.'

'No, Joe, he let his pride get in the way of common sense.'

'You'd have done the same if you'd been reduced to a sergeant on grounds that were obviously unfair.'

'I wouldn't have let myself get into that mess in the first place,' said Marmion, vehemently, 'because I'd have been careful to consider the consequences. Syme never did that. Simply because the commissioner didn't do what he wanted him to do, he went over his head to the Home Secretary and did actually get his suspension reversed.' He leant closer to Keedy. 'Can you hear what I'm telling you, Joe?'

'Yes – you just don't like Syme.'

'Given the choice between him and Sir Edward Henry, I know which one I'd choose. When Syme got that offer from Churchill, he had, in a sense, won his case. Had he accepted reinstatement, he'd have been able to wear a police uniform again and the commissioner might have been forced to resign.'

Keedy gulped. 'Was it that serious?'

'Yes, Joe.'

'Sir Edward would have been a terrible loss.'

'Syme wouldn't care about that. His only interest was in himself. And now he's no longer in the police force, he has the gall to agitate against it. How did you get involved in NUPPO?'

'Someone gave me a copy of their advertisement.'

'Throw it away.'

'But it made me think.'

'NUPPO consists of a couple of hundred officers with a grievance against the police. In Syme's case, there are *lots* of grievances. He's one of those self-appointed martyrs. Forget the union, Joe. They're all hotheads. Don't get mixed up with them.'

'But I support their policy of demanding higher pay.'

'We all want that,' said Marmion, raising his voice, 'but most of us realise that we have to win a war first. You said earlier that unity is strength. I agree. We must all pull together. It's the only way to defeat the Germans and save this country from being run from Berlin. Isn't that a far more urgent need than putting a couple of pounds a week into the pockets of the bobbies of Britain?'

Keedy needed only a few moments to think about it.

'Yes,' he said, shamefaced, 'I suppose that it is.'

'Then let's hear no more about the union.'

'I didn't mean to upset you.'

'Well you did, so let's leave it there. You may not like the wages we get,' said Marmion, forcefully, 'but while they exist, we must get back to the case in hand and earn them.'

Arms folded, he turned away. Keedy was thoroughly sobered.

Griselda Fleetwood was both glad and relieved that she'd been able to reassure her husband that nothing untoward had ever occurred between her and her fiercest rival. When her husband had stormed into her suite, she'd been taken completely by surprise. Relations between the couple were usually harmonious and Fleetwood never had cause to shout at his wife the way he'd done earlier. It had rattled her. When he'd apologised for misunderstanding what Fraser Buchanan had told him, the two of them had a companionable drink together.

As soon as he'd finished his whisky and soda, he excused himself to go off to a meeting at his club. Pleased that they were now on good terms again, Griselda was nevertheless glad that he had to leave because she was conscious that she had not been entirely honest with him. Keen to make sure that he was no longer in the hotel, she went to the window and looked out. Her husband soon came out, got into his car and was driven off. She was about to turn away when she noticed a figure on the other side of the road. Dressed in a fur-collared coat and a Homburg hat, a man ambled along the pavement opposite. He stopped to take out a silver case, remove a cigarette from it and slip it between his lips. Putting away the case, he took out a lighter and ignited the cigarette. After taking a first puff, he glanced up at the hotel and saw Griselda framed in a first-floor window. He gave her a dazzling smile.

Raising his hat to her, Fraser Buchanan strolled calmly off.

The Master of the Old Berkshire Hunt lived just over the border in Oxfordshire. When they turned into the drive, the detectives could see a stable block to the right of what was a substantial Regency house. The car scrunched to a halt on the gravel forecourt and they got out. A servant opened the door to them and, when they identified themselves, he conducted them to the library and asked them to wait while he informed Major Garroway of their visit. Marmion and Keedy hardly had time to admire the painting above the fireplace before Garroway came marching in. He was a striking man in his sixties, tall, distinguished, straight-backed and with flowing grey locks. When introductions had been made, Garroway looked from one to the other.

'How did you know where to find me?'

'We're detectives, sir,' explained Keedy, smiling.

'We simply rang the chief constable of Berkshire,' said Marmion, 'and he kindly provided us with this address. I gather that you and he are good friends.'

'Yes, that's right. Hector rides out with us occasionally.'

'We won't intrude on you for long, Major. We're anxious to trace a lady who attended your hunt ball some four years ago.'

'Why?' asked the other, chortling. 'Didn't she pay for her ticket?'

'It's rather more serious than that.'

'Really?'

Marmion showed him the photograph and indicated the mystery woman. 'Do you by any chance recognise this lady?'

'No, but I recognise Sir Godfrey and Lady Brice-Cadmore. If you want to know who this lady is, why not ask Sir Godfrey?'

'That's no longer possible, I fear. He's been rushed to hospital and is in no condition to answer any questions. Besides, it was he who gave me this photograph,' said Marmion. 'I'm wondering if someone has the guest list for that particular ball.'

Garroway was curious. 'What exactly is going on, Inspector?'

'We're here in connection with a murder at a London hotel, sir.'

'Good heavens!' exclaimed the other. 'Are you telling me that this lady in the photo was the victim?'

'She might or might not have been a victim.'

'Don't you *know*?'

'I'm afraid not. Another lady was found dead at the hotel and this one disappeared. You can see why it's vital for us to find her.'

'I can indeed and, yes, there is someone who might be able to supply you with a name. She's been organising the ball for years and is frighteningly efficient. Don't be surprised if she's committed the names of all the guests at that particular ball to memory.'

'What's her name?' asked Keedy, taking out his notebook.

'Bunny Hassall.'

'Do you have her address, please?'

'I certainly do,' said Garroway. 'If anyone can help you, Bunny will. She's a remarkable woman. You'll see what I mean when you meet her.' He crossed to a desk and took out an address book. 'She lives no more than a few miles away. She'll soon point you in the right direction . . .'


Sorry to see her daughter go, Ellen Marmion stood at the open door and waved her off. Hours earlier, she'd been afraid to answer the door, but those fears had now disappeared. Thanks to Alice, she was no longer oppressed by demons. They'd been put to flight by some straight talking from her daughter who'd been appalled at the state that her mother was in. Ellen closed the door, came into the living room and picked up the book she'd borrowed from the library, certain that it would keep her absorbed for many untroubled hours.

Before she started to read it, however, she thought about Alice's future as the wife of a Scotland Yard detective. It would consist for the most part of a succession of lonely evenings, wondering whether her husband was safe and when he'd come back home. During the day, there would be no problem because Alice had a career of her own in the police. At the end of her shift, however, she'd be acutely aware of Keedy's absence. In order to have company, she might well decide to have a baby sooner rather than later. Ellen would have to take on a new role as a doting grandmother. She couldn't wait for that to happen.

She was still musing about her daughter's visit when she heard a noise. It was too distant to recognise. Even when it got slowly closer, she couldn't be certain what she was listening to. Ellen strained her ears. There was an eerie silence for a few seconds followed by a noise that she'd come to know only too well. It was the sound of enemy bombs being dropped on the capital. Another German air raid was taking place.

All of a sudden, the claims of William Le Queux and Quentin Dacey took on renewed credibility. Ellen blenched.

Could they be right, after all?

Lena Gosling was walking across the lobby when she saw a familiar figure coming into the hotel. She was surprised to see him.

'You're early,' she said.

'We have a crisis on our hands,' said Rogan. 'I want to do my bit to help. Also, I know that Mr Chell will be finishing early. It's important to have one man on duty here.'

'After what's happened, I couldn't agree more.'

'How is Millie?'

'She's still as nervous as a kitten. If truth be told, so am I but I'm not going to show it. Someone has to be calm and collected around here.'

'Have the police been back?'

'Inspector Marmion came to see Mr Chell about something. I don't know about the sergeant.'

'I do,' said Rogan, sourly. 'He came to see me at home.'

She was astonished. 'Why did he do that?'

'There's only one reason – I'm a suspect.'

'I can't believe that he'd think *you* were involved, Len.'

'Well, he does. Sergeant Keedy didn't put it into words but I could read that look in his eyes. He made me go through my statement line by line. I was dying to go to bed but he kept on and on at me.'

'I'm sorry to hear that.'

'I hope he hasn't said anything to Mrs Fleetwood. I need this job, Lena. If she knows I'm under suspicion, she might lay me off.'

'Mrs Fleetwood knows how reliable you are,' she said. 'And so does the manager. He spent the whole night here with you. Your job is safe. Mr Chell would speak up for you, I'm sure.'

'I'm glad that somebody would.'

'Cheer up, Len. You don't need to look so miserable.'

'That's exactly how I feel.'

'Then there's one way to put a smile on your face.'

Before she could tell him what it was, she caught sight of someone out of the corner of her eye. She turned to see Griselda Fleetwood coming down the stairs as fast as she could. Lena and the night porter greeted her in unison. Ignoring them completely, she brushed between the couple and went out through the front entrance.

Lowering his voice, Rogan spoke to Lena Gosling.

'What the hell's got into *her*?'

# CHAPTER FIFTEEN

Though they'd been warned to expect a remarkable woman, they were not really prepared for Bunny Hassall. Still in her fifties, she had a face that looked twenty years younger and had an almost youthful bloom on it. With sparkling eyes and a permanent smile, she seemed to radiate joy. The moment they met her, Marmion and Keedy felt inspired by the woman. Bunny was sitting in a wheelchair and, as soon as they'd been introduced, she went out of her way to explain that she bore the horse that had thrown her from the saddle no ill will even though it had led to her being paralysed from the waist down.

'It was my own fault,' she said, blithely. 'I asked Tosca to jump a fence that was far too high for her. She did try – God bless her – but the pair of us took an almighty tumble. Tosca recovered. I did not.'

They were in the living room of a rambling cottage with a thatched roof and overhanging eaves. Applewood was burning in the grate. The walls were adorned with paintings of horses. On the mantelpiece was a photograph of Bunny about to join the Boxing Day Hunt.

When she was told why they were there, she was delighted.

'You want me to help with a murder investigation?' she said with childish excitement. 'That's wonderful!'

'I'd like you to take a good look at this photograph,' said Marmion, handing it to her and pointing to the woman beside Sir Godfrey. 'We need to find out who this lady is and where we might find her.'

'I can tell you who's on the other side of dear old Godfrey,' she said. 'It's his late wife, Diana, such a delightful creature in every way. As for this other lady, I can't put a name to her, but I do recognise two other people here.' She picked each of them out with a delicate finger. 'This is Maurice and Gwendolyn Farrier. With a surname like that, you'd expect them to love horses yet neither of them has any interest. Their hobby is dancing so they never miss a hunt ball. How many years ago was it?'

'Four,' said Keedy.

'Then there's your answer.'

'I don't follow, Mrs Hassall.'

'I remember it clearly. The Farriers brought a guest with them and she is the lady standing next to Godfrey.'

'She's doing more than simply standing beside him,' Marmion pointed out. 'She's gazing intently at him.'

She tittered. 'Godfrey always was something of a charmer.'

'Had you ever seen this woman before?'

'No, Inspector. She was a complete stranger. But since I know who brought her, I'll be able to tell you her name.'

Without warning, she spun round in the wheelchair and propelled herself out of the room. Marmion and Keedy watched her go, amazed at her energy and total lack of self-pity.

'If a horse had done that to me,' said Keedy, 'I'd have wanted to kill, roast and eat it.'

'You can't blame the animal, Joe. Mrs Hassall doesn't. She knows that she was partly to blame, and she's come to terms with her disability. In her place, I wouldn't go near a hunt ball but she's happy to go on organising it as if nothing happened.'

'That takes guts.'

'It also takes a real love of horses. Even though it crippled her, she won't turn her back on that world.'

While they were waiting, they took the opportunity to look around the room. Horse brasses abounded and a horseshoe was nailed to one beam. There was also the faintest whiff of a stable in the air. Keedy looked at the framed portrait of Bunny Hassall, wearing a hard hat, hacking jacket, a pair of jodhpurs and some shiny boots as she sat astride her horse. In her hand was a glass raised in celebration.

'Is that what they call a stirrup cup?' he asked.

'I wouldn't know, Joe.'

'Do you think that's the horse that threw her?'

'It could be Tosca, I suppose.'

'How old do you think she is?'

'Are you talking about the mare or Mrs Hassall?'

'Mrs Hassall,' replied Keedy with a grin. 'She seems around my age, but she must be a lot older.' He looked around covetously. 'I'd love a place like this for me and Alice but – think of the cost.'

'Don't complain about police pay again,' warned Marmion.

'Sorry.'

They heard the sound of the wheelchair coming back and resumed their seats. When Bunny entered the room, she had a thick record book across her knees. Pulling up between them, she held the book up.

'This is the bible of the Old Berkshire Hunt Balls,' she said. 'If someone so much as put their head into the ballroom, their name will be in here.'

'Go back four years, please,' said Marmion.

'I would love to, Inspector. I had two legs in 1913 and used to ride out every day. Also, of course, there was no war on.' She flicked the pages of the book until she came to the right one. 'Here we are. The names are alphabetical so the Farriers are . . . yes, right here,' she said. 'They bought three tickets.'

'What was the name of their guest?'

'Vesta Lyle.'

'Miss or Mrs?'

'It doesn't say.'

'Could you give us the Farriers' address, please?'

'Yes, of course. I know it off the top of my head.'

As Bunny recited it, Keedy wrote it down in his notebook.

'Thank you,' he said. 'We'll go there immediately.'

'I do hope I've been able to help. I think it's unconscionable to steal someone else's name as this woman did at the hotel. No wonder Godfrey was so upset.'

'This photograph of his is valuable evidence.'

'I'm glad. Please give him my love when you next see him.'

'That may not be possible, I'm afraid,' explained Marmion. 'When I last saw Sir Godfrey, he was in a critical condition in hospital. They had grave doubts that he'd survive.'

'Oh!' she cried, a hand to her chest. 'I'm so, so sorry. We've been friends for forty or more years.' She turned away to hide her tears and only faced them again when she'd composed herself. 'Godfrey was not simply a friend,' she said almost dreamily. 'We were very close at one time. In fact, he once proposed to me. I was extremely flattered, of course, but I turned him down. If you adore horses, you don't want to spend all your time birdwatching. Diana was a far better wife than I could ever have been to him. She loved that festival they went to every year at some cathedral or other. That wouldn't have suited me. The best sound in the world, I believe, is the pummelling of hooves on grass when you ride hell for leather. That's music to my ears.'

Having left one hotel in a rage, Griselda Fleetwood had walked a hundred yards or so to another. When she reached the Unicorn Hotel, however, she stayed outside for several minutes to give herself time to control her temper. Only when she felt calm enough for a confrontation did she go into the building and walk over to the desk.

'I'd like to speak to Mr Buchanan, please,' she announced.

'I'm afraid that he's not here,' said the receptionist.

'He must be. Not long ago, I saw him only two streets away. I was certain I'd find him here.'

'He *was* here, it's true, but he had to leave.'

'Do you know where he went?'

'I believe he was returning to the Roath Court in Piccadilly.'

She glowered at him. 'I know very well where it is.'

'May I have your name, please?'

'Why do you ask?'

'I could tell Mr Buchanan that you were looking for him.'

'Don't bother,' said Griselda. 'I'll tell him myself.'

She hurried out of the hotel.

Claude Chatfield was responsible for deploying detectives on a number of cases and was adept at choosing the right men to investigate particular crimes. He was reading through a report of a daring robbery in Hatton Garden when he was interrupted by a visitor. Sir Edward Henry had just walked into the superintendent's office.

'I thought you'd still be with the Home Secretary,' said Chatfield. 'Your meetings with him tend to go on for hours.'

'I expected the same thing to happen today, but I was misled. Having been told that I'd be party to a discussion of some significance, I discovered that it had no significance at all.' His eyebrows arched in unison. 'Such are the ways of Cabinet ministers.'

'We're glad to have you back, Sir Edward.'

'Do you have any news for me?'

'If you're referring to the theft of thousands of pounds of jewellery, I have some excellent news. Three arrests have been made and all the property stolen from Hatton Garden has been recovered.'

'That's very commendable, Superintendent.'

'One of those arrested – you will not be surprised to hear – worked at the shop concerned. I wish every crime could be dealt with so swiftly.'

'So do I,' said the commissioner. 'It might stop the press hounding us the way that they do. What of this business at the hotel in Chelsea?'

'It's still in its early stages.'

'I'd hoped for some progress – and so had Harold Fleetwood.'

'You may tell him that Inspector Marmion is both diligent and tenacious. He won't give up until he's solved the murder and the disappearance of the hotel guest. In fact,' said Chatfield, 'he's driven to Berkshire in order to find out the real name of the lady who'd been staying in that room.'

'That could be a vital piece in the jigsaw.'

'There are still many other pieces to find, Sir Edward.'

'What about the victim herself?'

'She, alas, remains an enigma.'

'Has the newspaper appeal for help brought no information in?'

'There's been nothing of real value. It's very strange. You'd have thought that *somebody* would have noticed she was missing by now.'

'I don't envy Marmion. It's a baffling case.'

'Those are the ones he likes best, Sir Edward.'

'Typical of him – he's a first-rate detective.'

'That's because he's learnt from me,' boasted Chatfield. 'But even Marmion is by no means infallible.'

'Who is?' asked the commissioner. 'But we must make allowances for Marmion. His son ran away from home and they haven't a clue where he might be. That must prey on the inspector's mind.'

'I'm sure that it does in private. However, it won't stop him doing his job properly. When he's hunting down a killer, nothing else matters to him – not even his family.'


While Ellen thought every day about the disappearance of her son, it was her daughter she missed most at that moment. The sound of the air raid had awakened her dread. She needed Alice there to talk sense to her and to still her fears yet again. It was not to be. Her daughter was already on a bus somewhere on the other side of London. At least, that was what she thought. As she was hunched on the sofa, Ellen was jerked out of her foreboding by a loud knock on the door. Alice had come back, after all, to rescue her mother from her rising terror. Rushing to the door, Ellen opened it wide and got ready to give her daughter a grateful hug.

She was thwarted. Instead of Alice, it was Rene Bridger who was standing outside. Ellen felt a searing disappointment.

'Is anything wrong?' asked the visitor.

'I was . . . expecting my daughter.'

'Then I won't keep you long, Ellen,' said the other. 'I've been thinking about what you said earlier. You'd decided to go and hear that man speaking tomorrow.'

'I'm in two minds about it now, Rene.'

'Why is that?'

'It's a bit complicated. Look,' said Ellen, standing back, 'why don't you come in and have a cup of tea?'

'I thought you were expecting your daughter.'

'I was but . . . I doubt if she'll come now. She'd have had to cross London and that air raid would have put her off. Come on. I was just about to put the kettle on when you knocked on the door.'

'In that case . . .'


Darkness was starting to cover everything when they left Bunny Hassall's cottage and headed towards Wantage. They were both impressed by the way she'd coped with her disability and managed to keep so buoyant. The woman in the wheelchair was an example to everyone seriously injured by an accident. Robbed of many things in life, she was making the most of those that still remained.

'I don't think I could do that,' confessed Keedy.

'What are you talking about, Joe?'

'Mrs Hassall – she's so philosophical.'

'That was never your strong point. You're a man of action.'

'She was a woman of action until that fall. By the way, is Bunny her real name?'

'Anything is possible among horsey people,' said Marmion with a smile. 'They're a strange breed.'

Following the directions given to them, the driver took them to a small village and pulled up on a triangle of land outside a churchyard. Maurice and Gwendolyn Farrier lived in one of a cluster of houses nearby. The first thing that Keedy noticed was a pub further down the street. He turned hopefully towards Marmion.

'Don't even think about it, Joe.'

'I'm thirsty.'

'We're on duty.'

'Nobody will ever know.'

'I will,' said Marmion. 'Now let's find them, shall we?'

The Farriers lived in a rambling house with a large front garden. Built of red sandstone, its only external feature of interest was its solidity. Invited in, the detectives found the atmosphere slightly menacing. They were taken into a capacious but rather gloomy living room. Farrier saw them looking at the array of silver cups on the sideboard.

'Gwen and I are enthusiastic dancers,' he said, proudly. 'We've been lucky enough to win various competitions over the years.'

'That must keep you fit,' said Keedy.

'We do exercises every day.'

It was borne out by their appearance. Both in their late fifties, they were slim, well dressed and patently in excellent health. Keedy could just imagine them gliding effortlessly around a ballroom.

'Have you really come all the way from London?' asked Gwendolyn.

'Yes,' said Marmion. 'When you hear what's happened, you'll understand why.'

He gave them a highly edited version of events at the Lotus Hotel and told them about the visits to Major Garroway and to Bunny Hassall. Producing the photograph, he handed it over to Farrier.

'It was actually given to me by Sir Godfrey Brice-Cadmore,' he said, 'but it was Mrs Hassall who discovered that the lady next to him in the photo was a Vesta Lyle. Apparently, she was your guest at the Hunt Ball four years ago.'

'Yes, she was,' confirmed Farrier.

'Can you tell us about her, sir?'

'My wife is the best person to do that. Vesta is a relative of hers.' He passed the photograph to her. 'Or, at least, she was.'

'What my husband means,' said Gwendolyn, 'is that we haven't seen anything of Vesta for years. She turned up at short notice and . . . well, made herself at home. Technically, she's my cousin, but since she spent most of her time in France, I saw very little of her. We kept in touch with the odd birthday or Christmas card.' She studied the group photograph and picked out her relative at once. 'Yes, that's Vesta. I remember it being taken. I also remember that Vesta paid for a copy of it herself – heaven knows why. Most of the people in it were strangers to her. That was in 1913,' she continued, handing the photograph back to Marmion. 'After that, she just sort of drifted out of our lives.'

'Did she say why she'd come to see you?'

'Yes, her husband had died. He was French, incidentally, but she never took his name, which was Dufays – Alphonse Dufays. For professional reasons, she preferred to be known by her maiden name.'

'What sort of professional reasons?' asked Keedy.

'Vesta is an artist. For anyone with a serious interest in painting, she once told me, Paris was the place to be. She wanted to mingle in the Bohemian world of French painters. It sounded rather romantic.'

'I daresay there was a romantic appeal,' said Farrier, 'but Vesta had a realistic streak. She knew that most artists lived in abject poverty, so she looked for someone who'd support her financially. That's why she married Alphonse. She was quite honest about it.'

'What did her husband do?' said Marmion.

'He was something important in the French government. He adored Vesta and loved the idea of subsidising a talented artist. Nobody was more thrilled than Alphonse when her paintings began to sell for quite large amounts of money. I suppose he felt that he was getting a good return on his investment.'

'As she became more well known,' said his wife, taking over, 'Vesta travelled all over Europe. She even had an exhibition in Poland one year.'

'Did you ever see anything of her work?' asked Keedy.

'Oh, yes. She gave us one of her paintings when she was here.'

Keedy looked around. 'Is it hanging in here?'

'No,' said Gwendolyn. 'I'm afraid that it wasn't to our taste.'

'The truth is,' added Farrier, 'that it's up in the attic. It was a depiction of a picnic on the banks of the Seine. We could see that it had a lot of artistic merit.'

'Then why did you hide it away?' said Marmion.

'None of the people in the painting were wearing any clothes, Inspector. We felt that it was out of place in what was originally built as a vicarage.'

'Was the artist aware of your disapproval?'

'No, no, of course not,' replied Farrier. 'We told her how grateful we were. The irony is that the painting might be worth a lot of money, but we'd feel too embarrassed to offer it to a dealer. Also, of course, there's always the chance that Vesta might come back here.'

'That seems highly unlikely now, sir.'

'Do you think that she's dead?'

Marmion pursed his lips. 'We're ruling nothing out.'

Fraser Buchanan was working alone in the manager's office when the telephone rang. He was astonished to hear that Griselda Fleetwood was waiting in reception. Buchanan asked for her to be conducted to the office. He then got up, took his jacket from the hook on the back of the door and slipped it on again. After checking his appearance in the mirror, he opened the door wide. Griselda was only yards away. She responded to his warm smile with a ferocious scowl.

'Come on in, Mrs Fleetwood,' he said, standing aside then closing the door once she was in the room. 'This is a lovely surprise.'

'What are you playing at?' she demanded.

'I'm not playing at anything.'

'My husband came here earlier and you said something to upset him. He was furious.'

'Yes, he did get rather hot under the collar.'

'What did you tell him?'

'I told him the truth, that's all,' said Buchanan. 'You came to see me and, after a pleasant discussion, we were on first-name terms.'

'That's not strictly true.'

'Then our memories of the event differ.'

'I merely came to seek your advice.'

'And I gave it freely – do not open a hotel.'

'That wasn't what you said at first,' she reminded him. 'You were very interested in my idea. It appealed to you. Then I turned down your offer of putting money into the venture. Once I did that, you decided that you'd do your best to frustrate my ambition.'

'You were a rival, Griselda.'

'Don't you dare call me by my Christian name!'

'You can't expect me to encourage your fantasy.'

'It wasn't a fantasy when you saw its potential and offered to invest in it. You couldn't be nicer to me then.'

He smiled. 'I *like* being nice to you, Mrs Fleetwood.'

165

'It's too late to turn on your charm now. I've just come to tell you what a loathsome human being you really are. I've spoken to the police about you, so they're well aware of your dirty tricks.'

'I do not condone murder,' he said, seriously. 'I may have caused the Lotus some minor inconveniences but that's as far as I'd go. I give you my word of honour that I had nothing whatsoever to do with the problems besetting you.'

'Then why did you stop outside the hotel earlier on to gloat?'

'I just happened to be passing.'

'You're a liar, Mr Buchanan.'

'You can call me "Fraser" if you prefer.'

'I know what I'd *like* to call you, but I never sink to obscenities.'

'That's a sign of good breeding,' he said, smirking, 'though I suspect that your husband would have no qualms about showering me with expletives. Let me give you the same warning I gave him. If you wish to make an accusation against me, I'll call in the manager so that I have a witness. You might care to know,' he cautioned, 'that I have an exceptionally good lawyer. Slander and libel are his specialities.'

The conversation was over. The blistering anger that had taken her there was suddenly denied an outlet. Still convinced that he was in some way behind the murder at the Lotus, she realised that she'd have to be patient and wait for the police to prove it. Mastering her fury, she went across to the door and opened it.

'Goodbye, Griselda,' he cooed.

By way of reply, she went out and slammed the door behind her.

The conversation with Farrier and his wife had been a revelation. It altered the detectives' perspective on the case. In addition to the name of the missing guest, Marmion and Keedy had been given detailed information about her life and character. What didn't emerge was any explanation of why she'd signed the name of Lady Brice-Cadmore in the register at the Lotus Hotel. While staying there, she hadn't behaved like the Bohemian artist that she was alleged to be in real life. Nobody there had questioned Vesta Lyle's claim that she was a member of the English aristocracy. It was a part that she'd clearly played to the hilt.

While Gwendolyn had talked fondly of her cousin, her husband was less enthusiastic. He made no criticism of the artist, but he obviously had some reservations about the woman, not least the cavalier way that she'd turned up in the past with very little notice. There'd been little reciprocal hospitality. They had only once been invited to visit her in Paris but – because of her itinerant life – they only ever saw her on the rare occasions when she needed a bed for a few days in England. As they listened to Gwendolyn's reminiscences, all that Keedy could think about was the nude painting up in the attic. Marmion, however, was hoping for the chance to speak to Farrier alone because his memories of the woman might not be quite so sentimental. The opportunity eventually came when his wife went off to find some family photographs of her cousin. Marmion didn't have to prompt Farrier. Lowering his voice to a whisper, he spoke to them with urgency.

'There's something I must tell you,' he said. 'I've kept it from my wife because I don't wish to upset her by making her look at Vesta in a rather different light.'

'Go on, sir,' urged Marmion.

'I was a doctor before I took early retirement. As a result, I've always been an advocate of sound health in mind and body. It's one of the reasons we go dancing so much.'

'Better you than me,' said Keedy. 'I've got two left feet.'

'When she was last here, I discovered something about Vesta that troubled me a great deal. To be more exact, it disgusted me.'

'Why was that, sir?'

'I believe that the human body is a gift from God. Abusing it in any way is sinful. I won't go into the circumstances, but the upshot is this. I caught her injecting something into her arm.'

'Was it some form of medication?'

'It's not one I'd ever recommend to my patients,' said Farrier. 'The shameful thing is that it's been readily available from chemists for many years, as indeed have laudanum and arsenic. Only now is the medical profession waking up to the fact that these drugs are highly dangerous and, in larger doses, can be lethal. They should be strictly controlled by legislation.'

'What drug was she injecting into her arm?' asked Marmion.

'Cocaine.'

'We've seen the effect that can have if used too often.'

'It explained certain aspects of Vesta's behaviour.'

'Was the lady just dabbling with it?'

'No, Inspector,' said Farrier, 'she had a sizeable amount with her and admitted that she'd been taking it for years.'

'Surely, she was aware of the risks?'

'She's an artist. They live lives without boundaries.'

'I thought you said that her husband was a senior official in the government. He must have lived in a world of rules and regulations. He'd hardly sanction the use of cocaine by his wife.'

'Perhaps he was unaware of it. Vesta was very good at concealing the obvious symptoms. It was only because of my medical training that I realised something odd was going on.'

'I can see why you kept it from your wife,' said Keedy.

'With all her faults, Gwen liked her. Well, you've heard that note of nostalgia in her voice when she talks about Vesta. I'd hate to destroy the happy memories she has of her.'

'That's very considerate of you, sir.'

'I think that's why we haven't seen her for the last four years. Vesta was shocked at being caught in the act but not as shocked as my wife would be if she knew the truth.'

'It would shatter her image of the woman.'

'It would, Sergeant. She loves to boast about the famous artist in her family,' said Farrier, 'and enjoys impressing people. But nobody would be quite so impressed if they realised that Vesta Lyle is a cocaine addict.'

# CHAPTER SIXTEEN

Ellen Marmion had never been a close friend of Rene Bridger's because they had so little in common. If anything, she found the woman morose and apprehensive. Yet it turned out that there was another side to her, and Ellen was starting to see glimpses of it. As they sat in the kitchen and drank their leisurely cups of tea, Rene spoke more candidly to Ellen than she'd ever done before.

'It was my husband's fault our Alec joined up,' she confided. 'He egged our son on. Bert said that, because he was too old to fight himself, then someone in the family had to do it for him. I blame Bert.'

'When they brought conscription in,' Ellen pointed out, '*everyone* of a certain age would have had to join, including your son.'

'Our Alec wasn't allowed to wait for that. His father kept on and on at him until he went down to the recruiting station. It wasn't right, Ellen. The lad was barely eighteen.'

'Paul wasn't all that much older.'

'If only he'd waited until conscription, Alec might still be alive. As it was, he was killed at Mons in August 1914.'

'A lot of soldiers fell in that battle, Rene.'

'There's only one that matters to me,' said the other, eyes flashing. 'I've never been able to look at my husband in the same way since then. I believe he's got our Alec's blood on his hands.'

'That's unfair.'

'It's what I see. Bert sent him off to die when he could have waited a bit. Alec didn't want to go, and I did everything in my power to keep him safe at home, but my husband knew best.' Her lip curled back in a sneer. 'Husbands always do, don't they?'

'Harvey put no pressure on Paul to join up.'

'Then you were lucky.'

Iron had entered the woman's soul. Her anger was implacable.

'Why have you been having second thoughts about this meeting tomorrow?' asked Ellen, keen to steer her onto another topic.

'I found myself thinking about it. I wondered if this Mr Dacey really does have proof that the Germans have been sneaking into this country for years. Also,' added Rene, 'my husband said it was nonsense, but then, Bert says that about most things. So I thought I might go along just to annoy him.'

'I'm still hovering.'

'Earlier on you wanted to go.'

'Alice tried to talk me out of it.'

'She can't stop you, Ellen. It's your decision, not hers. What's the worst that can happen? If Mr Dacey can't do what he says in that advert, then we simply walk out of the meeting.'

'That's true.'

'On the other hand . . .'

'He might really have evidence to back up his claim.'

'That's why I decided to be there tomorrow. What about you?'

'Well . . .'

Ellen bit her lip and pondered.

Alice's journey back to her flat had been lengthened by the air raid. She was just about to change buses when she heard the distant buzz of the aircraft so she ran to the nearest Tube station for shelter. Like everyone else in London, she was getting used to daytime and night-time raids, and took the appropriate action. It meant that she was sitting below ground on a crowded platform for the best part of three-quarters of an hour. When she finally emerged with the others, she joined a bus queue and waited, conscious that it might be some time before the vehicle actually came. She let her mind wander.

After her visit home, she was worried about the way her mother had plunged into dejection after reading a novel. It was totally out of character. Ellen had always been such a sane, steady, level-headed woman who never let anything vex her for long. Yet a library book she'd borrowed had clearly shaken her to the core. Alice could only hope that she'd managed to restore her mother's confidence and dispel her fears.

When the bus finally came, she collapsed gratefully into a seat. Instead of worrying about her mother, however, she found that the person who monopolised her thoughts now was Jennifer Jerrold. Something about the policewoman's explanation for considering resignation did not ring true. Having believed her story when she first heard it, Alice now began to question the version she'd been given. Going on duty in the hours of darkness had introduced policewomen to the realities of life at night in the capital. Drunkenness, violence, prostitution and sexual assault were common sights, much of it accompanied by streams of profanities. It would have shocked Jennifer. as indeed it had shocked Alice at first.

Yet both of them had quickly adapted to the situation and learnt to take it in their stride. If Jennifer had told her parents what she'd been forced to experience, they'd have been outraged on their daughter's behalf. If that were the case, Alice asked, why had they waited for over a year before they did something about it and urged Jennifer to quit the force? People with a strong faith tended to react immediately to anything that ran counter to it. Mr and Mrs Jerrold would long ago have insisted that their daughter hand in her resignation. What had caused the lengthy delay?

The more she replayed the conversation she'd had with the other policewoman, the more Alice came around to the view that Jennifer had lied to her. Brought up in a God-fearing home, the woman was herself a committed Christian. Had she been so offended by the sight of drunken revellers vomiting in doorways, by the series of disgusting propositions put to her by lecherous off-duty soldiers or by the unmistakable sound of couples having intercourse in dark corners, Jennifer would have resigned at once. Instead of that, she'd put her sense of duty before her delicate sensibilities and remained in the Women's Police Force.

Alice began to wonder if she'd even mentioned to her parents the rigours of patrolling London at night. Knowing what their reaction would be, Jennifer might well have kept them ignorant of what their daughter routinely saw when wearing her uniform. Something else had forced the woman to resign. Out of friendship, Alice was determined to find out what it was.

The drive back to London was taken up largely by a discussion of what they'd learnt about Vesta Lyle. Claiming to be interested in her work,

Keedy said that it would have been helpful to see the example of it that was hidden away in the attic of the Farriers' house.

'It might have told us something about her character,' he said.

'Wanting to see that painting,' observed Marmion, drily, 'tells us something about *your* character, Joe.'

'You'd expect a man to paint that kind of scene, but not a woman.'

'Vesta Lyle sounds as if she's a very unusual woman.'

'I'm surprised that Mrs Farrier put up with her. Everything seems to have been done on her cousin's terms. She was *exploiting* them.'

'That's what artists often have to do. Most of them struggle to make a living so they sponge off friends and relatives.'

'But Vesta Lyle wasn't poor. Her paintings made money and she had a husband with a steady, well-paid job. She had exhibitions all round Europe. I wonder what her husband thought about that?' said Keedy. 'I'm looking forward to spending all my free time with Alice. What sort of husband and wife spend so much time apart?'

'It was their choice, Joe.'

They fell silent. Marmion was still weighing up the new evidence they'd gathered but Keedy was thinking about his earlier exchange between them. His intention of taking on another job had been well and truly quashed by Marmion and he accepted the wisdom behind his comments. As far as union activities went, however, Keedy hadn't been entirely put off by the inspector's harsh comments. He still believed that improved pay and work conditions could only ever by achieved by coordinated action from policemen throughout the country. War had increased their workload significantly, widening their range of responsibility as they enforced the dictates of the Defence of the Realm Act. DORA, as it was known, had empowered them to interfere in people's private lives in a way that was unthinkable before the war.

Yet there was no recognition in the pay structure of the Metropolitan Police Force of the additional and more dangerous duties they'd been compelled to take on. When the time came to demand more, Keedy vowed that he'd stand shoulder to shoulder with like-minded police officers, even if his companion didn't happen to be one of them.

Marmion ended the silence with an abrupt question.

'What was the most important thing we discovered today?'

'Don't make a horse jump something that's too high for it,' said Keedy, 'or you'll end up in a wheelchair like Mrs Hassall.'

'It's not something to laugh at, Joe. She was the one who came up with the name of Vesta Lyle and I'm eternally grateful to her for doing so. At a stroke, she gave this investigation the boost it needed.'

'At least we've got *something* to take back to Chat.'

'It might also help to appease Harold Fleetwood for a while,' said Marmion, 'though he won't be happy until the killer who caused all that trouble at his wife's hotel is dangling from the gallows.'

'He'd enjoy pulling the lever himself.'

'Yes – especially if the noose was around Buchanan's neck.'

'Do you think the Lotus can recover?'

'If anyone can breathe new life into it, Mrs Fleetwood can.'

Since a few guests had now left the hotel prematurely, it was reassuring to see a new one arriving that evening. She was a fleshy, middle-aged woman in an ocelot coat and a hat with ostrich feathers sprouting from it. The hotel's owner waited until the receptionist had booked her in before she moved across to speak to the newcomer.

'Good evening,' she said, sweetly. 'Welcome to the Lotus. I'm Griselda Fleetwood.'

'I've heard that name before.'

'I own this hotel.'

'Yes, that's right. Lady Carvington mentioned your name when she recommended this place to me. She stays here often, I gather.'

'That's true,' said Griselda, broadening her smile to conceal her animosity about their mutual friend. 'Lady Carvington has graced the Lotus many times.'

'She has such exacting standards. To gain her approval is a real achievement.'

'Thank you.'

'I had intended to be here earlier but the train from Derby was abominably late. Even in first class . . . it was also revoltingly dirty.'

'I'm sorry to hear that, Mrs . . .'

'Beech,' said the other, grandly. 'Mrs Amanda Beech.'

The receptionist pressed the bell on her desk to summon a porter, and a young man in a neatly pressed uniform appeared instantly. He picked up the suitcase that the taxi driver had brought in when he delivered his passenger. Mrs Beech sailed contentedly off in the wake of the porter. As soon as she was out of earshot, Griselda turned to Chell, who'd been watching from the other side of the lobby.

'How long do you think we'll be able to keep her?'

'She'll stay for one night, at least.'

'Not if Phyllis Carvington knows that she's here. She'll have her friend out of the Lotus in a shot.'

'Our troubles are only temporary, Mrs Fleetwood.'

'I'm beginning to doubt that.'

'Why?'

'It's just a feeling I have.'

'I wish I could share it. In launching his attack on us, Buchanan hoped to bring us down for good. If he's failed to do that,' said

Griselda, anxiously, 'he's bound to try something even worse. That's my greatest fear, Mr Chell. What *else* has he got up his sleeve?'

Fraser Buchanan was walking across the lobby of the Roath Court Hotel when someone stepped out from behind a potted palm and offered him an envelope. Taking it from him, Buchanan slipped it into his inside pocket.

'Thank you, Maitland,' he said.

He left the building with a smile of satisfaction.

'Tell me more about Vesta Lyle,' said Chatfield.

'You've heard all there is to hear, Superintendent,' said Marmion.

'Not quite,' added Keedy. 'You forgot to mention her gift to the Farriers of a nude painting she'd done. They felt too embarrassed to hang it on their wall, so it's hidden away in the attic. It's strange, really,' he went on. 'Mr Farrier was a doctor for many years. You'd have thought he'd be quite used to looking at naked bodies.' He turned to Chatfield. 'It was a painting of people having a picnic on a riverbank, sir.'

'I find the very notion offensive,' said the superintendent. 'What were they getting up to, that's my worry?'

'They were just sitting and eating, I suppose.'

'These people were *French*. They lack our social restraints. *Anything* could have happened and the idea that it was depicted by a woman makes the whole thing even more abhorrent.'

Marmion had delivered a comprehensive and measured report of their trip to Berkshire, emphasising that it had been well worth the time and expense to go there. Having listened carefully, Chatfield slapped his desk with the flat of his hand and made his decision.

'You've unmasked the killer,' he declared. 'Vesta Lyle's syringe was the murder weapon. She used it to give herself some kind of bizarre pleasure, but it could also inflict pain and death.'

'I'm afraid that I don't agree,' said Marmion.

'But it's so obvious, man.'

'What was her motive?'

'She must have hated the other woman enough to commit murder.'

'Most of us know when we're hated, Superintendent. We tend to avoid the people who pose a threat to us. If the victim was aware of the danger Vesta Lyle represented, why on earth did she agree to visit the woman in the privacy of a hotel room?'

'That's what I wondered,' said Keedy.

'Then you're both wrong,' said Chatfield, tetchily. 'In my opinion, our task is now much easier. Instead of looking for a third person who committed the murder, then abducted Vesta Lyle, we only have to search for the artist herself.'

'We believe that she might also be a victim, sir.'

'Then why hasn't her body turned up, Sergeant?'

'I can't answer that.'

'It's because she was actually responsible for the crime.'

'Once again,' said Marmion, 'I come back to the taxi she ordered.'

When he repeated his theory that Vesta Lyle would never have ordered a taxi if she didn't expect to use it, he at least had the reward of making Chatfield think twice. After referring to the notes he'd made during Marmion's report, the superintendent took a different line in the debate.

'Let's talk about that ball,' he said. 'What was Vesta Lyle doing there in the first place?'

'She was taking up an invitation from her cousin,' said Marmion.

'Surely it was one she'd be far more likely to refuse. Given her

178

predilection for the company of decadent artists, she'd have thought the event would be unbearably stuffy.'

'That was something I raised with Mr and Mrs Farrier. They belong to the county set. Their guest certainly didn't. She was most at ease in a world where the rules of behaviour are, as you suggest, a little more fluid.'

Keedy grinned. 'Nude picnics on the riverbank, for instance.'

'There wasn't any nudity at the Hunt Ball, Sergeant. You saw that photograph of it. There was an air of formality. Everyone was wearing their best bib and tucker.'

'Vesta Lyle wasn't. She had to borrow a dress from her cousin.'

'In other words,' said Marmion, 'she had to conform for once, and I don't think she enjoyed that. Why did she do it? The answer, I think, lies in that photograph. She chose to stand next to Sir Godfrey Brice-Cadmore and to look at him in that way. For his part, he couldn't, for the life of him, remember who she was when he singled her out of that group, but he felt that he somehow knew her. I do hope his relapse is only temporary. If and when he starts to recover,' he continued, 'the name of Vesta Lyle might somehow jog his failing memory.'

'Ah,' said Chatfield, face clouding, 'there's something you need to know, Inspector.'

'Is it about Sir Godfrey?'

'We had word earlier that he passed away in his sleep.'

Marmion felt a stab of grief. 'Oh dear,' he said, 'I am sad to hear that. I'm afraid that he's another victim of what happened at the Lotus Hotel. It shattered him to learn that someone was pretending to be his wife. He was such a help to us.'

'We can't expect any more assistance from him.'

'Then we must look elsewhere, sir.'

'In which direction?' asked Chatfield.

'We need to know much more about Vesta Lyle,' said Marmion, pensively. 'The Farriers told us a great deal, but they admitted that they had no idea where the woman was most of the time. There were occasions when cards they sent to her home address in Paris were returned unopened. It's apparent that she deliberately kept them in the dark about her movements, then popped up in this country when it suited her. Why did she do that?'

'Perhaps she wanted to shock them,' said Keedy.

'From what we've heard about her, I think she'd enjoy giving them an occasional jolt. Look at that painting she gave them.'

'I wish I could.'

'You told me that her husband worked for the government,' said Chatfield. 'What exactly did he do?'

'We don't know, sir,' said Marmion, 'but that's a good starting point. We need to find out a lot more about him and about the nature of their marriage.'

'What was his name?'

'Alphonse Dufays.'

'And was he a civil servant?'

'The Farriers were not sure. Having met him that once, they felt he must have been quite senior in the government. According to them, he was obviously well paid. He and his wife had a lovely house in the Paris suburbs, it seems. Is there any way we can get more detail about him from our French counterparts?'

'I doubt it,' admitted Chatfield. 'Since the war started, normal channels of communication have disappeared. Everything is controlled by military necessity now. The French police have neither time nor inclination to deal with any random requests.'

'They might if we stressed the importance our enquiry,' said Marmion.

'The information we got from them about Alphonse Dufays might help to solve a murder and explain what Vesta Lyle was doing in this country.'

'Her late husband was only one of thousands employed by their government. As far as they're concerned, he was a minor cog in a vast machine that is now straining all its sinews to fight a war. At this moment in time, nothing else matters to them.'

'That's a harsh truth but we may have to accept it.'

Keedy snapped his fingers. 'I've just remembered something.' The others turned to him. 'The murder victim was wearing clothing from Paris. Was she a friend of Vesta Lyle's who'd come over from France?'

'It's possible,' said Marmion.

'In my opinion, it's very possible.'

'That's why it's so frustrating,' cried Chatfield. 'We have too many possibilities and no real certainties.'

'We have one certainty, sir.'

'I'm not even convinced about that.'

'We have the name of the guest staying in that room at the Lotus.'

'Do we?'

'Yes, sir.'

'The hotel register describes her as Lady Brice-Cadmore, a woman she met at a hunt ball four years earlier.'

'Oh, I don't think Vesta Lyle had any time for the wife,' said Marmion.

'What do you mean?'

'She went to that ball specifically to see Sir Godfrey.'

'Why do you think that, Inspector?'

'It's because she asked for a copy of that photograph. Apart from the Farriers, everyone else in that group was unknown to her – with one exception. That's why she stood next to Sir Godfrey Brice-Cadmore.'

\* \* \*

181

Nervous at the best of times, Millie Jenks was now in a state of almost continuous apprehension. She was terrified to go anywhere near the room where she'd made the grisly discovery and feared that it would haunt her for the rest of her life. When she'd first secured the job at the Lotus, she'd been filled with pride, yet it now seemed like a prison. Millie had thought of leaving but that would mean she was letting down Lena Gosling and the other people who had faith in her. It would also upset her parents who'd been boasting about their clever daughter's job. In their eyes, even the tedious and unskilled work she did had a distinct lustre because it was in a hotel for the wealthy and titled. Fortunately, both her father and mother were illiterate so they wouldn't have been able to read news of the murder. Her one source of comfort was that Lena Gosling had looked at all the newspapers ordered daily by the hotel and found no mention of Millie in any of them. She had at least been spared that torture.

It was Lena who was still propping the girl up. When she found Millie loitering in the laundry room, she put an arm around her.

'It's no good hiding in here,' she said. 'If you have a problem, Millie, you simply have to confront it.'

'Oh, I couldn't, Mrs Gosling.'

'It's a challenge, I know, but I think you're brave enough to face that challenge, aren't you?'

'No, I'm not.'

'Would you do it if I was by your side?'

'I'm not sure.'

'That would be cheating, anyway,' said the older woman, dismissing the idea. 'It's something you have to do on your own.'

'I've tried,' whined Millie, 'I really have. I've been there two or three times and, as soon as I see the door to that room, I feel sick.'

'You have to fight against that feeling.'

'I can't, Mrs Gosling. My stomach starts churning and my legs turn to rubber. Then there's this pounding in my head.'

'All right,' said the other, unwilling to cause Millie even more distress. 'I won't press you. Just remember what I said. Stop treating that part of the hotel as if it's out of bounds. It's getting late now. You go off to bed and make sure you get a good night's sleep.'

'I haven't slept a wink since it happened.'

'Give it time, Millie. It will get easier.'

'But it hasn't, Mrs Gosling,' said the other. 'It's got worse.'

One of the perquisites of his rank was that Marmion had a police car to take him home. At the end of a very long day, he and Keedy were being driven to their respective addresses. Rain was bucketing down and a gusty wind was hurling it at the windows of the vehicle.

'It's a nasty night out there,' said Keedy.

'I know, Joe. It's in weather like this that I start wondering how Paul is getting on. Does he have shelter? Is he warm and safe? I hate the thought of him being huddled under a hedge somewhere and getting soaked to the skin.'

'Don't worry about him. He's a survivor. The army toughened him up. He'll pull through somehow.'

'I hope so. It's such a worry.'

'Then it's a credit to you that you never talk about it when we're at work. I'm not sure that I could block it out the way that you can, Harv. It would gnaw away at me.'

'I deal with it my way,' said Marmion. 'I'll make a bargain with you. I won't mention Paul if you promise not to talk about NUPPO again.'

'Fair enough,' agreed the other. 'But that doesn't mean that I've forgotten about the union.'

'I accept that, Joe.'

'Let's talk about Vesta Lyle. She fascinates me.'

'We must get more information about that husband of hers. They seem to have had a very strange marriage.'

'What do you think he made of her nude painting?'

'If he loved her enough to marry her, he must have approved of her work. Most husbands in his position would feel proud of his wife.'

'But very few of us would *be* in that position,' said Keedy. 'How would you like it if your wife disappeared to Poland for an exhibition?'

'If she earned a lot of money there, I think I could cope with her absence. She could pay to get our roof fixed before the winter.'

Keedy laughed. 'It was a serious question.'

'Then the serious answer is that I don't know. We're dealing with people from a different class, Joe, and the husband is from a different country. He and his wife have their own set of rules. It's not for us to sit in judgement on those rules.'

'Vesta Lyle lives with a man who obviously has a good income. Most wives in that position wouldn't even consider working.'

'She's the odd one out.'

'Why doesn't she use her married name?'

'I really don't know.'

'Do you think she's still alive?'

'I'm certain of it.'

'Why?'

Marmion shrugged. 'I can't explain it.'

'Maybe we'll get an explanation tomorrow,' said Keedy. 'Now that we've released her name to the press, everyone in the country is going to know that Vesta Lyle, a famous artist, is wanted in connection with a murder. We'll have the eyes of a nation looking for her.'

'I wish that were true. Unfortunately, it isn't. The eyes of the nation are too busy scanning the skies for the next air raid or looking at the Channel ports in case there's a German invasion. We're competing with the war, Joe. That's what people will read about tomorrow.'

Ellen Marmion was perplexed. After the unexpected visit of Rene Bridger, her decision to ignore the lecture by Quentin Dacey had been thrown into doubt. She was now tempted to go, after all. There was someone to accompany her now and that was reassuring. Rene had changed her mind completely and that had a strong effect on Ellen's judgement. Should she do the same? Her mind was like a pendulum, swinging to and fro at regular intervals. It was dizzying.

In a bid to get away from making a decision, she picked up her library book and started to read it, trying to shut out everything else. It was a well-intentioned failure. With one novel in her hands, she found herself thinking about the previous one she'd read. *The Invasion of 1910* kept forcing its way into her consciousness. There was no escape. After hours of wavering, she made a resolve. No matter how late her husband came home, she would stay awake to speak to him. Unable to make up her own mind, she would turn to him to do it for her.

When she went to bed, therefore, she put on her dressing gown, left the bedside light on and started on her library book again. Her plan worked. Now that she'd elected to discuss the situation with her husband, she was able to concentrate on her novel and enjoy its sunlit world of romance and drama. Ellen was at last content.

After dropping Keedy off at his flat, the police car drove on through the driving rain. It was well past midnight now, but Marmion was not weary. His mind was still buzzing with ideas relating to aspects of the case.

Though he didn't entirely agree with the inspector, Chatfield had more or less given him a free hand. Marmion could take whatever initiatives he wished. That was a positive bonus in an investigation where he had to think on his feet and make snap decisions. What made everything so difficult for the detectives was that he and Keedy were outsiders. They were dealing with a hotel frequented almost entirely by female members of the aristocracy, and searching for an artist whose way of life was a mystery to them. To make matters even more complicated, the artist, Vesta Lyle, had lived in France for years in a highly unconventional marriage. The case was mired in mystery.

When the car pulled up outside his house, Marmion thanked the driver, got out and dashed through the rain to the front door. Letting himself into the house as quietly as he could, he hung up his hat and raincoat then padded softly upstairs. Light was showing under the door of the bedroom. Opening the door gingerly, he saw that Ellen was fast asleep with an open book across her lap. He tiptoed across to her, removed the book gently from its position, then pulled the blanket up over his wife. He placed the book on the bedside table then reached under the pillow for his pyjamas.

It was a typical night at the Marmion household.

# CHAPTER SEVENTEEN

Though she usually slept soundly at the hotel, Griselda Fleetwood had a disturbed night and rose much earlier than usual. By six o'clock, she was already on the prowl. When she came down into the lobby, she saw Rogan seated behind the reception desk. At the sight of the owner, he leapt to his feet.

'Good morning, Mrs Fleetwood,' he said.

'Good morning.'

'I wasn't expecting to see you up at this hour.'

'I couldn't sleep. I know it must seem like closing the door after the horse has bolted but I simply had to get out of bed to check everything.'

'That's *my* job.'

'What sort of a night has it been?'

'It's been very quiet, Mrs Fleetwood.'

'Is there anything at all to report?'

'No,' he replied. 'I only had to let one guest in after midnight. I wish it was always like this. Mr Chell asked me to do my rounds more often and that's exactly what I did.'

'Good.' About to move off, she was nudged by a memory. 'Oh, I know what I meant to ask you. Have you seen anything of Maitland, the young porter we took on not long after we first opened?'

'I haven't seen Ian Maitland for years.'

'Mrs Gosling says that he's now working at the Roath Court.'

Rogan feigned surprise. 'Is he? I didn't know that.'

'So you've never seen him lurking around here?'

'If I had, I'd have reported it to Mr Chell.'

'Of course,' she said. 'By the way, as I was coming downstairs, I thought I heard the front door being unlocked.'

'Yes, Mrs Fleetwood, you did. The newspapers are delivered early. I brought them in.' Bending down behind the desk, he brought up a small pile of them and set them on the counter. 'I've barely had time to glance at the front pages, but I did notice that there was something about the Lotus on most of them.'

'Let me see,' she said, grabbing the first newspaper.

'They've found out the name of that lady who was staying here.'

Absorbed in a front-page article, she was no longer listening. The Lotus was given coverage second only to the latest war report. Griselda gritted her teeth as she read on. Casting one newspaper aside, she snatched up another then worked her way steadily through the pile. At length, she looked up in despair.

'They make this place sound like a death trap,' she protested.

'Ignore them, Mrs Fleetwood.'

'Don't they realise how much damage they can do to us by printing this kind of drivel? It's monstrous.'

'The police know who our guest really was, that's the main thing.'

'Vesta Lyle,' said Griselda, before tossing the last newspaper aside. 'Who the devil is she? And why didn't the police tell me as soon as they knew her name? It's a conspiracy, that's what it is,' she went on, cheek muscles taut. 'Fighting against the press is a hard enough job, but I have to take on the Metropolitan Police as well now. Just wait until I see Inspector Marmion.'

Unaware that his name was being taken in vain, Marmion was at that moment stirring in his sleep before coming fully awake. Through one bleary eye, he was just in time to see his wife putting a cup of tea on the bedside table. He murmured his thanks.

'I knew you'd want an early start,' she said.

'You should have had a lie-in, Ellen. I could have made the tea.'

'What time did you get home last night?'

'It was late.'

'I didn't hear you come in.'

'That was deliberate,' he said. 'If I wasn't a policeman, I reckon that I'd make a very good burglar.'

'There's no such thing. Burglars are all very bad.'

Dying to tackle him about her dilemma, Ellen knew that it wasn't the right moment. He needed time to drink a reviving cup of tea, visit the bathroom and get dressed. Postponing the discussion, she went off to prepare breakfast so that he had a good meal inside him as he set off on what would be another punishing day.

They were eating the last of the toast when she finally spoke up.

'Harvey . . .'

'Yes, love.'

'There's something I've been meaning to ask you.'

'If it's about the wedding, I'd rather hear it another time. I really am in a rush now.'

'Rene Bridger wants me to go to a lecture with her,' she said, adjusting the facts slightly. 'It's about the threat of German spies.'

'There isn't one.'

'This man claims that there is.'

'What's his name? It's not Quentin Dacey, is it?'

She was surprised. 'Why – do you know him?'

'I know *of* him, Ellen. He's a scaremonger, trying to spread fear among us. He's been to Scotland Yard quite a few times, demanding police protection.'

'Does he need it?'

'Dacey thinks so, but the commissioner doesn't. Besides, he can't spare men to go on protection duty. Our manpower is at full stretch. We've had to recall retired officers to increase our numbers.'

'So it's a waste of time me going to the lecture, is it?'

'Go along, if you fancy,' said Marmion, 'but make sure you ask him where his evidence is. German spies have not infiltrated this country. They're all behind barbed wire on the Isle of Man. I know, I went there with Joe. That's why I think Quentin Dacey is a fake.'

Ellen sighed. She was more confused than ever now.

Alice's concern for Jennifer Jerrold had grown. Something had happened to make the latter tell her an obvious lie. It was very unusual for someone like Jennifer to deceive anyone. She was known for being honest and straightforward. Only something serious would make her act so uncharacteristically. Since she knew which bus the other policewoman would take to work, Alice made sure that she was at the stop to meet it. Jennifer was the last of a dozen people who got off the bus. When Alice fell in beside her, she was taken aback.

'Good morning,' she said.

'I won't pretend that I'm here by accident,' said Alice. 'I've been thinking about what you told me yesterday.'

'Oh, I see . . .'

'We both know that you're not really planning to resign because your parents are forcing you to do it. Had that been the case, you'd have left long ago. Am I right Jenny?'

'Why are you so bothered about it?'

'You're my friend. Caring about someone is what friends do. Also, you're a very good policewoman – better than me, in fact.'

'Oh, I don't know about that. It's in your blood, Alice.'

'Forget about me. Let's talk about you.'

'I've decided it might be time to leave, that's all.'

'No, it's not. A big decision like that needs a big reason. I'd like to know what it is.'

'Look,' said Jennifer, 'it's very kind of you to take an interest in me but there's no need. You've got much more important things to worry about than me – your wedding, for instance. I heard about that.'

Alice put a hand on her arm to stop her. 'What is it, Jennifer?'

'I'm within my rights to resign, aren't I?'

'This is nothing to do with your rights, is it?'

Alice looked deep into her eyes and saw mingled pain and anxiety. Jennifer was suffering yet reluctant to confide in anyone. She shifted her feet uneasily. Wanting to turn away, she was held captive by the intensity of Alice's gaze. At length, tears began to form.

'There is something,' she admitted.

'Is somebody bullying you at work?'

'No, no, it's nothing like that. I get on well with everybody.'

'Then what's the problem?'

'It's a man.'

'Who is he?'

'That's the trouble. I don't know.'

'Is he bothering you?'

'He keeps following me,' said Jennifer, voice quavering. 'It's been going on for months. I just don't know how to cope with it, Alice. That's the real reason I'm leaving. This man is making my life a misery.'


As a rule, Harold Fleetwood returned to his house in St Albans at the end of each day but the crisis relating to the Lotus Hotel kept him overnight in London at his club. When he got to his office that morning, he found his wife waiting for him. The moment he walked into his office, she was ready to fire the first question at him.

'Have you seen the newspapers?' she asked.

'Not yet, Griselda.'

'The police have identified our missing guest.'

'Who is she?'

'Her name is Vesta Lyle and she's an artist of sorts who lives in France. What is she doing in England? Why did she pick on the Lotus? And why use a false name?'

'You should be asking the police.'

'I would've done that if they'd had the courtesy to tell me what was going on. But they didn't. Nobody from Scotland Yard bothered to tell me about this latest development. If I hadn't opened a newspaper this morning, I'd still be unaware of it.'

'That's totally unacceptable,' he said, angrily. 'You should have been the first to know.'

'It's the way that the news has been presented that annoys me, Harold. The reports seem to imply that the Lotus is at fault. They show the hotel in a very poor light.'

'Editors need their heads banging together.'

'You have more influence with the press than I do,' she said. 'Most of them find the concept of a successful businesswoman hard to stomach. That's why there's been that campaign of innuendo against me.'

'Yes, and we know who orchestrated that.'

'Buchanan.'

'He's always had some tame reporters in his pocket.'

'Leave it to me, my love,' he said, taking her by the shoulders. 'I'll cancel the morning's appointments and get across to Fleet Street at once. By the time I've been through it like a whirlwind, they'll have to name it Fleetwood Street.' They shared a laugh. 'When I've dealt with them, I'll have another crack at Buchanan.'

'No, no,' she said in alarm. 'Leave him be. The police are looking into his involvement. You made your feelings known to him and that will be enough. He's probably shaking in his shoes already.'

Fraser Buchanan stood at the counter and scrutinised the proof copy with great care. Only two slight emendations were necessary. He handed the sheet back to the printer.

'I'll need four hundred of them,' he said with a broad grin.

Marmion and Keedy climbed into the back of the police car and settled down. The vehicle moved off through the thickening traffic.

'It's the third visit to Berkshire for you,' observed Keedy. 'You'll soon know your way around blindfolded.'

'We may come again before we're finished, Joe.'

'That suits me. Putting distance between us and Chat is always a pleasure. What are we hoping to find out today?'

'We need as much detail about Vesta Lyle's private life as the Farriers can dredge up. Now that they've had time to go through old letters and cards from her, they should be able to tell us a lot more.'

'Why did she stay at an expensive hotel in London when she could have had free accommodation in Berkshire?'

'That's one thing they can't tell us.'

'Pity.'

'The Farriers didn't even know that she was in this country.'

'Yet the strange thing is that they weren't upset,' said Keedy. 'If I had a cousin in France who came to this country, the least I'd expect was a warning of her visit.'

'As we found out, they just accept her weird behaviour.'

'It's not weird, Harv – it's downright rude.'

'There is something we ought to remember.'

'What's that?'

'She wasn't here as Vesta Lyle,' said Marmion, 'but as Lady Diana Brice-Cadmore.'

'Maybe she felt she needed a title if she was staying at the Lotus. She wanted to be on equal terms with the aristocracy.'

The car suddenly came to a juddering halt as a horse-drawn cart swerved into its path. They took time to manoeuvre their way past it, then pressed on.

'Have you seen any of the papers this morning?' asked Marmion.

'I had a glance at one of them.'

'Mrs Fleetwood will be hopping mad.'

'That's nothing new.'

'When I offered to contact her yesterday evening, Chat said that he'd take care of it, but he was hauled off to a long press conference then had a couple of hours with the commissioner.'

'Do you think he had time to send word to her?'

'I doubt it.'

'But he's so efficient, as a rule.'

'Even the best horse stumbles.'

'That means he'll get another visit from Mrs Fleetwood.' They traded a knowing glance. 'By the way, Alice called in to see her mother yesterday. Because you're tied up with this case, she was at a loose end.'

'Don't rub it in.'

'Ellen was fast asleep when I got back but we did have a proper conversation this morning. She surprised me.'

'Why?'

'She wants to hear a lecture by Quentin Dacey.'

Keedy laughed. 'Was she *serious*?'

'Oh, yes – a friend of hers asked Ellen to go.'

'Does either of them know what a fraud Dacey is?'

'Obviously, they don't.'

'That man will do anything to get publicity.'

'He has a following, Joe.'

'Is Ellen going to listen to him?'

'My advice was to stay well clear of him,' said Marmion, 'but I can't stop her and Rene Bridger going, if they really want to. I did remind Ellen what we saw on the Isle of Man.'

'That's the only place you'll find any German spies.'

'I suggested that she told that to Dacey.'

Ellen Marmion had decided to take her husband's advice. He had reinforced what Alice had told her mother. Both of them had been strongly against her interest in attending a lecture by a man with such a questionable agenda. Of the two, Alice had been the more forceful, fearing that someone as suggestible as her mother would come away from the lecture with notions that would only cause unnecessary disquiet. At a time when Britain and her allies were suffering reverses on the battlefield, people on the Home Front needed something to soothe them. Quentin Dacey would never deliver it. He was bent on sowing fear and panic.

When her friend called for her, Ellen had her excuse ready.

'I'm not feeling well, Rene,' she said.

'What's the matter with you?'

'I feel a bit off colour, that's all.'

'It didn't stop you brushing the front path a short while ago,' said Rene Bridger, suspiciously. 'I watched you.'

'Why don't you go on your own?'

'It's because I prefer company. I've never been to a lecture before and, to be honest, I feel a bit nervous about it. Having you beside me would settle me – and I'd do the same for you.'

'That's true,' admitted Ellen.

'Your husband told you not to go, is that it?'

'No, it isn't. Well, that's not exactly what happened, anyway.'

'Bert tried to stop me,' said the other. 'He said that only morons would listen to a man like Mr Dacey. So I told him that he was married to a moron and walked out.' Rene cackled. 'That shut him up.'

'Harvey said that Mr Dacey was a terrible nuisance to the police. He claims that, because he speaks the truth about Germans, they're out to kill him.'

'That shows you how brave he must be.'

'If he was that brave, he wouldn't keep begging for protection.'

'All right,' said Rene, resignedly. 'I can see what you're trying to tell me. You're scared to hear the truth.'

'I just don't believe that's what we'd hear.'

'How do you know if you're stuck at home, pretending to be ill?'

'I'm sorry I said that. It was a silly excuse. But I feel so uneasy about the whole thing, Rene.'

'So do I, but it doesn't put me off going. I'm just glad of an excuse to go into the West End. If I get bored with Mr Dacey, I can go and look at the shops instead. You'd enjoy doing that, wouldn't you?'

'Yes, I suppose I would.'

'When did you last see what the big stores have got to sell?'

'It must be months ago.'

'Then give yourself a treat and come with me.'

'I don't know, Rene . . .'

'Yesterday, you were keen to go. Today, you've lost your nerve. Don't you want to *know* what's really going on in this war?'

'In one way, I do.'

'Then stop shilly-shallying,' said Rene, brusquely. 'Put on your hat and coat and come with me. Why not go as far as Leicester Square before you finally decide? If you're still afraid to listen to the lecture, I'll go in there alone.' She smiled. 'But I fancy that you'll stay with me somehow.'

'I might . . .'

With a long list of things to do that morning, the last person that Claude Chatfield wanted to see was the owner of the Lotus Hotel. When she was shown into his office, she was obviously primed for attack. He could almost see steam rising from her. Jumping up behind his desk, he came across to her and gestured towards a chair, manufacturing a pale imitation of a smile as he did so.

'How nice to see you again, Mrs Fleetwood,' he lied.

'Inspector Marmion ought to be here as well.'

'That's out of the question, alas.'

'Why?'

'He and the sergeant are busy gathering information.'

'Is it the kind of information that *I* might get told about?' she asked, pointedly. 'Or will I have to wait until it appears in the press?'

He cleared his throat. 'I owe you an apology, Mrs Fleetwood,' he said, penitently. 'There's been an unfortunate oversight on my part.'

The journey to Berkshire seemed quicker than on the previous day and it was also far less contentious. There was an unspoken agreement between the two of them to refrain from any mention of additional jobs or union activity. Once Keedy had confessed that he'd been thinking about work as a nightwatchman, he saw how unrealistic the idea was. Since he already had a taxing job, he'd have little energy left for secondary employment. More importantly, he might imperil his career in the Metropolitan Police. Marmion might have won the argument on that score, but he knew that he'd failed to stamp out Keedy's interest in NUPPO. He was also aware of growing unrest among the rank and file, leading to an increase in the numbers joining the union. His future son-in-law was not the only police officer with serious complaints about the pay structure and the terms of employment. One day – Marmion knew – it would come to a head. All that he could do was to hope that it didn't happen until the war was finally over.

Since they'd been warned that the detectives might return, Maurice and Gwendolyn Farrier had prepared some refreshments. All four of them sat around the table, drinking tea.

'As requested,' said Gwendolyn, 'I've had a good search up in the attic.'

'What did you find?' asked Marmion.

'As I warned you,' she continued, 'letters from Vesta were rare events, cards even more so. I could only find these.' She handed him a small pile, tied up in blue ribbon. 'Some of them have little drawings that Vesta added to amuse us.'

'Thank you, Mrs Farrier. I'll enjoy looking through them.'

'What sort of drawings are they?' asked Keedy.

'They're just squiggles, really,' she explained.

'If she's that good as an artist, they might be worth something. I read somewhere that even signatures of famous people can be bought and sold for lots of money.'

'I've been thinking about her wedding,' said Marmion. 'Was your cousin a Catholic?'

'No – but she converted to Catholicism.'

'Was that a necessary condition?'

'No, I don't think so. Alphonse was not the sort of man to force her into any commitment as serious as that. Vesta acted out of a sincere belief in the precepts of the Roman Catholic Church. Notwithstanding her liberal inclinations,' she went on, 'Vesta had a spiritual side to her as well. Indeed, I think that part of Alphonse's appeal for her was that he loved church architecture.'

'Was he a devout man?'

'He was too good-looking for that,' said Farrier.

'Maurice!' chided his wife.

'It's true, Gwen. He was almost devilishly handsome and he knew it. Mind you, pride was the only one of the seven deadly sins of which you could accuse him – and it was a very subdued pride, at that. All in all, he was an unusually reserved man. He let his wife monopolise the limelight.'

'I don't suppose you have a photograph of him, do you?' asked Marmion.

'As a matter of fact, I have,' replied Gwendolyn, undoing the ribbon and extracting an envelope. 'This is a picture taken at their wedding. Needless to say, we weren't invited – very few people were.'

'That's rather unusual.'

'It's a time when families come together,' said Keedy.

'The sergeant speaks from experience,' said Marmion. 'He's due to marry my daughter next year.'

'Congratulations!' said the Farriers in unison.

Gwendolyn produced a small photograph from the envelope and gave it to Marmion. He examined it before passing it on to Keedy.

'I see what you mean about him being good-looking,' said the latter. 'I hadn't realised how much older he was than his bride – older and slightly shorter than she is.'

'Vesta was always attracted to older men,' said Gwendolyn, 'and they were clearly delighted in each other.'

'Where was this taken?' asked Keedy.

'It was at a little church in a Paris suburb.'

'The sun was obviously shining on them.'

'Vesta told me that that was a good omen.'

'And so it proved,' added her husband. 'When she was last with us, she couldn't stop telling us how contented they'd been, even though they spent so much time apart.'

Marmion took the photograph back from Keedy and studied it again. It looked like a conventional picture for a wedding album. Nobody else was visible. Bride and groom gazed devotedly at each other.

'You told us that he worked for the government,' said Marmion, 'but you weren't quite sure in what capacity.'

'That's right,' said Farrier. 'When it came to talking about his work, Alphonse was very self-effacing. One thing was apparent, however. He was a highly educated man and had a job commensurate with his intelligence.'

'If he was that important, there'd have been obituaries.'

'Vesta didn't send any of them to us.'

'How was she in the wake of his death?'

'She was a lot quieter than usual.'

'And yet she was keen to attend the Hunt Ball,' recalled Keedy.

'I think she saw it as a break from the tedium of being stuck in a rural backwater like this,' said Gwendolyn. 'We love this kind of gentle existence, but Vesta is very much an urban creature.'

'Thank you, Mrs Farrier,' said Marmion. 'You and your husband have been very helpful. Could you possibly give us a few minutes so that we can take a look at these letters and cards?'

'Yes, of course.'

'We may have more questions afterwards.'

'Maurice and I will be happy to answer them, especially if it helps you to solve this terrible murder. Do you have any idea who the victim really is yet?'

'Frankly, we don't.'

'But we will eventually,' said Keedy.

'We just have to be patient and then – truth will out.'

'It always does in the end.'

Opening the first of the envelopes, he took out a letter.

Chatfield dodged most of the verbal blows aimed at him by his visitor and he deflected the rest by shifting his position slightly. Griselda Fleetwood railed at him for ten minutes before he was allowed to make an abject apology. Instead of calming her, it only set off a fresh relay of metaphorical punches. Chatfield rode them skilfully.

'I accept all that you say, Mrs Fleetwood,' he conceded, both palms aloft in a pacifying gesture, 'but you are ignoring positive signs.'

'There aren't any, Superintendent.'

'We now know the real name of your missing guest – Vesta Lyle. To find that name, Inspector Marmion has been driven all over the county of Berkshire. At this very moment, he is there once more in search of additional information regarding this lady.'

'What about the murder victim?'

'She has yet to be identified.'

'Two whole days have passed.'

'Two whole years have not been enough to solve some murder cases,' he warned.

'Two *years*!' she exclaimed.

'Evidence has to be chiselled out slowly like gold nuggets.'

'Is that how long I'll have to wait? Two weeks will be enough to kill off my hotel. Guests have already started to leave as if the place is filled with a nasty smell.'

'I'm very sorry to hear it.'

'And today's newspapers will send even more of them scurrying for another hotel. Why don't you do what I told you at the very start?'

'We are continuing our scrutiny of Mr Buchanan.'

'I want him arrested,' she howled.

'I'm quite sure that you'd like him hanged, drawn and quartered into the bargain,' he said, 'but we can't arrest anyone unless we have firm evidence of his wrongdoing.'

'I can give you dozens of examples, Superintendent.'

'But will they stand up in court?'

'They ought to – the man is evil incarnate.'

'Our investigation has so far found that he has a good reputation as a hotelier and has won a number of awards.'

'You don't know how low Fraser Buchanan will stoop.'

'We were told he sent you a bouquet of flowers out of sympathy.'

'I had them thrown out instantly.'

'Wasn't that a trifle intemperate?' asked Chatfield.

'It was the only response he deserved. That's why your attitude towards him is so infuriating. My husband has already been here once to complain. If we don't get clear progress in this investigation soon, I'll let him loose on you again.'

'I sincerely hope that won't be necessary.'

'Go after Buchanan!' she demanded, bunching a fist. 'That's the way to solve this case. He's sworn to destroy the Lotus. Stop him, Superintendent, or my hotel is doomed.'


The secretary was seated at the desk with a box of envelopes. Buchanan gave her a list of addresses and a thick pile of printed letters.

'I want these in the post as soon as possible,' he said.

# CHAPTER EIGHTEEN

It did not take long for the detectives to sift through the correspondence. The letters were uniformly short and the postcards very often had no more than a few words scribbled on them. While the correspondence was mostly in English, Vesta did lapse into French from time to time. When they'd finished the whole pile, Keedy looked up at Gwendolyn.

'Is this *all* you got in almost twenty-five years?' he asked.

'I'm afraid so. Vesta always claimed that being on the move left her little time for correspondence. As you can see, those postcards came from a variety of countries. She was a true cosmopolitan.'

'We were rather in awe of her,' said Farrier. 'Compared to Vesta, we were very provincial. We've only been to the Continent twice and neither of us has ever bothered to learn a foreign language.'

'My cousin could speak French and German fluently.'

'And she'd met so many important people in the course of her work. In some countries, a high-ranking public figure would open her exhibition.'

'What did you think of her letters, Inspector?'

'Some of them were rather . . . too frank,' said Marmion.

'Vesta loved to shock.'

'She certainly shocked me when I first met her,' confessed Farrier. 'I wasn't used to such forthright conversation from a woman. To be quite honest, I didn't like her at all, but she soon won me over. Anyway, I hope that reading her letters was of some help to you both.'

Keedy nodded. 'The more we know about her, the better.'

'What puzzles me,' said Marmion, 'is that there are two sides to her that don't seem to fit together. On one side, there's the free-thinking artist who chooses to live a life without any rules; on the other side is a practising Roman Catholic who sends you postcards that always have pictures of cathedrals on them.'

'She revelled in that dichotomy,' said Farrier.

'Which one was the real Vesta Lyle?'

'Only her husband could have told you that.'

'When she was with Alphonse,' said Gwendolyn, 'she was always on her best behaviour. On the occasions when they were together in Paris, they went to Mass in Notre Dame every Sunday.'

'Besides,' added her husband, 'art and religion are not diametrical opposites. Look at the great painters of the Renaissance. They were religious by nature and often specialised in Biblical scenes.'

'How many of those great painters were women?' asked Marmion.

'That's a good question, Inspector.'

'None that I can think of,' said Gwendolyn. 'And even if there were any, they wouldn't be anything like my cousin. She's highly individual, which is why she had such success abroad – though not, oddly enough, over here. She's virtually unknown in Britain.'

'Let me switch to something else,' suggested Marmion. 'When she went to that Hunt Ball with you, why was she so keen to be photographed with Sir Godfrey Brice-Cadmore?'

'We're not sure, Inspector.'

'She can't have known him, surely?'

'It's very unlikely.'

'Yet she bought that photo of him standing next to her.'

'I told you that she was attracted to older men and Sir Godfrey did have a charm and nobility about him. But he might not be the reason she wanted a copy of the photograph. It also included Maurice and me. Vesta might simply have wanted it as a memento of a happy occasion.'

'It's possible,' said Marmion, dubiously. 'By the way, I have to pass on some distressing news. Sir Godfrey died yesterday in hospital.'

'Oh dear!' sighed Gwendolyn. 'What a sad way to end a long and distinguished life. We only saw him once a year at the ball, but he always acknowledged us. When she was alive, Sir Godfrey and his wife were a fixture at the event.'

'I had a long chat with him once,' remembered Farrier. 'It was about the joys of birdwatching. I tried to get in a word about the pleasure of dancing, but I had no chance. He talked on and on.'

'Did he and his wife have any children?' asked Marmion.

'No, Inspector – neither did Alphonse and Vesta, of course.'

'Why was that?'

'Who knows?'

'Vesta told me that neither of them liked the idea of children,' said Gwendolyn. 'Looking back, it's just as well they didn't change their minds. Having a family would have hampered their careers.'

'It didn't hamper *my* career,' said Farrier, complacently, 'and we had three children. We also had a nanny, of course, and she took most of the strain. The secret is being able to organise your time.'

'My cousin could never do that. Vesta was too chaotic.'

'You couldn't say that about her husband, Gwen.'

'No,' she agreed, 'he gave the impression of being very much in charge of his life. Chaos versus control – their marriage was a perfect example of the attraction of opposites.'

'Thank you,' said Marmion, getting up. 'We're sorry to have intruded on your hospitality a second time. It was very kind of you to show us the letters from your cousin. We understand her a lot more now.'

'We'll do anything we can to help you find her.'

'At least we now know the sort of person we're looking for,' said Keedy. 'That makes a big difference.'

'What's happened to the hotel where she was staying?'

'It's in trouble, I'm afraid. Murder is bad for business.'

'It's not only the guests who were upset,' said Marmion. 'They have the choice of leaving. It's the staff I feel sorry for. They'll have been terrified by what happened and they have to go on working there.'

In the wake of the calamitous event at the Lotus Hotel, the manager had called the entire staff together and told them to carry on as if nothing had happened. His well-intentioned advice was much easier to hear than to put into practice. No matter how much they tried, they couldn't forget the heinous crime that had taken place there and it was bound to affect their behaviour. Most of them were nervous, hesitant and wary. Millie Jenks remained close to hysteria.

Mindful of Lena Gosling's comments, she made extra efforts to feel and act normally. To that end, having a fixed daily routine was an advantage. She did her duties with clockwork precision. Yet she never went near the room where the murder had occurred. During a short lull, she decided to try once again to conquer her fears. Walking down the corridor as she'd done days earlier, she got within a few yards of the room before hitting an invisible barrier. While her body turned to ice, her mind was a raging furnace of memories. They were so vivid that they made her head pound.

Unable to move in any direction, all she could do was to stand there and suffer. It was agonising. In the room just ahead of her, she'd touched a dead body and made it topple onto the carpet. All she wanted to do now was to run away but she was rooted to the floor. Millie feared that she would be stuck there in perpetuity. Her eyes lost focus, her body began to shake and the pounding in her head was unbearable. She was on the point of collapse when a gentle hand was placed on her shoulder from behind.

'Come away,' said Lena Gosling. 'Try again later.'

Alice Marmion had to bide her time before she could catch her friend alone. It came when they had a break from their respective beats. Seeing Jenny Jerrold heading for the canteen, Alice intercepted her and took her aside to a quiet corner.

'I've been thinking about what you told me, Jenny.'

'You don't need to. It's my problem.'

'But it's one you can't run away from,' argued Alice. 'If this person is really determined, he'll probably have followed you home. There's no escape there.'

'It's only at work I've had the feeling of someone watching me.'

'Have you ever asked yourself why?'

'No, Alice, I just have this terrible urge to get away from him.'

'You shouldn't let him frighten you off. What he's doing is wrong. The obvious thing is to report him. We're in the police, after all. Our job is to stop this kind of thing happening. For goodness' sake,' said Alice, 'if a friend of yours was in this situation, you'd want to help them.'

'Yes, I suppose I would.'

'Then why not turn to one of us?'

'It's difficult to explain, Alice.'

'Keeping it bottled up means you've been suffering in silence.'

Jennifer turned her head away in embarrassment and Alice was reminded of Iris Goodliffe's plight. She, too, had kept her troubles to herself for a long time. The difference was that Iris knew who her tormentor was. In Jennifer's case, he was anonymous. That made him more sinister and unnerving.

'I just didn't want anyone else to know about it,' said Jennifer.

'There must be a reason for that.'

'Well, the simple truth is that . . . I felt ashamed.'

'Of *what*, for heaven's sake?' asked Alice. 'You're not to blame, Jenny. He's the offender here.'

'I know but . . . oh, I'm beginning to wish I never told you now.'

'You should be very grateful you did speak out, because I intend to do something about it.'

'Don't tell anyone else,' begged Jennifer. 'I couldn't bear that.'

'This is between you and me. Nobody else needs to be involved. Well,' she added, '*one* other person will be involved when we find out exactly who he is and why he's been pestering you.'

* * *

When they got back into the car, Keedy expected it to return to London but Marmion gave the driver instructions to go in a different direction.

'Where are we going?' asked Keedy.

'I want to pay a second visit to Mrs Hassall.'

'Why?'

'She may be able to help us, Joe. There's something she told us that may turn out to be far more important than it seemed at the time.'

'What are you on about?'

'Wait and see. Meanwhile,' said Marmion, 'you can tell me what we learnt from our visit to the Farriers.'

'We discovered that Vesta Lyle was even more peculiar than we thought. The woman was so selfish. Only people as kind-hearted as the Farriers would have put up with her.'

'Is that all?'

'She obviously had some kind of charm. Farrier disliked her at first, but she soon won him over.'

'Tell me what else we learnt.'

'There wasn't anything.'

'Oh, I thought there was a lot more. Look at the facts. She married a man who was much older than her yet spent very little time with him. Mr and Mrs Farrier met him only once, then they were deliberately kept well away from Alphonse Dufays.'

'That's true.'

'Then there's this cloak of secrecy around Vesta Lyle,' said Marmion. 'Those letters and cards she sent to the Farriers gave nothing away. There was no hint of affection for her cousin in them. The most interesting things about them were the postmarks.'

'They were sent from all over Europe.'

'That's because of her reputation as an artist. As a result, she was invited here there and everywhere.'

'Ah,' said Keedy, realisation dawning, 'I'm beginning to read your mind now.'

'Vesta Lyle spoke fluent French and German.'

'It sounds as if she was far more European than British. And she was able to mix with people of influence wherever she went. Because of her paintings, she was in a privileged position. I daresay she went to all kinds of civic receptions.'

'Meanwhile, her husband was working for the French government but keeping very quiet about what he actually did. I can see why now. My guess would be that he was in their secret service.'

'What about his wife?'

'She was only a wife in name. I don't believe that either of them wanted a normal marriage, Joe. At heart, they had so little in common. They settled for an arrangement that suited each of them. It's the reason they were happy to spend so much time apart.'

'That would explain why they never considered having children.'

'So what brought them together in the first place?'

'We were told that. Vesta Lyle chose a precarious profession. She married him to have some financial stability.'

'When her paintings began to sell, she had plenty of money to support herself. I'm wondering if it may also have been supplemented by an income from the government. Don't let's jump to any conclusions,' warned Marmion, 'or we may be going off in the wrong direction altogether, but I think it's possible that both she and her husband might have been engaged in some sort of espionage.'

\* \* \*

From the moment she left the house, Ellen knew that she'd go to the lecture, after all. For all her protestation, she was keen to hear what Quentin Dacey had to say on the subject of *The Unseen Hand*. Her husband and daughter need never even know that she'd been to central London with her friend. On the bus journey there, she and Rene Bridger speculated on what they might be told. Because they were so engrossed in their conversation, the journey seemed to flash by.

The hall in which the lecture was being given was in a side street off Charing Cross Road. Since they were among the first to arrive, there was a wide choice of seating for them. Rene nudged her.

'Let's sit in the front row, Ellen.'

'Oh, no,' said the other, nervously.

'I thought you wanted to ask him a question. The best place to do that is when you're very close.'

'We can sit further back, Rene.'

'What are you afraid of?'

'I don't know.'

'Look at your hands – they're shaking.'

'If we decided to sneak out before it's finished,' said Ellen, 'it would be much easier to do that nearer the back. It won't be quite so obvious then.'

'The more obvious, the better, I say. If he talks rubbish, he needs to be told. In any case,' continued her friend, 'we may not have to leave at all. Mr Dacey may be right in what he says. If that's the case, I hope you'll be grateful that I talked you into coming.'

'I *am* grateful, Rene.'

'Then prove it by sitting in the front row with me.'

Ellen felt trapped.

\* \* \*

During her visit to Scotland Yard, Griselda Fleetwood had only been slightly pacified by Chatfield. As she took a taxi back to her hotel, she was still seething. When she got there, bad news was waiting. Rex Chell took her into the privacy of his office to break it.

'I'm afraid that Mrs Beech has left us,' he said.

'But she was due to stay for three days.'

'Unfortunately, she read one of the morning papers.'

'Oh dear!'

'If guests order one, Mrs Fleetwood, we can't really hide the newspapers away. As it happens, we were lucky. Mrs Beech simply made a polite excuse and checked out. Someone else might have shouted at us for not warning them about the murder – then refused to pay the bill.'

'Yes,' she said, gloomily, 'and they'd be right to do so.'

'What happened at Scotland Yard?'

'Ha! The superintendent is blind. The evidence against Buchanan is staring him in the face and he refuses to see it.'

'Aren't they doing *anything* about him?'

'He claims that they're "looking into" his activities. It's another way of saying that he doesn't really believe what I told them.'

'*Cui bono?*'

'What does that mean?'

'"Who stands to gain?" It's a Latin phrase.'

'Buchanan will gain from our losses. I've told them that.'

'Mrs Beech is a prime exhibit,' said Chell. 'When she left here, she went straight off to the Unicorn. Sadly, she's not the only guest of ours to do that.'

'The papers are largely to blame. I've set my husband on to them. He may not speak Latin, but he has a few choice phrases of his own.

We can't let editors get away with trying to ruin us. It's a flagrant misuse of power.'

'I couldn't agree more, Mrs Fleetwood. However, all may yet be well if Inspector Marmion tracks down the killer.'

'How can he do that when he's driving around Berkshire on a pleasure trip? That's what hurts me the most, Mr Chell,' she hissed. '*Nobody* has shown the slightest interest in saving us.'

Hoping to see Bunny Hassall again, the detectives were obliged to wait because she was not there. As they looked out through the windows of the living room, they soon saw her, sitting in a trap and urging the pony on with a flick of the whip. No longer able to ride, she could obviously still take pleasure from being around horses. When she disappeared into the stable yard, they waited in silence.

It was fifteen minutes or so before she finally wheeled herself into the room and showered them with apologies.

'We should be saying sorry to you, Mrs Hassall,' said Marmion, 'for barging in here without warning.'

'You're very welcome, Inspector.'

'Thank you.'

'Why don't you both sit down?'

The visitors exchanged pleasantries with her as they took their seats on the sofa. Marmion then used a sentence that he'd employed many times when breaking bad news to bereaved parents. He lowered his voice and spoke with due solemnity.

'I'm afraid that I have sad tidings for you.'

'What is it?'

'You may remember that I told you about Sir Godfrey's condition.'

'Please don't tell me that he's died,' she said, hands clasped. 'I've been praying for him to recover. He was such a resilient man. He'd always enjoyed rude health in the past.'

'He passed away in his sleep yesterday.'

'God rest his soul!'

She closed her eyes tightly and recited a silent prayer. Marmion and Keedy had no choice but to sit there and wait. Her reaction had been very different to that of the Farriers. They had been sorry to hear the news, but it had not moved them deeply. Bunny Hassall, on the other hand, was devastated. When she eventually opened her eyes again, she changed the subject.

'Did your visit to the Farriers yesterday bear fruit?'

'Yes, it did,' replied Marmion. 'As a matter of fact, we came on here after calling on them for a second time.'

'You must be getting to know Berkshire quite well.'

'I wish we had time to enjoy its delights.'

'It's lovely to be out in such beautiful countryside,' said Keedy. 'The air is so much cleaner here than in London.'

'That's why we all live so long in the country, Sergeant. Sir Godfrey was in his eighties, you know. But for this cruel business, he might have survived for many more years.'

'We'll never know, Mrs Hassall.'

'Alas, we won't.' She looked quizzically from one to the other. 'What brought you back here?'

'It was something you told us the last time,' said Marmion.

'What was that?'

'This may not be the right moment to put such a question to you. Given what I've just told you about Sir Godfrey, you may not wish to dwell on your friendship with him.'

'Oh, it was more than friendship, Inspector. We were close.'

'I see.'

'And don't think I'm too grief-stricken to talk about him because I'm not. As for the past, I have no regrets about what happened between us. It was simply not to be.'

'You said that he proposed to you.'

'Well, he did and he didn't,' she said with a light laugh. 'Godfrey was like that. He made it sound like a joke, but I knew that he was being serious. At the same time, I realised that we were simply not made for a lifetime together. Years later, he thanked me for turning him down.'

'Had he met his future wife by then?'

'Good lord – no! Godfrey was courting someone else.'

Keedy stared. 'He seems to have been very—'

'You don't need to say the word, Sergeant,' she said before he could complete the sentence. 'Think it, if you wish, because it's true. If you'd seen him in his declining years, you'd never have imagined that Sir Godfrey had had such a wild life in his younger days. There was no time for watching birds and listening to music then. His father was to blame.'

'Really?'

'He had this idea that his son's education would be incomplete if he didn't go on what used to be called the "Grand Tour". He expected Godfrey to be swept away by the beauty of European art and architecture, and to come back singing the praises of Mozart, Beethoven and Brahms.'

'Is that what happened?' asked Marmion.

'To some extent, it did, but there was an interim period that really upset his father. Godfrey didn't follow the prescribed itinerary.'

'What did he do instead?'

'He stayed months longer in one place than he was supposed to.'

'And where was that?'

'Paris.'

Marmion's ears pricked up. Keedy's mouth fell open.

'Freedom of the press is a noble concept, ladies and gentlemen, and we British delight in boasting that we enjoy it in this country. Nonsense!' said Quentin Dacey, eyes suddenly alight. 'Utter nonsense! It's a mirage. Instead of telling you the truth, the British press is hiding it from you. Every publication is censored. Several have been banned altogether. Why is this? It's because the government doesn't want you to know the ugly truth about this war. They doctor reports of casualties in battle so that we don't know that our troops are being massacred. They give the impression that we are slowly winning the war when, in fact, it's already been won by the Germans. How do I know this? Let me tell you . . .'

It was strange. Quentin Dacey had an unusually high voice and a slight lisp, yet he had his audience spellbound. Much shorter than Ellen had imagined, he nevertheless embodied authority. Everything he said seemed to be undeniably true. Rene Bridger was also captivated by his manner and his delivery. Having come to the lecture with a certain amount of cynicism, she had no doubts now. Like Ellen, she was at the mercy of Dacey's charisma.

'Where *are* these spies?' he asked. 'Let me show you.'

Moving to a large map of London, he pointed to a series of small black crosses that he'd placed in various locations.

'German agents were living here, here and here,' he said, 'until I discovered their addresses. I informed the police at once, of course, but by the time they raided these houses, the enemy had flown. What can we deduce from that, ladies and gentlemen?' he asked, voice soaring to an even higher octave. 'The answer is unavoidable. Those agents were warned in advance that I'd traced them to their lairs. And who warned them? It can only have been someone in a senior position in the Metropolitan Police Force.'

He paused to let the information sink in. Everybody was shaken by the revelation but Ellen was horrified. The idea that anyone in the force that employed her husband could be a German agent shocked her beyond measure. She'd planned to ask a question of Dacey, but her mouth was suddenly so dry that she was unable to speak. In the event, it was Rene Bridger who acted on her behalf. After waiting until the end of the lecture, she shot up her arm. Dacey pointed to her.

'Yes?'

'We were told that all German spies were rounded up at the start of the war,' she said. 'What do you say to that?'

'I'd say that you were deliberately deceived,' he replied.

Rene indicated Ellen. 'My friend's husband saw the camps on the Isle of Man where they are kept.'

'Then he was woefully misled.'

'You can't mislead a man like him.'

'Why not?'

'It's because he's too experienced.'

'What was this man doing on the island?' asked Dacey with a sneer. 'Was he there on holiday or did he work there?'

'No,' said Ellen, stung by his gibe and finding her voice at last. 'He's a detective inspector from Scotland Yard and he was there in an official capacity. And let me tell you that I don't believe there are any German agents in the Metropolitan Police Force because it's filled with people like my husband who are doing a very dangerous job out of love for their country. They'd *never* betray it, so don't you dare say that they would. You should be ashamed.' Rising to her feet, she turned to her friend. 'Come on, Rene. We're leaving. I'm not listening to any more of his lies. He's a disgrace.'

As the two women made their way to the rear of the room, there was a smattering of applause that grew steadily in volume. Other people got up to follow them out.

Dacey was well and truly silenced.

When Claude Chatfield reported to the commissioner, he saw the pile of newspapers on his desk. Sir Edward Henry's frown was eloquent.

'Yes, I know,' said Chatfield. 'Instead of congratulating us on the progress we did make, the papers are sniping at us because we haven't solved the murder. What do they expect in so short a time?'

'They expect miracles, Superintendent.'

'Then they need to look elsewhere.'

'We get criticism and our backs are broad enough to bear it. The real victim of these articles is the Lotus Hotel. Would *you* want to stay there after reading this coverage?'

Chatfield was amused. 'I wouldn't be eligible to stay there,' he said, 'because I'm neither female nor aristocratic, but I take your point. It was made very clearly by Mrs Fleetwood when she called to see me earlier on. The hotel is suffering badly.'

'What can we do to relieve that suffering?'

'To be candid, there's very little. Only an arrest and conviction will dispel the gloom over the Lotus.'

'I can imagine the state Mrs Fleetwood must be in.'

'The trouble is,' said Chatfield, 'that she's already identified the culprit. According to her, a rival hotelier is behind the murder, but we've found no evidence to support that theory.'

'Yes, her husband told me about the vendetta with Mr Buchanan. I didn't realise there was so much bad blood in the hotel trade.'

'It's been an eye-opener to me as well, Sir Edward.'

'What's the inspector doing today?'

'He's following up a lead in Berkshire. I can only hope that it turns out to be of real value. He's convinced that there was a link in the past between Vesta Lyle and Sir Godfrey Brice-Cadmore.'

'I can't think what it could be.'

'Neither can I,' said Chatfield, 'but if it's there, Marmion will certainly find it.'

When she pressed them to stay for some refreshments, Marmion and Keedy agreed readily so that they could listen to her reminiscing about Sir Godfrey Brice-Cadmore. Talking about him gave her such immense pleasure and fleshed out the portrait that the detectives had of him. As a young man, he had clearly relished the joys of Paris and returned to the city time and again until he finally married. On the drive back to London, they were able to review what they'd learnt.

'Who would have thought that he'd turn out to be like that?' said Keedy. 'Mrs Hassall was far too nice a woman to put it in so many words, but he obviously went abroad to sow his wild oats.'

'You can see why his father took a dim view of it.'

'I wish I'd had a chance to travel.'

'We don't live in that world and we have to accept it. You and I were born to work. He had the luck to go where he wanted at his father's expense. Dad couldn't afford to send me to Brighton, let alone to the capitals of Europe. The farthest he'd ever been out of London was to Coventry and that was only to his brother's funeral.'

'Don't you feel deprived sometimes, Harv?'

'Of course, I do, but I always count my blessings. I've got a difficult job maybe, but, when I get things right, it gives me a thrill that lasts for days. I'm enjoying that sensation right now.'

'I wish that I could.'

'Look at what we heard today.'

'It could just be a coincidence.'

'I don't think so.'

'The dates may not fit.'

'The simple fact is that Sir Godfrey could have been in Paris at the same time as Vesta Lyle. According to Mrs Hassall, he loved to spend his evenings in Montmartre. That went on until he was into his thirties. Judging by what the Farriers told us, Vesta was only eighteen when she left home to study in Paris. We know that he was attracted to younger women. He eventually married one. Just think of the two of them meeting. He must have been bewitched by this promising young English artist and, on her side, she'd have been dazzled by the fact that he would one day inherit his father's title.'

'Do you think they got close?'

'They must have done, Joe. She was an earlier version of Mrs Hassall. He might even have proposed to her – though you can see that his parents would never have accepted her as a daughter-in-law. Who knows?' Marmion went on. 'She might have nursed the desire to be his wife for years and, when their paths eventually crossed again, she made sure that she stood next to him in that photograph.'

'But the sad thing was he no longer recognised her.'

'Distant memories fade when you get to his age.'

'Vesta must have felt so upset that he'd forgotten her.'

'She got what she wanted in the end,' said Marmion, piecing it slowly together. 'When she deliberately chose to stay with the upper crust in the Lotus Hotel, she pretended that she was every bit as good as them by posing as Lady Diana Brice-Cadmore. It gained her respect and deference from the staff. The name was chosen with great care,' he decided. 'After all these years, she was finally able to be his wife.'

# CHAPTER NINETEEN

When they walked out of the lecture, Ellen and her friend felt a quiet sense of triumph. By way of celebration, they went straight to a Lyons Corner House and treated themselves to tea. Rene Bridger couldn't stop praising Ellen.

'You were wonderful,' she said. 'I've never heard you speak like that before, Ellen. There was such passion in your voice.'

'I wasn't going to let him sneer at the police.'

'You were quite right.'

'He just caught me on a raw nerve,' said Ellen. 'Until then, I'd been hypnotised by him. His argument was very convincing. If he hadn't said that about the police, I'd have gone home believing every word of it.'

'I'm the same. Mr Dacey had me in the palm of his hand, then, all of a sudden, I saw him for what he was – a nasty little man who likes to frighten people and who can't stand anyone disagreeing with him.'

'Oh, I'm so glad I went, Rene. It's cured me of believing all that stuff about German agents flooding the country.'

'When you challenged him, you shook him rigid.'

'Good.'

'And when we left and got a round of applause, some other people walked out behind us. That will have hurt him. Quentin Dacey is just a scaremonger. My husband was right about him, after all. He talked rubbish.'

'Are you going to tell that to Bert?'

'Yes – even though he'll crow over me for days.'

'I'm not even sure if I ought to tell Harvey that I went.'

'If *you* don't,' said Rene, 'then I will. Your husband ought to know about the way you stood up and defended him against those lies we had to listen to. He'd be proud of you.'

'Maybe I will tell him, then.'

'If it was me, I'd boast about it for a week.'

They giggled. Ellen was so pleased at the change in her friend. Rene Bridger had somehow shaken off the misery that usually made any conversation with her such an effort. For once, she hadn't mentioned her son or lapsed into bitterness. As for Ellen, she'd forgotten about Paul for a while. They were no longer two women weighed down by their respective tragedies. Temporarily, they'd both been liberated from their obsessions and had the warm satisfaction of upsetting Quentin Dacey. All in all, the trip to central London had been a success.

'So, what is it to be, Ellen?' asked Rene.

'I don't follow.'

'Are you going to tell your husband or not?'

'Oh, I think I ought to tell Harvey,' replied Ellen, 'but I don't think I'd dare to say anything to my daughter.'

'Why not?'

'Alice was very annoyed at me for even thinking of going to that lecture. She remembers the time when Joe risked his life in the Isle of Man in search of what he thought was a German spy. She feels that people like Mr Dacey only belittle what the police have done to make us as safe as they can. I'm relieved that Alice didn't come with us today.'

'What do you mean?'

'All I did was to give Dacey a rude shock. If my daughter had been there, she'd probably have assaulted him.'

As she walked in step with her partner around their beat, Alice reflected on the difference between Iris Goodliffe and Jennifer Jerrold. One had yearned for male attention and, when someone finally showed an interest in her, had been only too willing to respond. The other was shy by nature and wholly inexperienced in dealing with the other sex. Jennifer shied away from men. Her life revolved around the church. Now that she was being stalked, she'd lost her nerve and simply wanted to run away, even if it meant losing a job she coveted. Iris had shown no signs of doing that. She was more robust than Jennifer, eager to carry on in the Women's Police Force, despite the fact that it might bring her into contact with the very man who'd molested her.

The only thing that the two women had in common was the urge to keep their respective anxieties hidden. Because she cared about both of her friends, Alice had managed to draw a confession out of each of them.

'I'm so grateful to you,' said Iris.

'Why?'

'Everything is different now. Since you let me talk about my fears, they don't seem too bad. When I leave the house, I don't have to grit my teeth any more.'

'Was it really that difficult?'

'I was afraid that he'd . . . try again.'

'There's no chance of him doing that, Iris. I think Doug Beckett feels guilty at what he did – and so he should. You won't be bothered by him again.'

'The awful thing is that . . . I was so fond of him.'

'You can't carry on being fond of a man who treats you like that.'

'I know that now.' They turned a corner and strolled on. 'Did I see you talking to Jenny Jerrold earlier?'

'Yes.'

'Has she told you why she thinking of resigning?'

'Jenny said that it was because of her parents. When they heard about some of the incidents she's had to deal with on night duty, they were horrified. What they really objected to was the bad language.'

'You have to close your ears to that.'

'Mr and Mrs Jerrold are very puritanical. They think that their daughter will be corrupted by the terrible things she sees and hears.'

'Is that what Jenny told you?'

'Yes, Iris.'

'And do you believe her?'

'Of course,' said Alice. 'Can you imagine her ever telling a lie?'

Relieved to see them back at Scotland Yard again, Chatfield sat behind his desk and listened to what the detectives had learnt in the course of their visit to Berkshire. Because of his seniority, Marmion did most of the talking, with Keedy making occasional interjections. With an inbred respect for anyone from the upper classes, the superintendent was profoundly shocked to hear that, in his younger days, Sir Godfrey had been something of a roué. He did, however, accept Marmion's argument that he could well have met Vesta Lyle during his regular visits to the artists' quarter.

'What I can't believe,' he said, 'was that she never got over whatever kind of liaison she may have had with him.'

'Why else would she claim to be his wife?' asked Marmion.

'Let me finish, Inspector.'

'I'm sorry, sir.'

'One of the most interesting things about this woman is that she chose to become a Roman Catholic. People don't do that lightly. It's a big decision to make. Vesta Lyle willingly subscribed to a religion that gave her life a moral purpose and a definite structure. Neither of those things,' said Chatfield with a sniff, 'could you easily associate with a community of artists.'

'She only converted to Catholicism when she was about to get married,' said Keedy. 'Perhaps she lived by different rules after that.'

'So I would hope, Sergeant. As you both know, I was brought up in the Catholic religion and it's shaped my whole life. Over the years, I've been very struck by what you might call the zeal of the convert. When someone becomes a Catholic, they can sometimes tend to be even more pious than the rest of us.'

'Oh, I think you're pious enough, sir.'

'What I'm trying to say is that, when she went through a service of holy matrimony, she would have accepted the heavy commitments laid upon her. Any relationships she'd had with other men would have been wiped from her mind completely.'

'I disagree, sir,' said Marmion.

'We take our vows seriously, Inspector.'

'I'm sure that's true of you and Mrs Chatfield, but yours is a much more conventional marriage. Vesta Lyle seemed happy enough to become

Madame Dufays, yet she never used her husband's surname. Nor did she spend a great deal of time at home. Mrs Farrier told us that her studio was a long way from the house. She couldn't understand why her cousin didn't work in one of the rooms in what was a very large house.'

'There are all sorts of reasons for that.'

'Yes,' said Keedy. 'Perhaps she wanted to stay close to other artists because it's where she got her inspiration from.'

'Possibly,' said Chatfield. 'Or it may be that her husband didn't want the chaos and smell of an artist's studio anywhere near him. From what you've told me about him, Alphonse Dufays sounds as if he might have been rather fastidious.'

'That's exactly what he was, sir,' confirmed Marmion, 'and it leads me to believe there may be another explanation.'

'What is it, Inspector?'

'When Vesta Lyle and her future husband first met, they must have seemed a rather incongruous couple. Each had a profession and was happy to continue in it independently. The wedding may have taken place in a Catholic church,' he continued, 'but I wonder if the union only existed on the surface.'

'But they took solemn vows,' Chatfield insisted.

'I doubt very much if they kept them, sir. What I think they agreed to share was a marriage of convenience.'

Rex Chell had great admiration for Griselda Fleetwood but, whenever he was in a room with her, it seemed to shrink in size because of the sheer force of her personality. That afternoon, her husband chose to visit the Lotus Hotel so husband and wife were both in the manager's office with him. Chell began to feel a touch of claustrophobia.

'What did the editor say?' asked Griselda.

'He was full of apologies,' replied her husband, 'and claimed that he'd had no intention of damaging your business. I got much the same reply from the others. They all lied through their teeth.'

'It's a credit to you that they agreed to see you,' said Chell. 'If most people go to Fleet Street to protest, they rarely get through the outer door. I know that because I'm one of them.'

'My name carries weight,' said Fleetwood.

'And so it should,' added his wife. 'You've been an outstanding public benefactor over the years, Harold. You've got influence. I just wish that some of it rubbed off on me.'

'You're one of the most influential women in London.'

'I don't feel it.'

'You're an example to others, Griselda.'

'Oh, I don't think that any woman would be misguided enough to change places with me at the moment. When this hotel was launched, I won plaudits for my enterprise. There's no sign of them now.'

'You were praised for your originality, Mrs Fleetwood,' said Chell, 'and this hotel will always reflect that. As soon as the police catch the killer, the Lotus will recover instantly.'

'The killer owns a hotel two streets away,' she howled.

'Have the police hauled in Buchanan for questioning yet?' asked Fleetwood.

'No, they haven't.'

'Then I'll have to speak to Sir Edward again.'

'Leave it for a while, Harold. I tackled Superintendent Chatfield earlier and left him in no doubt about my disgust with the way the investigation is going. I also pressed him to go after Buchanan.'

'It won't be easy. He's too cunning to have left a trail.'

'Mrs Fleetwood was wondering what he'll do next,' said Chell.

'He's bound to exploit the unfortunate situation we're in.'

'It's one he created for that very purpose,' she snapped. 'Buchanan wanted us laid low so that he can kick the life out of us.'

'He won't get away with that,' said Fleetwood.

'Who's to stop him?'

'I am, Griselda.' He slapped his thigh. 'There's no time for delay. I'm not prepared to wait a moment longer. I'll get over to Scotland Yard right away and demand to see the commissioner. By this evening,' he promised, 'Fraser Buchanan will be in police custody.'

Buchanan was seated behind the manager's desk at the Roath Court Hotel when there was a knock on the door and it was opened by Ian Maitland.

'You sent for me, sir,' he said.

'Ah, yes.'

'I gave you something yesterday.'

'Why, so you did,' said the other, rising to his feet and taking out his wallet, 'and I was very grateful. What was your name again?'

'Maitland, sir – Ian Maitland.'

'I'll remember that name.'

'Thank you, sir.'

'Meanwhile, I want you to have something for services rendered,' said Buchanan, opening his wallet and taking out some five-pound notes. 'That's all I have at the moment. There'll be lots more to come when I've been to the bank. Here you are, Maitland,' he said, handing the money over. 'You've earned it.'

'I was very glad to help, sir.'

After discussing the case from every possible angle, they came back once more to the murder victim. Chatfield let his dismay show through.

'We've learnt a lot about Vesta Lyle,' he said, 'but we still have no idea who the murdered woman was or how she came to be in the Lotus Hotel.'

'I've been thinking about that, sir,' said Keedy.

'And what's the result?'

'I've settled for a possible answer.'

'Carry on.'

'She was in that hotel room because she was invited there by the woman calling herself Lady Brice-Cadmore.'

'That could well be true,' said Marmion.

'Why invite someone to a room,' asked Chatfield, 'and then disappear? I accept that it's unlikely Vesta Lyle was the killer, but what proof is there that the murder victim was, in fact, a guest?'

'Think about the hotel register, sir,' said Marmion, realising what Keedy had worked out.

'I've never seen the thing.'

'Well, I have and the first thing I noticed was that Lady Brice-Cadmore – as she claimed to be – had stayed there before. She may well have stayed at other hotels, of course, but she chose the Lotus because it was more suited to her purpose.'

'And what was that purpose, Inspector?'

'I'm not sure, but I can hazard a guess.'

'What is it?'

'Let's go back to the post-mortem report.'

'Yes, it's that detail about the French clothing that intrigued me,' said Keedy. 'I wondered about that. Then I remembered how many French people fled to this country in search of safety. It could well be that the murder victim was one of them.'

'It's conceivable,' agreed Chatfield. 'It would explain why we've had no success with our appeal to the public for help to identify the woman. Had it been carried by French newspapers, we might have had more encouraging results. I'm sorry, Sergeant,' he said, 'I'm holding you up. Please go on.'

'This is all supposition, of course,' warned Keedy, 'and I may be way off course, but the most telling detail for me in the post-mortem report was the fact that the deceased was a virgin.'

'That startled me as well. She was a married woman.'

'Was she?'

'You saw the wedding ring,' said Chatfield, 'and she wore other rings that must have been gifts from her husband.'

'That was the assumption we both made,' recalled Marmion.

'Suppose that we were wrong?' asked Keedy.

'It wouldn't be the first time.'

'Suppose that she was not married at all?'

'Then where did she get that wedding ring from?'

'I'm just coming to that, sir. Forgive me if I'm going slowly but the truth is that I'm thinking this through as I speak. I'm also chiding myself for being so easily misled.'

'By what?'

'By lots of things.'

'If you have a theory,' said Chatfield, tetchily, 'spit it out.'

'It's still forming in my mind, sir.'

'Hurry up, man.'

'Where would you find a virgin with a wedding ring?'

'I've got no time for guessing games, Sergeant, especially one that descends into vulgarity.'

'Let him speak, sir,' advised Marmion.

'I thought that must be it,' declared Keedy. 'It has to be the answer. You'd find her in a convent with a ring that signified she was the bride of Christ.'

Chatfield was affronted. 'Are you claiming that she was a nun?'

'I think she might have been in the past.'

'No, I refuse to accept that. To enter a convent is the most solemn undertaking possible. And if this woman was French, she must almost certainly have been a Roman Catholic. No member of an order would be permitted to dress the way that she was.'

'That's why I'm suggesting she might no longer be a nun.'

'Think of that expensive French apparel,' said Marmion. 'They'd never be allowed to wear that – or to have those rings. When they go into a convent, they renounce temptation of any kind.'

'They probably wear hair shirts,' said Keedy.

'Don't be facetious.'

'Well, it wouldn't surprise me, Superintendent.'

'I think that this conversation has taken a distasteful turn,' said Chatfield, 'so I'd rather not continue it. I refuse to believe that someone who pledged herself to an order of nuns would ever betray its sacred principles. Tell me this, Sergeant,' he demanded. 'What possible reason would she have to sneak into a hotel in the middle of the night?'

'Perhaps she wished to be with the woman she loved, sir.'

Chatfield came close to blushing.


When the bus brought them out of central London, they were in a buoyant mood. Rene Bridger couldn't wait to tell her husband what had happened at the lecture. As soon as they reached their stop, she more or less bounded off. Ellen didn't go straight to her own house. She walked instead to the public library and combed the shelves until she found the book that she was after. When she opened *The Invasion of 1910*, she saw that the handbill advertising Quentin Dacey's lecture was still there. After slipping it into her handbag, she replaced the book on the shelf and left the library. The first thing she did when she got back home was to tear the handbill into tiny pieces and washed them down the drain. The photograph of Quentin Dacey disappeared into a watery grave.

It was an unusually busy afternoon that left Alice and Iris little time for conversation. They were very happy to deal with so many incidents because it made the time fly past. When they got back to their base, they had a great deal to report. Inspector Gale was impressed with their work. Having dismissed Iris, she detained Alice for a private word. Fearing a rebuke, Alice was immediately on the defensive. Ever since she'd joined the Women's Police Force, there'd been an underlying tension between her and the inspector and it had led to a series of uncomfortable moments.

Thelma Gale directed her withering gaze at Alice.

'Did I see you talking to Jerrold earlier?' she asked.

'Yes, Inspector.'

'Are you and she close friends?'

'I wouldn't say that,' replied Alice, 'but we get on well together.'

'You do know that she's talking about leaving us, don't you?'

'I do, Inspector.'

'Has she discussed it with you?'

'Jenny did mention it.'

'Is her mind really made up?'

'I think so.'

'I feel that it isn't,' said the other. 'Something is forcing her to go, yet I sense that she doesn't really want to leave. I've questioned her about it, but she keeps saying that her parents disapprove of the sorts of things she has to deal with sometimes. Jerrold should have been hardened against all that by now.'

'I'm sure that she is.'

'So why did she decide to resign?'

Alice hesitated. Having given her word to Jennifer that she wouldn't divulge details of what had passed between them, she felt duty-bound to keep it. At the same time, she was tempted to tell the inspector the truth in the hope that she'd be able to solve her friend's problem. At length, she chose to side with her friend.

'I heard the same reason as you, Inspector.'

'Were you convinced by it?'

'I had no cause to disbelieve her.'

'Jerrold has the makings of a good policewoman,' said the other, seriously. 'That's why I hate to lose her. If you could persuade her to stay, I'd be very grateful. Let me be brutally frank,' she went on, 'there are one or two women under my command that I'd like to see the back of, but Jerrold is in a different class to them. She's got real promise. That's why I'd hate to lose her. Do you think you could ask her to reconsider?'

'I'll certainly try, Inspector.'

'If she still insists on leaving us, at least find out the real reason for her desire to resign. I'm sorry to ask you to spy on a friend but it's in the interests of this force. Jerrold could be an exceptional police officer,' said the inspector. 'In fact, she could be almost as good as you.'

Thelma Gale walked off and left Alice in a complete daze.

Sir Edward Henry was a man who never let friendship influence his decisions. Knowing the importance of impartiality, he judged every case on its individual merits and tried not to interfere. When he had a second visit from Harold Fleetwood, however, he could see how deeply upset his friend was at the way his wife was being treated. With the future of her beloved hotel in the balance, she was forced to learn significant facts about the investigation by reading the morning newspapers. That, the commissioner agreed, was indefensible. After placating his visitor with a promise of action, he went straight off to the superintendent's office.

Marmion and Keedy were still there and had the rare pleasure of watching Chatfield being criticised by the commissioner. Squirming in his seat, the superintendent admitted that he'd been at fault and that he'd apologised to Griselda Fleetwood earlier in the day. To deflect any further censure away from himself, he said that they were making headway in the case and signalled to Marmion that he should take over.

The inspector was quick to do so. Instead of discussing his belief that the murder victim was in the hotel at the invitation of Vesta Lyle, he concentrated on another aspect of the artist's life.

'I have a theory that her husband was employed by the French secret service and that he might have recruited his wife to work as an agent for them.'

Chatfield snorted. 'That's even more far-fetched than the sergeant's conjecture about what happened in that room at the Lotus Hotel on the night of the murder.'

'Let's hear the inspector out,' said the commissioner.

'Vesta Lyle was an artist feted all over Europe,' said Marmion, 'and, as such, she was in a unique position to meet people of importance in a variety of countries. It would have been fairly easy for her to gather intelligence wherever she went, then feed it back to the secret service.'

'Are you claiming that she's another Mata Hari, using her charms to ensnare her chosen targets?' asked Chatfield in disbelief.

'No, sir, she was no exotic dancer. She didn't need to use her body to gain what she wanted. Her paintings did that for her. They brought her admiration. Public figures came to her exhibitions. Wherever she went, she was trusted.'

'I agree with the inspector,' said Keedy. 'It took me time to accept it, but I can see how it must have happened now. Vesta Lyle wasn't trying to gather state secrets from foreign countries. She simply reported what she saw and heard, helping to build up files on respective nations.'

'That makes sense,' observed the commissioner. 'Female agents are not uncommon. All nations make use of them, if they have any sense. Women often have access to people and places denied to men. Mata Hari was the most notorious and she paid the price for it. As you all know, she was shot by a French firing squad only last week.'

'Quite rightly – she was a German spy.'

'It's a dangerous occupation, Sergeant. It requires bravery.'

'No,' said Chatfield, 'I still can't see the French government using a British artist to gather intelligence for them. They'd have female agents of their own.'

'She was a very clever woman, remember,' said Marmion, 'and lived in France from the age of fifteen. She might even have a French passport. As for Dufays, I'm convinced that he worked in the secret service.'

'That's pure supposition, Inspector.'

'It would explain how Vesta Lyle came to be used in that way.'

'I have no difficulty in believing that,' said Sir Edward, stroking his moustache. 'A glance at history is instructive here. France was a proud and powerful country until it was defeated by the Prussian army in 1870. As a result, they suffered humiliation and had to witness the unification of their neighbours into what we now know as Germany. In the wake of the disaster, the *Deuxième Bureau* was formed.'

'What's that?' asked Keedy.

'Its full title was the Second Bureau of the General Staff and it was the country's external military intelligence agency. I wish that I could praise its success, but its record has not been illustrious.'

'You're thinking about the Dreyfus Affair,' said Marmion.

'Indeed, I am.'

Keedy shrugged. 'That was before my time.'

'It was a shameful episode,' explained the commissioner. 'Captain Dreyfus was wrongfully arrested and found guilty of espionage and treason. Instead of being executed, he was sent to Devil's Island, a prison in French Guiana. Because he was Jewish, a wave of virulent anti-semitism broke out in France. It took eleven years and a public outcry before his innocence was finally acknowledged and the charges against him were dropped.'

'What happened?' asked Keedy.

'Dreyfus was exonerated, promoted to the rank of major and given the Legion of Honour. It was a vindication of sorts, but imagine what eleven years in a hostile climate did to his health.'

'I'm amazed that he came through the ordeal alive.'

'My worry,' said Marmion, 'is that their secret service has gone on making mistakes like that. It's a real cause for alarm because the outcome of the war depends on sound intelligence.'

'Oh, things have improved markedly since then.'

'Yes,' said Chatfield, 'they employ people like Vesta Lyle now.'

'Don't be cynical, Superintendent.'

'We've no proof whatsoever that her husband was working for the secret service. He could just as well have been employed as an advisor to a cabinet minister or as an expert on road and rail transport.'

'There's one way to find out, sir,' said Marmion.

'I don't see it.'

'We could ask.'

'That's a ridiculous idea, Inspector. They wouldn't listen to us. The French government is far too preoccupied with survival to answer casual enquiries.'

'It's an enquiry that may lead to the arrest of a killer.'

'You're taking us into the realms of fantasy once again.'

'Is that what *you* think, Sir Edward?' Marmion asked the commissioner. 'If the superintendent tried to get the information we need, the likelihood is that he'd be turned down?'

'It's not a likelihood, it's a certainty.'

'Then the request needs to come from the top. Working through our own intelligence service, the commissioner might be able to get some cooperation from the French.'

'That's just possible,' said Sir Edward.

'Then please act on our behalf.'

'What do you wish to know exactly?'

'The most important thing is whether or not Alphonse Dufays worked for that organisation you mentioned earlier.'

'The *Deuxième Bureau*?'

'That's right. Dufays died three years ago.'

'It's a waste of time,' said Chatfield. 'Intelligence agencies never disclose confidential information. Have you forgotten the trouble we had with our own secret service when we needed details of internees on the Isle of Man? It took us ages to get cooperation.'

'We got it in the end, sir.'

'The French will turn us down.'

'Nevertheless,' said the commissioner, 'we must try – even if I have to work through the Foreign Secretary. Unlike you, Superintendent, I believe that the inspector might well have found the key to unlock this baffling case. I say that with guarded optimism, mark you,' he added, 'because I know that he's relying on a fair amount of guesswork rather than on hard evidence.'

'It's a mixture of both,' said Marmion.

'Then leave it with me.'

'Thank you, Sir Edward.'

'Yes, thank you,' said Keedy.

Claude Chatfield remained resolutely silent.

# CHAPTER TWENTY

Alice Marmion was so astonished at the unexpected compliment from Inspector Gale that she wanted to tell someone about it. The obvious person was Iris Goodliffe but, if she knew what Alice had been asked to do, she'd realise that her friend had lied to her earlier on. There was the additional problem that Iris's already low opinion of herself as a policewoman would plummet even further. She'd be walking every day beside someone who'd actually been singled out for praise by Gale Force, who never stopped criticising Iris. It would destroy what little self-esteem she had, and Alice wanted to avoid that at all costs.

The strange thing was that the inspector had asked her to do something that she'd already decided to do. What set them apart was their choice of method. Thelma Gale wanted Alice to use her powers of persuasion on another policewoman to convince her that she should stay in the force. Knowing the real reason behind Jennifer Jerrold's resignation, Alice wanted somehow to get rid of the person who'd become such a menacing presence in her friend's life. How she would manage to do that, she was unsure, but the obvious first step was to identify the man.

She'd planned to get off early so that she was well ahead of Jennifer but the conversation with the inspector had delayed her. When they parted, therefore, she ran quickly down a backstreet so that she could rejoin the main road near the bus stop that Jennifer used. Alice had not told her friend of her intention because she knew it would make her uneasy and self-conscious. From a vantage point on a corner, she was just in time to see Jenny striding towards the bus stop and glancing over her shoulder from time to time. Alice pitied her. Feeling that she was under constant surveillance, Jennifer was patently on edge.

Yet there was nobody else following her. Someone might be lurking in a house and watching from a concealed position, but Alice saw no curtains being tugged. Could it be that Jennifer was imagining the whole thing? Not long after they'd got to know each other, Iris had told Alice that she'd love to arouse enough interest in a man to make him follow her out of sheer desire. What appealed to Iris was quite terrifying to Jennifer – if indeed there really was a stalker. Alice was beginning to doubt his existence.

She scolded herself for doing so. Jennifer Jerrold was a good, honest, intelligent young woman who'd volunteered to take on a daunting role in the Women's Police Force. If she felt that she was being followed, then she was right. Someone had taken an unhealthy interest in her. It might be that he was now at work and unable to keep an eye on her. That was not a conclusion that Jennifer herself had reached. Alice could see how nervous she was. As far as her friend was concerned, the man was there.

The bus eventually came, and Alice watched her get on. As it pulled away, she could see Jennifer peering apprehensively out through the window as if expecting someone to pop up and leer at her. Alice stepped out from her hiding place and asked herself what sort of man would watch Jenny week after week, even though it caused her visible distress. At what point would his fixation with her move from merely looking, to a desire to touch, caress, then grope at will?

The face of Douglas Beckett suddenly came into her mind.

The first phone call came when Rex Chell happened to be in reception. No sooner had he put down the receiver than he had to pick it up again as a second, then a third woman rang to give him the same information as the first. What was at first an irritation soon became something far more serious. A handbill was slipped through the letter box. Since she was passing it at the time, Millie Jenks picked it up and took it straight to the manager's office. After thanking her and sending her on her way, Chell read the handbill with a blend of alarm and anger. It was time to summon Griselda Fleetwood from her room on the top floor.

When she came into his office, she had no idea what to expect.

'Is it good news or bad?'

'It's neither, Mrs Fleetwood, because it's not news at all. It's exactly what we'd expect of him.'

'Buchanan?'

'He got someone to deliver this.'

He gave her the handbill and watched her face slowly change shape and colour as she read the neatly printed advertisement. It drew attention to the fact that a murder had occurred at the Lotus Hotel and made it a place to avoid because its security was defective. The Roath Court and the Unicorn were held up as examples of places that offered everything that the Lotus had, with a guarantee of safety for its guests because both hotels had retired policemen on patrol. Before she'd finished reading it, Griselda scrunched up the handbill and hurled it into the wastepaper basket. She turned angrily to Chell.

'We've had three phone calls from regular guests of ours,' he said, 'warning us that they received this handbill today in the post. I fear that there'll be several more before the day is out.'

'This is deplorable!'

'I can think of a stronger word than that, Mrs Fleetwood.'

'My solicitor must see it immediately.'

'The damage has already been done. It's quite obvious that a copy of this has been sent to our regular clientele with the express purpose of denigrating the Lotus.'

'There's only one way Buchanan could have done that.'

'Precisely – he somehow acquired the names and addresses of our guests. We have a traitor in our midst.'

Griselda glowered. 'Who the devil can it be?'

Leonard Rogan sat impatiently in the pub and nursed the remains of a pint of beer. When his friend eventually turned up, Rogan was curt.

'I expected you half an hour ago.'

'I was held up.'

'That's twice you've kept me waiting.'

'Don't make such a fuss about it,' said the other. 'I bring you glad tidings, Len.' He took out an envelope and handed it over. 'That's half of what we agreed. I'll give you the rest tomorrow morning when I get the rest of what he owes me. Meet me near the Roath Court.'

'I will,' said Rogan, counting the money. 'I had to take chances to get what you wanted.'

'Mr Buchanan was very grateful.'

'Does that mean he has a job for me?'

'There's no hurry. We don't want to give the game away.'

'You promised me.'

'Yes, I did, and I always keep my promises.'

'When would I start?'

'It'll be when you're told and not before. Mr Buchanan is pleased with me,' said Maitland, airily. 'He said that he'd remember my name. That means I can get you a job at the Roath Court any time I like.'

After their discussion in the superintendent's office, Marmion and Keedy went off to the canteen. They were still savouring the way that Chatfield had been routed.

'Did you see the look on Chat's face when the commissioner sided with us?' said Marmion. 'He was like a burst balloon.'

'He'll get his own back on us in due course.'

'I know. He bears grudges.'

'We can only hope that the French secret service cooperates.'

'Keep your fingers crossed.'

'It's not been Chat's day, has it?' said Keedy. 'He was obviously embarrassed when you came up with that explanation of what the murder victim was actually doing at the Lotus.'

'That woman was there by invitation. I'm certain of it.'

'And so you really think that she and Vesta Lyle . . . ?'

'It's a strong possibility.'

'But how could the two of them have met in the first place?'

'Well, it probably wasn't at an art exhibition. Seriously, most nuns are not allowed near anything of that kind. They'd regard it as profane. Vesta Lyle would have had to go to a convent, I suppose.

Some of them operate as a retreat for women who want seclusion.'

'Is that what she was after?'

'Even if it wasn't a close marriage,' said Keedy, 'she must have been upset by the death of her husband. And we know that she converted to Catholicism. Why did she do that? Was it out of a sense of need?'

'What sort of need?'

'I can't say, Harv, but the church seemed to provide it. Nobody would attend Mass in the most famous cathedral in France unless they were staunch Catholics.'

'Why was their wedding held almost in secret?'

'That was their choice.'

'It's as if they didn't want people to know.'

'Perhaps they didn't,' said Keedy. 'I saw it as proof of what an intensely private man Alphonse Dufays really was. That's why I believe your theory about him working for the secret service.'

'Chat didn't think much of that theory.'

'I'd put my money on you, Harv.'

Marmion grinned. 'Have you got any money?'

'Well, no, not really . . .'

'Then don't try to get it by working as a nightwatchman. It'd be the ruin of you. I'm not letting my daughter marry someone who can't even keep his eyes open because he's worked for eighteen hours a day. And on the subject of money,' said Marmion, 'don't forget that the bride's father is supposed to pick up the bill for the wedding. You don't have to search for a second job.'

'It was just a thought.'

'What about NUPPO?'

'I've forgotten all about it,' said Keedy, dismissively.

'Thank goodness for that.'

They munched their food and washed it down with hot tea. After a few minutes, Keedy remembered something.

'You said that the murder victim was no longer a nun.'

'Yes, I did.'

'How do you know?'

'It's because she had such freedom of movement. I always thought that nuns didn't have that. It's one of the things they renounce, surely?'

'What made you think she was a French nun?'

'If she'd been in a British convent, someone would have reported her missing. They might also have recognised the description we gave of her in the press. I'm sure that Mother Superiors take a sly peak at the newspapers so that they can keep abreast of worldly affairs. Even people who withdraw from normal life want to know how the war is going on.'

'She wouldn't be reported missing if she'd already gone back on her vows and left the convent.'

'I still think there's a French connection somehow,' said Marmion. 'Mind you, it's a pity the murder victim wasn't still a nun.'

'Why?'

'They're usually clothed from head to foot in black – apart from the white wimple, that is. What better way to slip unnoticed into the Lotus Hotel?' he joked. 'She could have walked right past the night porter in the dark and he'd have been none the wiser.'

Keedy laughed. 'You think of everything.'

'One of us has to.'

They were interrupted by a detective constable who handed Marmion a letter from the superintendent. When he read it, he puffed his cheeks.

'One of us needs to get across to the Lotus.'

'What's happened?'

'They've had more trouble from Buchanan.'

'Would you like me to go?'

'I'll handle it, Joe. You can check on how much information has come in from the public since we released the name of Vesta Lyle. If there's any running around to do, leave it to me. You've got something else to do later on.'

'Have I?'

'Yes, you've got to find a way to get in touch with my daughter before she forgets what you look like. Alice loves surprises. I'm sure you'll get a warm welcome.'

'That's an offer I can't refuse.'

'It's not for your benefit – it's for *hers*.'

When Alice took a sympathetic interest in Jennifer Jerrold's plight, it was not out of simple kindness. She knew what it was like to be stalked. Alice had been followed back to her flat one night by a man who'd been trailing her for days. She knew that someone was there, but she'd been unable to see him and was not ready for his attack. Alice was lucky. Joe Keedy had been waiting outside her flat and he was able to intervene. As a result, the stalker was given a good hiding. After that, he never dared to trouble Alice again.

Unfortunately for Jennifer, there was no detective sergeant in her life. In fact, there was no reliable male friend to whom she could turn. As one of three sisters, she'd been brought up in a house that set great store by respectability. None of the three daughters was allowed to go out alone with a man. The parents saw to that. Since men were kept resolutely at arm's length, Jennifer had no idea how to relate to them. What she did recognise, however, was the sense of threat a man could represent. It was poisoning her life. Alice could identify with that feeling.

Jennifer clearly felt that, in leaving the police force, she would be escaping from the unwanted attention of a stranger, but Alice began to have doubts. If someone had been following her so often and for so long, it was almost certain that he knew where she lived. That being the case, Jennifer's bid for freedom was illusory. All that she'd be doing was to shift the location of the stalking to the area near her home.

Eager to rescue her friend from her crippling fear, Alice came to a decision. Since she knew where Jennifer lived, she resolved to get there the following morning well ahead of the time when her friend left. If there was a man loitering in readiness, Alice was determined to find out who he was. His obsession with Jennifer had to be nipped in the bud before it developed into something more dangerous.

As a result of the publicity about the murder, a number of people had come forward with information. Most of it was of no value at all and some of it was deliberately misleading. Those who came forward with the sole purpose of telling lies in order to get a share of the reward money were dealt with harshly. Yet some useful evidence did appear, largely in the form of letters.

One of the people in charge of collating it was Detective Constable Clifford Burge. He was a thickset man in his early thirties with a strong Cockney accent. Joe Keedy liked the man and was not put off by his rather unsightly features. Aware of his outstanding work in dealing with the problems of juvenile delinquency, Keedy had the greatest respect for Burge. When he went to the room where the man was reading through a pile of correspondence, he was given a broad grin by the detective constable.

'How's it going, Cliff?' he asked.

'It's not the most exciting job I've ever had, Sergeant,' said the other, 'but it does mean I'm working on a murder investigation at last. That's always been my dream.'

'What you're doing may seem like drudgery but it's important.'

'I hope so.' He indicated a small pile. 'These are the only letters worth reading. I've weeded out the obvious false claims and the hoaxes, of course. One man insisted that we'll find the evidence we need in the cellars of the Houses of Parliament. You can guess what name he signed.'

'Guy Fawkes?'

'You're right first time.'

'I was cheating. He's one of our regular correspondents. Whatever the crime we need help to solve, he always sends in his advice.'

'These are more genuine,' said Burge, handing over the small pile of letters. 'To start with, they all have an address. Two of them are of particular interest.'

'Why is that?'

'They tell more or less the same story. The first one is from a man who was returning home after being on the night shift. He claims that he saw a man and a woman getting into a taxi close to the Lotus Hotel at around four in the morning.'

'That would certainly tie in with the likely time of the murder.'

'He only remembers them because of something unusual.'

'What was it?'

'The woman was carrying the luggage and the man was hurrying her along. That seemed odd. He couldn't see their faces in the dark.'

'This sounds promising,' said Keedy.

'The other letter was written by someone who was actually on his way to work and walked within a few yards of the couple. He says that the man more or less bundled the woman into the taxi, then got in after her. Here's the interesting bit,' said Burge. 'He heard them speak.'

'What's so interesting about that?'

'They were talking in French.'

Marmion arrived at the Lotus Hotel to find its atmosphere reassuring and its mood tranquil. Beneath the surface, however, it was a different story. In the manager's office, the owner of the hotel was enraged and even the normally unruffled manager was letting his disgust show. Marmion invited them to vent their anger in turn. Griselda Fleetwood went first, gesticulating wildly and spitting out her words like so many brass tacks. Chell's account was more articulate and less inflamed. He gave the inspector the handbill.

'A copy of that has gone to everyone on our mailing list,' he said.

'How many people would that involve, sir?'

'It's almost four hundred.'

'We need you to arrest Buchanan,' ordered Griselda.

'I'd need a good reason to do that.'

'You're holding it in your hand, Inspector.'

'What proof do you have that the handbills were sent out by Mr Buchanan? Yes,' he went on, 'I'm sure you'll tell me that it's typical of him and in line with his previous manoeuvres against you.'

'Arrest him at once. Force him to confess.'

'The days of the rack and the hot poker are long gone, Mrs Fleetwood. A court of law expects cast-iron evidence.'

'That handbill maligns my hotel.'

'Actually, most of it relates to Mr Buchanan's hotels.'

'Doesn't that tell you he must have printed it?' she asked, losing her patience. 'I'm going to sue him for this.'

'I'm not certain that you can do that,' said Marmion, reading the handbill again. 'The language has been very carefully chosen. There is a mention of the Lotus, it's true, but there's no direct attack on it. Only a solicitor could tell if you'd be likely to win a libel case. What I will do, in the first instance,' he said, trying to mollify them, 'is to find out who printed this handbill. He's been careful to leave his name off it, but we'll track him down somehow.'

'At least you'll do *something*, then,' she said, resentfully.

'You and Mr Chell are best placed to get to the root of this, Mrs Fleetwood. The list of your guests was leaked to Mr Buchanan, or whoever it was who had those handbills printed and distributed. The real villain may be under this very roof.'

'Don't you think we know that?'

'It's an obvious assumption,' said Chell, 'and I made it myself when I had the warnings by telephone. I went through the names of every one of the people employed here and thought hard about their individual characters and their record of service.'

'Our staff love to work here,' boasted Griselda. 'That's why we never have a problem with recruitment. We trust them and they repay us with loyalty and dedication.'

'It's all part of the ethos we've created here,' said Chell. 'I've trained them with care. In most hotels, members of staff are always on view. Here they are largely invisible until they're actually needed. They never rush down corridors – they glide. They treat the guests as if they were royalty and that's not as peculiar as it may sound, because some of our patrons are actually connected in some way with the royal family.'

'You don't need to sell the Lotus to me, Mr Chell,' said Marmion. 'Its virtues are clear. Nevertheless, confidential information was patently taken from here and given to a third party who used it to your disadvantage.'

'We must have been robbed,' concluded Griselda.

'There was no report of a break-in and you have a night porter on duty at a time most likely to entice burglars.'

'Then the matter is in your hands, Inspector. We expect action.'

'You've every right to do so,' said Marmion. 'I've told you that one of my detectives will root out the printer responsible for the handbill. But my focus – as you'll understand – must remain on the murder inquiry. Once that's been brought to a satisfactory conclusion, you won't have to worry about handbills like this one because the Lotus will be restored to its deserved place among the hotels of the capital. I know you were outraged when you saw what had been written about you,' he continued, 'but don't forget that some of your patrons rang to warn you about the attack on the Lotus. That shows the high regard in which they hold it.'

'I never thought about that,' she said.

Griselda smiled for the first time that day.

Ellen's delight slowly evaporated. Having enjoyed thinking about the way she'd confronted Quentin Dacey, she decided to make some early decisions about the guest list for the wedding. Since her daughter wasn't yet ready to do so, Ellen felt that she'd take the first step on Alice's behalf. Seated at the kitchen table with a pad, she started with the names of the immediate family then branched out. In no time at all, she had over thirty people pencilled in for an invitation.

One name, however, was missing and it created a chasm in the list. If Paul were not there, his absence would overshadow the whole event. At the same time, if he turned up in the surly mood that had made him leave home in the first place, there'd be a nasty atmosphere at the wedding. Ellen was once again torn between wanting him back and accepting that he had effectively deserted the family. The longer he stayed away, she believed, the less chance there was of his ever coming back. Hopes that he might be present at his sister's wedding were futile.

Ellen felt a pang of regret and used the pencil to cross out every name on the page. Making plans for the wedding was far too painful.

Chelsea was known for its hospital, its barracks, the quality of its housing and its literary associations, but not everyone there lived in style. Gordon Wale and his family occupied the ground floor of a terraced house in a dingy backstreet. The first thing that Keedy noticed when he got there was that the people who rented the upper half of the house were very active. There was a constant thud of feet above his head. Wale was used to it, but the sergeant found it distracting. After introducing himself, Keedy explained that he'd come as a result of the letter sent to Scotland Yard.

'What were you doing out and about at that time of night?'

'I work as a storeman in a factory,' said Wale. 'It's in operation twenty-four hours. I have to walk over a mile to get there.'

'Well, I'm very glad you took that route. What you saw could turn out to be valuable evidence in a murder investigation.'

'That's why I wrote to you, Sergeant.'

Wale was a chunky man in his fifties with a rough beard and bushy eyebrows that all but obscured his eyes. It was clear from his letter that he was not well educated. There were several grammatical errors and a number of words were misspelled. It didn't detract from the importance of his testimony. Keedy asked him to recount what had happened.

'I was walking along the street,' said Wale, 'and I saw this taxi pulled up at the kerb. Next minute, two people came towards it. The woman was carrying a suitcase and a handbag, and the man was hurrying her along.'

'How close did you get to them?'

'They brushed right past me.'

'And you heard them speak French – is that right?'

'I *think* it was French. I don't speak the language myself.'

'How old were they?'

'Oh, they were not young, Sergeant. They deliberately kept their heads down when they passed me but, from the way they moved, I'd say they were as old as me, if not older.'

'What did they do when they reached the taxi?'

'The man opened the door and put the suitcase in, then he more or less shoved the woman after it. As I carried on walking, the taxi started up and drove past me. That's it,' said Wale. 'I thought no more of it until someone at work mentioned later that there'd been a murder nearby that night.'

Keedy probed for more detail until he realised that there was nothing left to learn. After thanking the man, he made for the door.

'Is there any chance of a reward?' asked Wale, hopefully.

'No,' said Keedy, 'I'm afraid not. There's a long way to go yet before we solve this crime. Your contribution has been small but very useful. Thank you, sir.'

Since there was a new development in the case, Marmion was duty-bound to report it to the superintendent. He went to Chatfield's office in the knowledge that he might well be chastised by his superior because of what had happened at their last encounter. Marmion showed him the handbill received by the Lotus Hotel.

'And who do you think put this through the letter box?' asked the superintendent, malevolently. 'Was it a French nun of dubious character? Or do you think it might have been a member of the secret service who died three years ago? Don't let us rule out a German spy posing as an exotic dancer.'

'Very funny, sir,' said Marmion.

'I look forward to listening to more of your bizarre suggestions.'

'In this case, it seems certain that Mr Buchanan is involved. He owns the two hotels mentioned in the handbill.'

'And what does it actually say here?' Chatfield read the text quickly then looked up. 'If Buchanan really is behind this, it's an example of sharp practice.'

'I agree, sir, but is it actionable?'

'We can leave that to Mrs Fleetwood's solicitor to decide.'

'With your agreement, I'll get the printer tracked down so that we can confirm who employed him. A more difficult problem is finding the person who somehow got hold of the guest list from the Lotus.'

'Perhaps the handbill is accurate,' said Chatfield. 'Security at the hotel must be woeful. If someone can walk in there blithely in the middle of the night to commit a murder and abduct a woman, then it must be equally easy to steal confidential records.'

'That's very unfair, sir. The Lotus prides itself on its safety record. It's had five years without any incidents that might qualify as even petty crimes. How would it have kept its illustrious clientele if it wasn't the haven it claims to be?'

'You're quite right, Inspector,' apologised the other. 'My sneer was uncalled for.'

'Since the hotel first opened, Mrs Fleetwood has had to fight a running battle with Mr Buchanan. That handbill looks as if it's the latest grenade he's thrown at her.'

'Let me know as soon as you have clear proof of that.'

'I will, sir.'

'If Buchanan is behind this disgraceful handbill, then it's about time I had a word with the gentleman.'

'Oh, he's no gentleman, I can assure you.'

'Why do you say that?'

'He has no idea how to treat a lady, sir. Ask Mrs Fleetwood.'

Alice Marmion felt guilty. Having spent so much time thinking about Jennifer Jerrold, she'd largely forgotten her mother. She wondered if she'd really won the argument about the lecture by Quentin Dacey or if her mother had decided to attend it despite her daughter's objections. The very fact that Ellen had fallen prey to the ideas put out by Dacey and William Le Queux showed how lonely and vulnerable her mother was. There was little help from her father. He was rarely available to talk to anyone in the family. Alice was bound to blame herself for leaving home, but she'd seen it as an absolute necessity. Had her independence been bought at the price of her mother's isolation? Should her first duty be to the family?

It was getting late, but she hadn't even undressed yet. After an involuntary yawn, Alice began to unbutton her blouse. Suddenly, there was a sharp crack. It made her fly to the window and pull back the curtains. Keedy was standing below with a grin on his face. He'd thrown a small stone up to attract her attention. When he beckoned her with the crook of his finger, her heart lifted. She grabbed her coat and left the room on tiptoe.

Ten minutes later, they were sitting on a bench in the nearby park and ignoring the autumnal chill. With his arm around her shoulders, Alice felt warm and happy.

'I wasn't expecting you, Joe.'

'Is that a complaint?'

'Don't be silly.'

'The person to thank is your father,' he said. 'He more or less ordered me to see you before you forgot what I looked like.'

'I'd never do that,' she said with a laugh.

'How are you?'

'I'm fine now.'

'Does that mean you weren't until I turned up?'

'It does, actually.'

'Have you been having trouble with Gale Force again?'

'No, she's decided that I'm a model officer now.'

'That makes a change,' he said.

'It's all to do with Jenny Jerrold,' she explained. 'Jenny's a friend in the force. I'm keen to help her with a nasty problem, but I'll have to do some detective work first.'

'What a coincidence!' said Keedy. 'Not so long ago, your father was saying that you'd make a good detective. Can I help?'

'Afterwards . . .'

She snuggled up against him and felt his arm tighten around her.

Night continued to be a torment. If she actually managed to fall asleep, Millie Jenks would wake with a start after a short while. She knew that she'd never escape her nocturnal dread unless she did what Lena Gosling had advised and confronted her fears by going back to the room where she'd discovered the gruesome scene. There'd be no need to enter it and the room was in any case locked, but in making the effort to reach the door and put her hand on the knob, she'd be achieving a vital stage in her recovery. Until that happened, her despair would continue.

Getting out of bed, she put on her dressing gown and slippers before letting herself out. Millie knew the geography of the hotel well enough to be able to find her way around in the gloom, so she headed for the room where her terrors had all begun. When she got there, she was conscious of the fact that there was no Lena Gosling to come to her aid this time. Millie was alone now.

Summoning up all of her courage, she got within a yard of the door and reached out for the knob. Then she heard a noise from inside the room. It petrified her. As she looked down, she saw a ray of light flash across the bottom of the door before disappearing.

Her courage deserted her now. Hearing the approach of footsteps, she leapt back and dived into an alcove. The door opened soundlessly, and a figure emerged. By the light of his lamp, she saw his face.

# CHAPTER TWENTY-ONE

With something important to tell him, Ellen was determined to stay up for her husband. When the police car finally dropped him off, she was sitting on the sofa in her dressing gown and reading a novel. Marmion let himself into the house, intending to sneak past the living room to go quietly upstairs. He was surprised to see his wife wide awake.

'Still up, then?'

'I don't feel tired.'

'Has something happened?' he asked. 'You look so . . . cheerful.'

'I feel cheerful, Harvey. I went to that lecture I told you about.'

'That's a shame. I thought I put you off.'

'Rene Bridger more or less forced me into it,' said Ellen, 'and I'm very grateful. I made a speech there.'

'That's not like you, love.'

'I was so angry with him, it just came out.'

'What did you say?'

'I defended you and everybody else in the police force. Mr Dacey claimed that he sent details of German agents to Scotland Yard and nothing had been done about them. When Rene told him what you'd said about all the spies being sent to the Isle of Man, he sneered. I wasn't going to let him get away with that,' said Ellen, stoutly, 'so I told him we should be grateful to the police instead of insulting them. As I marched out with Rene, some people clapped and others followed us.'

'Good God!' he exclaimed. 'You have been having fun.'

'I went into that hall believing Mr Dacey and I came out hating everything he'd told us. Rene said I was wonderful.'

He kissed her. 'I told you the same thing years ago.'

'That was different.'

'It seemed to work at the time.'

She jabbed him playfully. 'How have you got on?'

'We're inching steadily along.'

'Is that all?'

'No, it isn't,' said Marmion, 'we've made more progress than we realise. More to the point, we got the commissioner to take our side against Chat.'

'Was the superintendent upset?'

'He was like a wounded animal, looking for someone to bite.'

'Well, I hope it wasn't you.'

'Come on,' he said. 'Let's go to bed.'

'You look as if you need sleep, Harvey. You can barely stand up.'

'Save your sympathy for Joe.'

'Why?'

'I'm off duty now. He's still hard at work.'

'What can he possibly be doing this late?'

'First of all, I hope, he was talking to our daughter. By now, he'll be in Chelsea, talking to taxi drivers. We've had information from a man who was walking near the hotel around the time we believe the murder took place. Joe spoke to him. As a result,' said Marmion, 'he's out in the cold in search of a driver who works late at night.'

The blackout turned London into a ghostly city. Light of any kind was either hidden or dimmed. Streets were dark and pedestrians had to pick their way along them with care. The most common complaint was that the invisible kerbs were a menace. Even after some of them were painted white, people kept tripping over them. Most of the capital was shrouded by night but the West End was an exception. Albeit subdued, lights still flickered there to advertise clubs and pubs to the scores of fun-seeking soldiers on leave from the front. Only when the rumble of German aircraft could be heard were lights swiftly extinguished at the heart of London.

His visit to Alice had revived Keedy. They'd been able to kiss away the time they'd been apart, and he felt inspired when he left her. The first place he went to in Chelsea was the Lotus Hotel, now no more than a dark silhouette against the sky. Nothing in its shadowy exterior hinted at the turmoil within. As he headed for the main road, he was reminded of one of the strictly enforced edicts that had been brought in. Whistling was forbidden because it might be confused with an air raid signal and cause unnecessary panic, so he hummed a tune quietly to himself.

He reached the taxi rank to find that there were no vehicles there. When a few started to arrive, none of the drivers remembered picking up a man and a woman at four o'clock three nights earlier. Keedy had to loiter there for a long time before his luck changed. A taxi drew up and the driver poked his head through the window. Keedy took out his warrant card to show to the man.

'I'm Detective Sergeant Keedy from Scotland Yard.'

'I've done nothing wrong,' bleated the driver. 'I'm properly licensed.'

'I'm sure you are. I just want you to tell me about the two people you picked up not far from here two nights ago. You contacted the police about them.'

'Ah yes, I know what you're talking about now.'

'Is it true that a man and a woman got in here talking French?'

'So that's what it was. It was gobbledegook to me.'

'Tell me what happened.'

The driver coughed and Keedy became horribly aware of his bad breath. He was a diminutive man in his sixties with a flat cap on his head and a cushion under his backside so that he could see through the windscreen. Taking out his notebook, Keedy jotted down the details as they came.

'Well,' said the driver, 'I was waiting right here when they came.'

'From which direction would that be?'

'It was over there – around that corner.'

Keedy was excited. The Lotus was located in the same street.

'Then what happened?' he asked.

'I was glad. You don't get many fares at that time of night. The woman was carrying a suitcase and swaying all over the place. The man kept urging her on.'

'I was told he more or less bundled her into the taxi after the luggage.'

'It was something like that. All I know is that he was angry and she sounded as if she was drunk.'

'Have you any idea what they were saying to each other?'

263

'Don't ask me, Sergeant. I couldn't understand a bleeding word.'

'How old were they?'

'I couldn't see. It was too dark.'

'Did they walk as if they were young and fit?'

'No, she was struggling. I did get a glimpse of her and I suppose she'd be around my age. Never saw his face.'

'Can you remember where you took them?'

'Of course,' said the driver as if insulted by the question. 'I never forget a destination.' He tapped his skull. 'They're locked away up here forever . . .'

'Right,' said Keedy. 'Take me there.'

The driver eyed him suspiciously. 'Are you serious?'

'Take me there now.' He clambered into the taxi, but the man still hesitated. 'Go on – you'll get paid.'

Alice was delighted that her plan had been approved by Keedy, even if it meant that she had to get up very early. The consolation was that she had free access for once to the bathroom she shared with three other female lodgers. As a rule, she had to wait her turn, but she was out of the house before the trio of women had even woken up. Getting across to Jennifer Jerrold's house involved taking two separate buses then walking over three hundred yards. Alice got there in plenty of time to choose her hiding place. Light rain was falling so her umbrella was able to serve as a means of concealment.

She had a good view of Jennifer's house, a corner property of some size, but saw nobody lurking nearby. People were too busy setting off for work to stand out in the rain. When her friend eventually came out of the house, Alice realised why Jennifer felt safe there. She was accompanied by her father who walked all the way to the bus stop with her before waiting until the vehicle arrived. Jennifer had a chaperone. She also had a stalker. When the bus pulled away, a man came out of the shop doorway from which he'd been watching her and stared after the bus until it was out of sight. There was something about the intensity of his interest that alerted Alice.

Keedy had warned her not to accost the stalker in case he turned violent, but Alice was too angry on her friend's behalf. The man on the opposite side of the road had caused Jennifer so much grief that she was on the point of resigning from the police. Seeing him walk off in the opposite direction, Alice ran across the road and went after him. He was tall and angular. He wore a raincoat and a wide-brimmed black hat.

When she got near him, Alice called out for him to stop, intending to challenge him about what he'd been doing. As he turned to look at her, the words died in her throat. Instead of looking at his face, she was transfixed by something he was wearing. It was a clerical collar.

Notwithstanding his late night, Keedy was ready to be picked up when Marmion arrived in a police car. The sergeant was as smartly dressed as usual and was bubbling with enthusiasm. Marmion was puzzled.

'What's got into you, Joe? Have you been drinking?'

'All I had was my usual cup of tea.'

'Something seems to have cheered you up.'

'I tracked down that taxi driver.'

He told Marmion about his visit to Chelsea and how the driver had picked up a man and a woman who'd been arguing in a foreign language. Keedy had been driven to the same destination as the couple.

'When I realised that we were on Cromwell Road,' said Keedy, 'I thought at first they'd gone to the French embassy, then we turned into a side street and stopped outside a small hotel called the Paradise. The night porter let me see the register. Vesta Lyle and the man stayed the night there under the name of Baker.'

Marmion started. 'An *English* name.'

'The man must have been fluent in English and have had documents to prove his identity. According to the night porter, the woman wasn't at all well when they arrived back after midnight. She had to be helped out of the taxi by the man. The couple left late in the morning without even bothering to have breakfast. That's all I can tell you, Harv. My guess is that they headed for somewhere like Dover.'

'Well, they won't be able to sail back to France. Chat made sure of that. All ports were sent a description of Vesta Lyle. If she tries to sneak out of the country as Mrs Baker, someone will spot her.'

'Then they must be holed up on the south coast somewhere.'

'You did well, Joe.'

'Thanks.'

'We've finally got a sniff of her. I'm interested in the fact that she seemed to be drunk. The murder victim had a lot of alcohol in her blood as well. Had Vesta Lyle been drinking heavily, or had she taken a bit too much cocaine?'

'I don't know,' said Keedy. 'I can tell you what the effects are of having too much beer, but I've never tried cocaine or any other drug.'

'Keep it that way.'

'I tell you what I can't work out. However did the man get inside the hotel to kill one woman and drag another one out? There was an obvious way to get the murder victim in there. Vesta Lyle could have let her in through one of the rear entrances in the early hours. When I took the first statement from the night porter, he told me that he patrolled the hotel at set times.'

'Vesta Lyle could easily have discovered that,' said Marmion. 'It may be the reason she'd stayed in the Lotus before. It needed to be a hotel into which she could smuggle her friend.'

'The man who took her out was no friend,' Keedy pointed out. 'The taxi said how roughly he spoke to her when he pushed her into the cab. There's something else as well. Mr Baker, as he called himself, was quite old. I can't see him forcing his way into the Lotus somehow. I'd love to know how he did it.'

'Sooner or later, we'll find out. Meanwhile, we've got a nice titbit to feed Chat. Well done!'

Millie Jenks wasn't quite sure that what she'd seen was real. Since the murder, she'd been so on edge that she kept making simple mistakes. She was also at the mercy of strange dreams. Had she really gone to the room at night where the crime had occurred? Or was it an illusion? And even if she had gone there, did she need to say anything about what happened? The fear of getting herself into trouble made her keep it to herself. As a consequence, she felt guilty for holding something back that the manager ought to know. It had an effect on her work.

'Come into my room,' said Lena Gosling.

'Yes. Of course,' said Millie, following her. 'Have I done anything wrong?'

'I'm afraid that you have. It started with you collecting the wrong bedlinen from the laundry room and went on from there.'

'I'm so sorry, Mrs Gosling.'

'Your mind just isn't on your work this morning. After what happened, we've made allowances for you, but we can't keep doing that.' Lena took her by the shoulders. 'What is it, Millie?'

'It's nothing . . .'

'I know when you're not telling the truth.'

Lena was determined to find out why the girl's concentration had deserted her. She waited until Millie eventually confided in her. When she heard what had happened, Lena fixed her with a stare.

'Are you quite *certain* about that, Millie?'

'Yes, Mrs Gosling.'

'It's a serious allegation. Are you ready to stand by it?'

'Well . . . I don't want to get anyone into trouble,' said the other. 'But I've told you the truth, honestly. I couldn't understand why he used a torch when he could've switched on the light.'

'All the light bulbs were removed.'

'Why?'

'Mr Chell will explain that. We need to see him at once.'

Alice was surprised to realise that she was talking to a priest but the man himself was utterly astounded when accosted by a policewoman. He backed away in embarrassment. He was a middle-aged man with an unusually pale face and he wore a pair of spectacles.

'You were watching her, weren't you?' she asked him, putting as much authority into her voice as she could muster. 'You were hiding back there so that you could keep your eyes on Jenny.'

'She's a parishioner of mine.'

'Does she *know* what you've been doing?'

'Frankly,' said the man, asserting himself, 'that's none of your business. Who are you, anyway?'

'My name is Alice Marmion. I'm a friend and colleague of Jenny's. She told me about the anguish it's caused her.'

'What anguish?'

'That's what she feels when she's being followed everywhere by someone who never shows his face. It's frightening.'

'I meant no harm,' he said, defensively.

'Well, you certainly caused it. Because of you, Jenny has been thinking of leaving the police. She can't stand being watched like that. It's shattered her confidence.'

'That's terrible. I had no idea she was even aware of me.'

'Who are you, anyway?'

'My name is Father Howells. I'm the curate at Jenny's church. We see each other every Sunday. We're good friends. She never shies away from me.'

'That's because she can *see* you,' said Alice. 'She knows that she can trust you. When she can't actually see you – and doesn't know who you are – then you become a threat to her.'

'Do I?' he said, genuinely distressed.

'It's cruel of you, Father Howells.'

'I would *never* deliberately cause her any pain.'

'Nevertheless,' said Alice, 'she feels it. Jenny was such a happy person when she joined us, but she's now scared to go home at the end of her shift because someone is dogging her footsteps.'

'I just enjoy . . .' His hands fluttered. 'I just enjoy . . . looking at her.'

Alice could see the love in his eyes. He was no menacing stalker with designs on her friend. Father Howells simply liked to watch the young woman he adored. During his pastoral work, he would have helped many of his parishioners to cope with their troubles. Ironically, he'd only created a problem for Jennifer Jerrold. When she saw the remorse in his eyes, Alice was tempted to feel sympathy for him, but her first duty was to her friend.

'It has to stop,' she said, firmly. 'I must ask you to give me your word that you'll never stalk Jenny again.'

'I give it willingly. I feel so ashamed.'

'That's your problem, Father. My only concern is to help Jenny escape from the fear that's ruining her life.' She saw him wince. 'That's how bad it is from her point of view. You claim to be her friend, but friends don't do what you've been doing to Jenny all this time.'

'But she wasn't expected to *know*,' he argued.

'That's no excuse.'

'You're right – it isn't.'

After taking a deep breath, he buried his face in his hands.

Marmion had faith in Keedy's belief that the couple posing as Mr and Mrs Baker would be keen to head for France and put distance between them and the ghastly crime that had taken place in Chelsea. He spent some time on the telephone, talking to the chief constable of Kent and reinforcing the importance of finding the pair before they vanished beyond British jurisdiction. After being promised full cooperation, Marmion put down the receiver and turned to Keedy.

'If they *are* on the south coast,' he said, 'they won't get through customs. If they're that keen to go to France, they'll have to swim there.'

'In their place, I'd prefer to hide over here. The moment they get to the coast, they'll be able to hear the guns pounding away. Does anyone in their right mind really want to head for a war zone?'

'If one of them committed a murder, they might have to.'

'Good point,' said Keedy.

'By the way, did you manage to see Alice last night?'

'Yes, I did. My visit was short and sweet because I had to get over to Chelsea at a time when that taxi driver was likely to come back on the night shift. Alice was in good spirits. She told me that she was following in her father's footsteps.'

'Oh?'

'She's doing some detective work for a friend.'

'That sounds like my daughter,' said Marmion with a smile. 'I had a surprise when I got home last night. Ellen was not only waiting for me, she was wide awake and dying to tell me about her triumph.'

He told Keedy about the lecture given by Quentin Dacey and the way that Ellen had lost her temper with the man and spoken up in defence of the police.

'At least it cured her of believing that the streets of London were populated by German spies. If they really did exist, they'd have killed Dacey by now just to shut the idiot up.'

At that moment, the door opened and Chatfield marched in. He was just in time to hear the last half-dozen words and they made him scowl.

'Show respect for senior officers,' he demanded.

'We always do, sir,' said Marmion.

'It didn't sound like it, Inspector.'

'Ah, you heard what I said, but I wasn't talking about you, sir. The sergeant and I were discussing Quentin Dacey. My wife went to hear a lecture he gave yesterday. Fortunately, she saw how misguided he is.'

'I agree with Mrs Marmion there,' said Chatfield, relaxing. 'I'm all for free speech but Dacey abuses the privilege. He's getting to the dangerous stage. Anyway,' he continued, 'let's put that troublesome fool to one side. I've come to report a small success.'

'What's that, sir?' asked Keedy.

'Everyone who's stayed at the Lotus Hotel was sent a handbill that drew attention to its supposed lack of security.'

'The inspector told me about that. It sounds like Buchanan's work.'

'It was. We have proof of that now.'

'How did you get that, sir?'

'The inspector got someone to contact London printers in turn and we soon got the name of the company we wanted. They do all of Buchanan's printing, apparently. It gives me an excuse to speak to the man directly.'

'Is there any point, sir?' asked Marmion.

'Of course there is.'

'I'm not convinced that it's a police matter at all. Why not let Mrs Fleetwood's solicitor fight it out with Buchanan's?'

'Aren't you forgetting something, Inspector?'

'What do you mean?'

'Mr Buchanan is, technically, still a suspect in a murder case.'

'Not in my book, sir.'

'Nor mine,' added Keedy. 'You read my report, Superintendent. The man who hustled Vesta Lyle out of the Lotus that night was French. He has nothing whatsoever to do with Buchanan.'

'That remains to be seen.'

'You'll be going into a cul-de-sac.'

'Do you dare to question my judgement?' said Chatfield, sharply.

'No, no, sir,' said Keedy, backing off.

The telephone rang and Marmion picked it up. They could see from his expression that he'd been told something of real interest. When he put down the receiver, he beamed at them.

'Mr Farrier is here. He has something to show us.'

It was worth it. Because she had to wait for a bus, Alice arrived late and was reprimanded by Inspector Gale in front of the other policewomen. The harsh words bounced off her. Alice was in such high spirits that she felt impregnable. As they formed into pairs, she looked across at Jennifer Jerrold, who offered a sympathetic smile. Alice replied with a wink.

* * *

272

Seeing how nervous Millie Jenks was, the first thing that the manager did was to ask her to sit down. Lena Gosling sat beside her, ready to prompt the girl. Chell smiled at Millie to put her at ease then asked what she had to report. As she described what had happened the previous night, he watched her carefully. He made no comment until she'd finished.

'Mrs Gosling tells me that you're a truthful girl,' he said.

'Oh, I am, sir. I've been brought up that way.'

'What did you think was going on?'

'I didn't really know, sir. I went to an empty room and I suddenly saw a light under the door. It sent shivers through me.'

'Are you quite certain that it was the night porter?'

'Yes, I am.'

'Did he see *you*?'

'Oh, no – I'd have fainted if he'd spoken to me.'

'I told Millie that the light bulbs had been removed,' said Lena. 'I said that you'd explain.'

'Willingly,' said the manager. 'You see, Millie, some people, I fear, have a ghoulish disposition. If there's a serious road accident or a house on fire, they love to stare at other people's disaster. Most of our guests would never dream of doing such a thing, mind you, but one can never take chances. There might be someone who'd want a perverted thrill out of standing in the middle of a murder scene.'

'That wasn't why I went there, Mr Chell,' said Millie, hurriedly. 'I never meant to go in. I thought it would be locked.'

'And so it should have been. But Mr Rogan has a master key.'

'He was obviously counting on the fact that nobody would be about at that time of night,' said Lena. 'It was sheer chance that Millie turned up.'

'I wish that I hadn't now,' cried Millie, close to tears. 'I never want to go through anything like that again. I still feel sick.'

'You're excused duties until you feel better.'

'Thank you, Mrs Gosling.'

'And you mustn't say a word of this to *anyone*,' instructed Chell.

'I won't, sir, I promise.'

'You can leave me to deal with Rogan. Were he still here, I'd tackle him myself, but he went home some hours ago. I'll need to tell Mrs Fleetwood what happened and take her advice. But I'm so glad you had the courage to come forward, Millie,' he said, gently. 'It was very brave of you and your account might turn out to be far more valuable than you imagine.'

When he arrived in Marmion's office, Maurice Farrier was carrying a parcel wrapped up carefully in swathes of brown paper. He was introduced to the superintendent, who indicated the parcel.

'You've brought something for us, I gather.'

'Yes, I have,' said Farrier. 'It was my wife's idea, really. We've had one of her cousin's paintings up in our attic since she gave it to us. Gwen wondered if it might be of interest to you.'

'It certainly would,' said Marmion.

'Hopefully, it might tell you something about Vesta.'

'Any scrap of information about her is welcome,' said Chatfield. 'But why didn't you show the painting to my detectives when they came to see you in Berkshire?'

'To be candid,' admitted Farrier, 'we've always been rather embarrassed by the gift. You'll soon see why. We felt that the attic was the best place for it until my wife wondered if it might be evidence of some sort.'

'We're very grateful to Mrs Farrier,' said Marmion, 'and to you, of course, for bringing it here.'

Taking out a penknife, Farrier used it to peel away the brown paper layer by layer. The painting was roughly two feet by eighteen inches and enclosed in a simple wooden frame. When the final piece of paper was taken off, Farrier set the object on a chair and stood back out of the way. Reactions differed.

'Goodness me!' exclaimed Chatfield.

'That's fascinating,' said Marmion.

'It's so beautifully painted,' observed Keedy.

What they were looking at was a group of eight people reclining on the bank of a river. All were completely nude and most of them were female. The figures were well drawn and the use of colour was arresting. At the centre of the group was a woman flat on her back on the grass with her arms outstretched. When he looked at her face, Marmion was the first to notice the similarity.

'The one in the middle looks very much like our murder victim,' he said. 'In fact, I'd swear that it *is* her.'

'So would I,' said Keedy. 'There's no question about it. But look what she was wearing.'

Everyone seemed to have discarded their clothes at random. They lay scattered on the grass. Beside the figure who'd caught the attention of the detectives was a wimple and a nun's habit.

Chatfield was mesmerised. Marmion couldn't resist a dig at him.

'There you are, sir,' he said. 'The woman was a nun, after all.'


It wasn't until their break that Alice had the opportunity of speaking to Jennifer Jerrold. She took her friend aside to explain why she hadn't been upset by the earlier reprimand from the inspector. Jennifer was amazed to hear that Alice had gone to such trouble on her behalf, standing out in the rain for a long period and making herself late for work. She was also perplexed.

'But there was no point, Alice,' she said. 'I'm safe when I'm at home. It's only when I leave here that I feel a pair of eyes on me.'

'The same man watches you leave home every morning and get on the bus. Because he's able to control his time, he waits for you outside here when you leave work.'

Jennifer was startled. 'You *saw* him?'

'I did more than that, Jenny. I talked to him.'

'Who is he?'

'Before I tell you,' warned Alice, 'I must stress that there was never any real threat to you. I know that you felt hunted but that was not his intention at all. He just liked to look at you.'

'I just want to know who he is,' said Jennifer, anxiously.

'You see him at church every Sunday. To be more exact, Jenny, *he* sees you. Do you realise who I'm talking about?'

'Oh, no . . . it's not him, surely?'

'When I challenged him, he admitted it.'

'Father Howells?'

'He promised to write a letter of apology to you.'

'But he's such a kind, caring man. He's our new curate. Since he joined the ministry team, he's made a real difference.'

'He told me that he used to pray for Sunday to come so that he could talk to you instead of being forced to peer at you from hiding places all the time. He loves you, Jenny.'

'But he's so much older than me.'

'He's very much aware of that,' said Alice. 'His wife died years ago and his life has been very empty since then. Without realising it and without wanting it, you helped to fill that emptiness.'

Jennifer was at once relieved and alarmed. She was glad that her stalker had finally been unmasked but disturbed to learn who it was.

It would now be very uncomfortable for her to go to church.

'Don't worry, Jenny,' said Alice. 'Father Howells realises the awkward position he's put you in. He'll be leaving the parish as soon as it can be arranged.'

'I don't want to drive him away, Alice.'

'He's doing it for his own benefit as much as yours. Look on the bright side, Jenny. You won't have to leave here in fear every evening and the Women's Police Force will retain a first-rate officer.' She smiled. 'You won't have to resign now, will you?'

On hearing what had happened, Griselda Fleetwood's immediate reaction was to confront Leonard Rogan in person. He had no reason to be in a room that had been sealed off from the rest of the hotel. Rex Chell pointed out that the night porter would be at home in bed and it was not her responsibility to chase after him. He advised her to contact Scotland Yard to see what Inspector Marmion made of the information. Reacting quickly to the telephone call from her, the inspector sent Keedy off to investigate. The latter had the use of a car to take him to the grimy little house in Paddington.

It was Mrs Rogan who answered the door. She recognised Keedy.

'Len isn't here,' she said.

'How long is he likely to be?'

'I don't know. He told me he had to see Ian about something.'

'Ian?'

'Yes,' she replied. 'Ian Maitland. He's a good friend of Len's. He works at the Roath Court Hotel.'

The arrival of Vesta Lyle's painting had told them a great deal about her. While Marmion had reservations about her choice of subject, he could see that the artist had extraordinary talent. The fact that she'd featured her friend was significant. To be given a central position in the painting, the woman had to have an important role in her life. After thanking him, Marmion had waved Farrier off and asked him to pass on his thanks to his wife. Shortly after that, he'd taken the call from the Lotus Hotel and, as a result, sent Keedy off to Paddington. He was now seated alone in his office, thinking once again about Vesta Lyle and wondering who had abducted her and how the man had possibly got into the hotel in the first place. There was a knock on the door and it opened for the commissioner to enter. As Marmion jumped to his feet, his visitor raised a palm to ease him back into his seat.

'There's no need to get up, Inspector.'

'Thank you, Sir Edward,' said Marmion. 'What can I do for you?'

'It's more of a question of what *I* can do for *you*. As I'm sure you recall, you wanted me to find out about Alphonse Dufays. Thinking that he might be part of the French secret service, I felt that I had little chance of getting any information about him.'

'None of us really held out much hope.'

'We were all wrong. To begin with, Dufays was nothing to do with any of their intelligence organisations. He spent his whole career in the French finance ministry.'

'Was he still employed there when he died?'

'That was the other surprise, Inspector. He's not dead. Alphonse Dufays retired from government service three years ago. His sense of timing was admirable. He left just before war broke out. Given what's happened since,' said the commissioner, 'he's probably glad to be clear of the chaos that must have descended on the financial affairs of France.'

'Wait a moment,' said Marmion. 'Mr and Mrs Farrier were told that

Dufays had died. It was the reason that his wife had come to stay with them. She even talked about his funeral.'

'Then she was obviously lying to them.'

'If Dufays is still alive, where is he?'

'I wasn't given any address, Inspector.'

Marmion thought about the information that Keedy had gleaned from the taxi driver. A Frenchman had more or less pushed a drunken woman into the vehicle.

'I think I know where he may be at the moment,' he said.

'Do you?'

'Yes, Sir Edward. He's here in England and I have a feeling that he came for one purpose. Probably against her will, Vesta Lyle has been reunited with her husband.'

Keedy didn't have long to wait. Seated beside the driver, he watched from the car as Rogan came walking jauntily along the street. When the night porter caught sight of the police car outside his house, he slowed to a more cautious place. Keedy got out of the car to confront him.

'Good day to you,' he said.

'What do you want, Sergeant?' asked the other, warily.

'I've got a few things to discuss with you.'

'You've already taken two statements from me.'

'That was to do with the murder. I now want to ask you about something indirectly connected with it.'

'You'd better come in,' said Rogan, gruffly.

'I'd rather stay out here, if you don't mind.' Keedy took a step closer. 'How was Ian Maitland?'

'Never heard of him.'

'Your wife told me you'd been to see him. One of you is lying and

I don't think it's Mrs Rogan. You know full well who Maitland is. He used to work at the Lotus.'

'Ah,' said Rogan, 'I vaguely remember him now.'

'Then you've got a very poor memory,' said Keedy. 'You've completely forgotten a man you were talking to a little while ago. Let's try another question.'

'I'm tired,' pleaded Rogan. 'I've been up all night.'

'And how did you spend some of your time? I'll tell you, in case that's slipped your memory as well. You went into the room where the murder took place.'

'That's not true!'

'We have a witness.'

'Then he or she is lying through their teeth.'

'There was no mistaking who you were. So,' said Keedy, 'let's do without any pointless denials, shall we? It will save us a lot of time.'

Rogan took a moment to consider his position. When he was ready, his manner changed completely. He opted for a degree of honesty.

'All right,' he confessed, 'maybe I did just pop my head in there. Someone like you is used to seeing murder scenes. I'm not. I was curious, that's all. That's not a crime, is it? I was only in there for a minute or so.'

'Hotel guests and staff were forbidden to enter that room.'

'What harm did I do?'

'You disobeyed orders,' said Keedy. 'Both the manager and Mrs Fleetwood were very upset to hear that. They got in touch with us. That's why I'm here.'

'Look, Sergeant, I swear on the grave of my mother that I was doing nothing wrong by putting my head into that room. I couldn't even see the place properly. Mr Chell had the light bulbs taken away.'

'I can see why he did that now. It was to thwart people like you.'

'I'm sorry – okay? I shouldn't have done it. I'll apologise to the manager when I go on duty tonight. Now will you please let me get some shut-eye?' begged Rogan. 'I'm exhausted.'

'You haven't told me about Maitland yet.'

'There's nothing to tell.'

'I rather fancy that there is. Your wife gave me the impression that you were a friend of his. Since you're so tired, why bother to see him when you'd obviously rather be in bed?'

Rogan yawned. 'Can I go now, Sergeant – *please*?'

'I'm afraid not,' said Keedy. 'When you arrived at work last night, you'd have become aware that somebody had been sending out handbills to former guests of the Lotus. It's caused Mrs Fleetwood a great deal of anguish. She was bound to ask how the person who had them printed could send them to the correct addresses. We both know the answer to that question, don't we?'

'I had nothing to do with it,' protested Rogan.

'Then perhaps it was all Maitland's fault.'

'He has no connection with the Lotus any more.'

'Yes, he does. He has a friend who's the night porter there.'

'Maitland is . . . just someone I know.'

'I think the pair of you are much closer than you'll admit,' said Keedy. 'That's why I'm taking you to Scotland Yard for questioning.'

'I can't go with you,' shouted Rogan.

'It's not an idle request.'

'What about my wife?'

'I don't think we'll need to trouble her.'

'Let me at least speak to her.'

'There's no need.'

'Are you saying that I've been *arrested*?'

'We haven't got to that stage yet, but it may come. You won't be lonely, I promise you. When I get back to Scotland Yard, I'll send someone to fetch Ian Maitland from the Roath Court.' Keedy's eyes glinted. 'Then the three of us can have a nice long, cosy chat.'

# CHAPTER TWENTY-TWO

Harvey Marmion was in his office, poring over the plan of the Lotus Hotel. Knowing where the murder had taken place, he was trying to work out how the killer got to that room and was able to escape the attention of the night porter as he left the building. A new idea began to form slowly in his mind. It put a warm smile on his face.

Claude Chatfield then entered abruptly without bothering to knock.

'Sergeant Keedy is back,' he said. 'He's brought Rogan with him and is sending someone to get Maitland.'

'It sounds promising, sir.'

'He's established a link between the two men.'

'Then he's done well.'

'I was going to confront Buchanan, but I'll hold fire now until Keedy has questioned them. He may be able to supply me with ammunition that I can use.'

'You may need it when you meet Mr Buchanan, sir. I'm told that he's as slippery as an eel covered in best butter.'

'Best butter?' groaned Chatfield. 'When did we last taste that?'

'It disappeared along with lots of other things, including a decent glass of beer. I can't bear to drink it now that it's been watered. Anyway,' said Marmion, 'I just thought I'd pass on the warning about him.'

'It's quite unnecessary. I can handle dodgy businessmen.'

'I'm sure that you can, sir.'

'You know,' said Chatfield, thoughtfully, 'I've half a mind to sit in on the interview with the sergeant.'

'He's more than capable of handling it on his own,' said Marmion, eager to give Keedy a free hand. 'Besides, you have so many other things to do before you tackle Mr Buchanan.'

'That's true. I have to see the commissioner first.'

'Please thank him again for the help he gave us. I never thought he'd find out anything about Alphonse Dufays but he turned up trumps. What he wasn't able to establish, of course, was whether or not Vesta Lyle was working for their secret service. At least we now know that her husband had no link with it.'

'It's interesting to hear that Dufays was a financial expert, but who would have thought him capable of murder?'

'He was not the killer, Superintendent.'

'He must have been.'

'I've changed my mind about that.'

'He committed a murder then dragged his wife out of that hotel.'

'How did he get in there?' asked Marmion. 'And how did a man of his age overpower and inject a fatal poison into the victim?'

'There *has* to be an explanation for that.'

'There is, sir, and it's one we should have considered at the start. I've spent ages thinking it over and the conclusion is obvious.'

'Then why can't I see it?'

'The victim was not killed by a jealous husband,' said Marmion. 'In fact, she wasn't killed by a man at all. My belief is that she was murdered by another woman.'

'That's impossible.'

'Consider the evidence.'

'Is any woman capable of doing something like that?' asked Chatfield, struggling to accept the idea.

'This one was, sir. And there have been lots of female killers in history. Many of them chose poison as their murder weapon.'

'I still find it hard to believe.'

'What's the most striking thing about the Lotus?'

'It's owner – Mrs Fleetwood.'

'And what was her mission in opening the hotel?'

'It was specifically for female guests.'

'There's our answer and it explains why no man had to force his way into the premises at night. The killer was already there. She was a guest at the Lotus.'

'That would mean,' said Chatfield, taking the idea seriously at last, 'that she'd know in which room Vesta Lyle was staying. She was stalking her. But hold on a moment,' he added. 'Only two people were seen leaving the hotel that night – a man and a woman. If the killer really was a female, why didn't she take the opportunity to escape with them?'

'That would have drawn attention to her immediately, sir, and we'd have been told that she'd fled the hotel. Once she'd delivered Vesta Lyle to the husband, she retired to bed, stayed the night and probably left after breakfast the following morning without raising the slightest suspicion.'

'Well done, Inspector! You may have the answer.'

'The first thing I must do,' said Marmion, 'is to check the hotel register. The killer will not be stupid enough to have given her real name, but she'll have been seen by the manager and probably by Mrs Gosling as well. They'll be able to provide us with a good description of her.'

'But how can you pick her out from the register?'

'Mr Chell can help me to do that. Most of the guests staying there that night are regular patrons and many of them are quite advanced in age. We're after a younger woman who was able to carry luggage in one hand while helping the inebriated Vesta Lyle along with the other before handing her over to her husband. She'll stick out a mile.'

'The woman must be as cool as a cucumber.'

'She would still have been at the hotel when we arrived. In fact,' he went on, 'Sergeant Keedy may even have taken a statement from her.'

'Then he'd certainly remember her. He has an eye for younger women. Oh,' said Chatfield, realising, 'I didn't mean . . .'

'That's quite all right, sir. He's calmed down a lot since he knew that I was going to be his father-in-law. Those days are over.'

'You must get across to the hotel at once, Inspector.'

'I will, sir. The sergeant will be sorry he can't come with me.'

'Don't worry about him. Keedy has a very important job to do right here at Scotland Yard.'

It was the fourth time that Keedy had interviewed Rogan. The first had been at the Lotus where the night porter had answered the questions a little too confidently for the sergeant's liking. When he talked to the man in his home, he had Rogan on the defensive and, as a result, there were discrepancies during the second interview. Since the third was in the street outside the house, Rogan had been placed at even more of a disadvantage, concerned that his neighbours would see him being grilled on his doorstep. Keedy wanted to get the preconditions right for what he hoped would be the final confrontation. He therefore left Rogan alone in a bare, featureless interview room while he went off to arrange for Ian Maitland to be picked up as soon as possible.

When he returned to the room, Keedy found the night porter pacing up and down. Jaw tight, he rounded on the sergeant.

'You've got no right to keep me here.'

'I think you'll find that I have.'

'There are no grounds at all for an arrest.'

'They'll come in due course, I'm sure.'

'My wife will be worrying about me.'

'You told her where you were going before we drove you off. Mrs Rogan knows exactly where you are – if not exactly why.'

'Listen,' said the other, modifying his tone, 'I know that it looks bad, me sneaking into the room. But it's not as if I was trespassing, is it? I *work* there.'

'You did,' agreed Keedy. 'I doubt if you ever will again.'

'Who is the witness?'

'It doesn't matter.'

'It does to me. It matters a lot.'

'The other charge against you is more serious.'

'I'd never do anything to hurt Mrs Fleetwood. She gave me the best job I've ever had. I've told you before. I love the place.'

'I believe you. The problem is that you didn't love it enough.'

'There's never been any complaint about me.'

'There are plenty of them now,' said Keedy. 'Tell me something. Would you rather be interviewed by me in a quiet room like this or would you prefer to face Mrs Fleetwood and the manager at the hotel? In your shoes, I'd choose to be here.' He pointed to a chair. 'Why not sit down?'

After eyeing him with suppressed anger, Rogan eventually took a seat on one side of the little table. Keedy sat opposite him.

'There,' he said, 'that wasn't too difficult, was it? We can just sit here together in comfort until Ian Maitland joins us. He won't be long.'

Griselda Fleetwood and Rex Chell were astounded by what they'd been told. It all sounded too improbable to be true. Yet there was no denying the logic behind Marmion's deductions. The killer had been a guest at the hotel, staying there under a false name and pretending to be there to enjoy its much-vaunted facilities. Griselda feared the worst.

'This is terrible,' she said. 'We harboured a murderess.'

'You weren't to know what she was,' said Marmion.

'Nobody will *ever* want to stay here again.'

'That's not true at all. When this has blown over, you'll have a new lease of life as one of London's premier hotels.'

'I agree with the inspector,' said the manager. 'There will be some bad publicity, but we can rise above it.'

'I'm not worried about the press,' she told him. 'It's Buchanan that I fear. Imagine how he'll exploit the fact that we accommodated, fed and pampered a ruthless killer.'

'You can forget about Mr Buchanan,' promised Marmion.

'Why?'

'The superintendent is going to take him on in person. Now that we have proof that he ordered the printing of those handbills, we can put some real pressure on him.'

'He must have hired that woman as well, Inspector.'

'Let's be realistic, Mrs Fleetwood. I'm afraid that Mr Buchanan had nothing to do with that. The killer was in the pay of a man named Alphonse Dufays. He was the husband of the woman who was staying in the room where the murder occurred.'

'What was his motive, Inspector?' asked Chell.

'We've yet to find out, sir. And now I must ask for your help.'

'You want to see the register, don't you?'

'Yes, I do, Mr Chell.'

'Let me save you the time,' said the manager. 'The woman you're after stayed here under the name of Miss Charlotte Browne. Of all the people under this roof that night, she was the one most capable of doing what you believe she did. Miss Browne was younger than anyone else, for a start, and she had great self-assurance. Look at the register, if you wish, but you'll find nobody else who qualifies as a possible suspect.'

'Can you give me a description of her, please?'

'I'll be happy to do so, Inspector, and I daresay that Mrs Gosling may want to add a few details of her own. I know that she spoke to her when Miss Browne asked what the procedure was in case of a fire. Mrs Gosling took her to the rear of the building to point out the two exits.'

'That's fairly conclusive evidence of Miss Browne's intentions,' said Marmion.

'I shudder at the thought that we let this woman stay here,' wailed Griselda. 'Our other guests will have seen and perhaps even spoken to this fiend. What are they going to think when they realise that they were breathing the same air as a heartless killer?'

Chell was philosophical. 'Only time will tell, Mrs Fleetwood.'

'Criticism of our security could bring us down.'

'Ah,' said Marmion, 'that reminds me. You may need the services of a different night porter. Mr Rogan may be unavoidably detained.'

Alice was about to go back on duty when Inspector Gale swooped down on her and took her aside. The older woman was smiling.

'I just wanted to thank you,' she said. 'Jennifer Jerrold has had second thoughts and decided to stay with us, after all.'

'That's excellent news, Inspector.'

'It's hardly news to you, is it?'

'Well . . .'

'I fancy that you had something to do with the change of heart.'

'Is that what Jenny said?'

'No, she didn't go into detail.'

'Then I'd rather not do so.'

'That's all right by me,' said the other. 'The result is all that I care about. I do, however, suspect that your lateness this morning was somehow connected with Jerrold's decision to stay. Am I right?'

'You might be.'

'In that case, I'm sorry that I shouted at you.'

Alice grinned. 'To be honest, I hardly noticed.'

From the moment he entered the room, Ian Maitland made his intentions clear. He was going to talk his way out of an awkward situation. He was relaxed, friendly and apparently cooperative. An extra chair was brought into the room so that he could sit beside Rogan with whom he exchanged no more than a glance.

'I believe that you and Mr Rogan are friends,' began Keedy.

'We know each other, Sergeant, but we're hardly friends.'

'Then why did he come to see you this morning?'

'He wanted to ask me about the Roath Court,' said Maitland, smoothly. 'Knowing that Mrs Fleetwood was bound to blame Mr Buchanan for what happened at the Lotus, he was keen to know what sort of a man he was.'

'You're a close friend of Mr Buchanan, are you?' said Keedy in mock surprise.

'No, but I've got to know him well and have a lot of respect for him. I was able to tell Len that he'd never do anything illegal, let alone arrange a murder.' He turned to Rogan. 'Isn't that right?'

'Yes, it is,' said the other, taking his cue.

'We spoke for no more than a couple of minutes.'

'That's interesting,' said Keedy. 'Mr Rogan and I have talked for much longer than that but, for a reason known only to him, he never mentioned the fact that he wanted your opinion of Mr Buchanan. Why was that?'

'It was a private conversation, Sergeant,' said Rogan.

'Maitland is happy enough to talk about it. Why weren't you?'

'I can explain that,' said Maitland, cutting in.

'I'm sure that you can,' said Keedy, 'because you're ready to tell any lie – however outrageous – if it gets you and your friend out of trouble. But I'm glad you admit that you know Mr Buchanan well. It accounts for the fact that he turned to you when he needed the guest list from the Lotus Hotel.'

Maitland snorted. 'That's ridiculous!'

'He knew that you had a contact there, someone who had a master key that gave him access to the manager's office in the dead of night. Rogan was able to copy that list of names and addresses.'

'I wouldn't dream of doing that,' yelled Rogan.

'Shut up, Len,' said Maitland. 'Let me do the talking.'

'I do my job well.'

'Really?' asked Keedy. 'Then how is it that a murder took place at the hotel when you were on duty to guarantee the safety of everyone staying there? That's hardly proof that you do your job well.'

'Len's a decent, honest, hard-working employee,' said Maitland, coming to his friend's aid. 'He stays at the Lotus out of loyalty, even though he could get better wages elsewhere.'

'At the Roath Court, perhaps?' said Keedy, pointedly.

Maitland was at last silenced. He ran his tongue over dry lips. Rogan shifted uncomfortably in his seat. Keedy pressed home his advantage.

'How much did Mr Buchanan pay you both?' he asked.

'He didn't give us a penny,' replied Maitland.

'That was very mean of him. The two of you provided him with information that was used to cause Mrs Fleetwood great embarrassment. Surely, you deserved something for going to such trouble.'

'We did nothing wrong, Sergeant. You ask Mr Buchanan.'

'I'll leave that to the superintendent,' said Keedy. 'When I tell him that you're both party to the theft of confidential information from the Lotus Hotel, he'll have a lot of searching questions to put to him.'

Even though the manager had identified the woman, Marmion wanted to take a look at the hotel register. He saw that Charlotte Browne had booked into the Lotus for one night and given a home address in Leeds. With the manager's permission, he used the telephone to contact the police in Yorkshire. It took only a few minutes for them to confirm that there was no street in the city with the same name as the one in the register. Marmion put down the receiver.

'The address is fictitious,' he said.

'And so was her name,' said Chell.

He went on to describe her as an attractive, dark-haired woman in her thirties who seemed at ease in the luxurious surroundings. Well dressed and well groomed, she was full-bodied and of medium height. Out during the day, she spent the rest of the time in her room.

The manager had sent for Lena Gosling. As Marmion finished jotting down the description given to him, she arrived at the office. She was eager to offer what help she could. Lena remembered the woman well.

'It was strange,' she said. 'Miss Browne was a handsome woman, yet she wouldn't stand out in a crowd. I thought that she dressed to look a bit older than she really was.'

'I hear that she asked you about the exits,' said Marmion.

'That's right, Inspector. She told me that she had a fear of being caught in a hotel fire. It had happened to her once before and had been very upsetting. That's why she insisted on having a room on the ground floor. Yet funnily enough,' continued Lena, 'she didn't seem like the sort of person who'd be fearful. Miss Browne was very poised.'

'Did you see her in the wake of the murder?'

'Yes, I did. She was in the lounge with everyone else. Sergeant Keedy interviewed the guests one by one, Miss Browne included.'

'She certainly had nerve,' said Chell. 'Most killers would surely have wanted to get well away from the scene of the crime, yet she stayed here all night. What does that tell you, Inspector?'

'It suggests to me that the dead woman might not have been her first victim,' said Marmion. 'That degree of self-control usually comes from experience.'

'Oh, I've gone cold all over,' admitted Lena with a shiver. 'I can't believe that I stood right next to a woman like that. It's frightening. The Lotus is hardly the place where you'd expect to find someone prepared to commit a murder.'

'Perhaps not, Mrs Gosling, but the law of averages operates here as elsewhere. In any large group of people, you stand the chance of having the odd sinner among the saints. Even in the British aristocracy, there are those with criminal tendencies,' said Marmion. 'I should know. I've arrested a couple of them.'

'That may be so, Inspector,' said Chell, 'but it's certainly not the case here. Miss Browne was not a member of the aristocracy.'

'She was while she was at the hotel. You've both told me how she fitted in so easily. In fact, she and Vesta Lyle have that in common. Both of them enjoyed mixing with the cream of society, if only for one night. I suspect that it brought the two of them immense satisfaction – especially for Vesta Lyle.'

'Why is that?'

'She was able to be Lady Diana Brice-Cadmore.'

Vesta Lyle looked nothing like an aristocrat now. Pale, drawn, hollow-eyed and sorrowful, she was slumped in an armchair in an attitude of defeat. She extended a desperate hand and mouthed some words. The man who sat on the opposite side of the room looked up from the book he was reading and spoke peremptorily.

'No, Vesta. *I* control your supply now.'

'*Please* . . .'

'It's no good pleading. You've got to be slowly weaned off cocaine now. It's done far too much damage to you and to our marriage.'

'I can't live without it, Alphonse.'

'You'll have to.'

'And I don't want to live without *her*.'

'You have no choice. Colette came between us and had to go.'

'But there was no need to have her killed.'

294

'It was the only way I could own you again.'

Vesta was in physical and mental agony. Her body was yearning for the drug that she needed, and her mind was aflame. There was no escape. She was at his mercy again. Dufays would stop at nothing to reclaim her. He'd proved that in the most vicious way. She was married to a monster.

They were in a hotel room near the Kent coast. While she was in despair, he was savouring his triumph. He felt no sympathy. She'd deserved the punishment he'd meted out and so had her lover.

'When I first met you,' he recalled, 'you were a penniless artist with dreams of being famous and with a baby in your belly. Nobody else would have touched you – but I did. Do you remember?'

'Yes,' she said, 'you did.'

'But you came on certain conditions. The child had to be adopted and, as far as you were concerned, it ceased to exist. I provided food, shelter and a studio in which you could work. You were grateful to me in those days, Vesta. Or, at least, you pretended to be, and I was ready to settle for that.'

'I kept to . . . our agreement.'

'That's not what you were doing at that hotel.' She winced. 'That creature couldn't be allowed to come between us. You must appreciate that. Because of her, you violated the agreement. Colette Fournier had to be got rid of. You'll accept that in time.'

'I'll never forgive you,' she said with sudden venom.

'Then you'll never get cocaine ever again.' She let out a cry of pain. 'You look tired. Try to get some sleep. I want you awake when she comes this evening.'

Vesta was terrified. 'That woman is coming *here*?'

'Yes,' he said. 'She did me a good service. She expects to be paid.'

\* \* \*

295

Armed with an account of the interviews that Keedy had conducted with the two men, Chatfield sat behind his desk and dealt with paperwork. It was not long before his visitor was shown in. He rose to his feet to welcome and appraise Fraser Buchanan. The hotelier was exactly what he'd expected. When they'd shaken hands and gone through the niceties, they both sat down. Buchanan looked completely unperturbed.

'It was very kind of you to invite me here,' he said, smiling, 'and to send a police car to save me the trouble of summoning my chauffeur. But I would have thought you had far more important things to do than to chat to me. Unless,' he went on, 'Griselda has been making more unjustified accusations about me.'

'Mrs Fleetwood is livid with you, sir.'

'That's so disappointing! There was a time when I had the feeling that she admired me. Women can be so fickle.'

'She was very angry about those handbills you had printed. And before you deny it,' Chatfield added, 'let me tell you that we've been in touch with your printer.'

'Then you'll know that he takes care of all my advertising. That handbill was the latest example of it. I know that it ruffled Griselda's feathers,' he said with a grin, 'but all's fair in love and the hotel trade, Superintendent. There's nothing in that handbill that isn't true.'

'My interest is in the people to whom it was sent in the post.'

'It's not illegal to tout for business.'

'There is if it involves stealing from one of your rivals.'

'Do I look like the sort of man who'd stoop to theft?' he asked.

'As a matter of fact, sir, you do.'

Buchanan stiffened. 'I resent that, Superintendent.'

'Do you know a young man named Ian Maitland?'

'I don't believe that I do.'

'He's one of your porters at the Roath Court.'

'We have a large staff there. You can't expect me to know them all by name. What about this . . . Maitland, is it?'

'He used to work at the Lotus.'

'Then he was probably glad to escape. Can you imagine what it must be like, surrounded all day by those ferocious old she-dragons?'

'Correct me if I'm wrong, Mr Buchanan, but you were quite happy to send handbills to a large number of those ladies. As for Maitland,' said Chatfield, 'did you know that he was sacked from the Lotus?'

'Porters come and go. As a species, I've no interest in them beyond knowing that they can do the job for which they're paid.'

'Maitland obviously did the job for which *he* was paid.'

'You're being very enigmatic, Superintendent.'

'Then let me be more explicit,' said Chatfield. 'You employed Maitland to persuade a man named Leonard Rogan, the night porter at the Lotus, to get details of the hotel's guest list.'

'That's a laughable suggestion.'

'It's an established fact, sir. Earlier on, Sergeant Keedy spoke to Maitland and Rogan in one of our interview rooms. It took him less than ten minutes to get a full confession out of them. As a result, I'm faced with a choice. Do I believe two half-educated minions or do I believe you?' Chatfield smirked. 'All of a sudden, you've lost your voice, sir.'

Vesta Lyle's plight was becoming more intense. Desperate for another injection of cocaine, she was shaking at the prospect of meeting the woman responsible for the death of her dearest friend and for returning Vesta to the control of her husband. Alphonse Dufays had, to some extent, been right. He *had* made possible her career as an artist. Had he not rescued her when she was in such a dire predicament, she would have been homeless, forced to beg in order to buy food for herself and her baby. The man who'd fathered the child had long ago left Paris. When she wrote to him for help, her letters elicited no reply. She'd been shut out of his life entirely. Then she'd met Alphonse Dufays.

'How long will we be here?' she asked.

'It may be longer than I thought,' he replied. 'When I took you from that hotel, I thought that we'd be perfectly safe because nobody knew who you really were. You'd given a false name. I expected the police to be running around after their own tails. Yet somehow they discovered who you really were. When I read your name in the newspapers, it gave me a nasty jolt at first.'

'Do they know who you are?'

'They would do if they saw my passport. If they looked at yours, they'd know that you were Vesta Lyle, the famous artist, the woman who ran away from a hotel in Chelsea and left a corpse behind.'

It was too much for her to bear. Vesta burst into tears. He'd spoken so callously about the woman who'd replaced him. Dufays didn't even dignify her with a name this time. She was simply a corpse and he was the one who'd arranged for her cruel murder so that he could reclaim his wife. Vesta's future would be intolerably bleak.

'I wish she'd killed me as well,' she said, miserably.

'Oh, no, I wanted you alive. That was the whole point.'

'Do I *have* to meet that woman?'

'She's good company when you get to know her. Under different circumstances, you'd get on well with her.'

'She's a black-hearted killer!'

He smiled thinly. 'She was a means to an end, Vesta.'

\* \* \*

Marmion got back to Scotland Yard to find Keedy waiting for him. The sergeant was eager to pass on the news that he'd arrested and charged Rogan and Maitland, and that the superintendent had done the same to Buchanan. Marmion was duly impressed.

'And what's this theory of yours, Harv?' asked Keedy. 'Chat tells me that you believe that the killer was a woman.'

'I *know* that she was. I can even tell you the name she used when she stayed at the hotel.'

'What was it?'

'Charlotte Browne.'

'That name sounds oddly familiar.'

'So it should, Joe – you interviewed her.'

Keedy blanched. 'She *stayed* at the hotel after the murder?'

'Yes, nobody can doubt her audacity.'

'I must have taken a statement from her.'

While Keedy flipped through the pages of his notebook, Marmion gave him a description of the woman who was now their prime suspect. Keedy read through her statement.

'I remember her now,' he said. 'She was an attractive woman and had an educated voice. Unlike most of them, she didn't look down her nose at me as if I'd just emerged from the nearest swamp. Charlotte Browne, eh? I'd never have singled her out as the killer.'

'She claimed to have come from Leeds.'

'There was no hint of a Yorkshire accent.'

'She made up her home address. She probably picked the first city that came into her mind.' Marmion started. 'Wait a moment . . .'

'What's wrong?'

'Isn't there a Leeds in Kent?'

'There's a Leeds Castle, I know that.'

'And I daresay there's a village of the same name nearby. I'm starting to wonder if Miss Charlotte Browne may have slipped up when she gave that address. It would be interesting to find out.'

Ellen Marmion had had a day of celebration. Wherever she went, she learnt that Rene Bridger had been there before her and talked about the way that Ellen had challenged Quentin Dacey at the end of his lecture. Nobody else had ever heard of him but they liked the idea of someone taking on a scaremonger. At the sewing circle, Ellen got a patter of applause as she arrived. When she went home early that evening, she was floating on air. There was another treat to come. Seeing that there was a light on in the house, she knew that Alice must have let herself in. Ellen covered the last thirty yards at a gentle trot.

They were soon hugging each other in the living room.

'I've got something to tell you, Mummy,' said Alice.

'And I've got something to tell *you*.'

'Go on, then. What is it?'

'No,' said Ellen, 'you go first. I've already had too much attention today. It was starting to go to my head.'

'Very well – I'll take my turn.'

When they'd sat down on the sofa, Alice told her about her detective work on behalf of a friend. Her mother was full of praise for the way that her daughter had gone to such trouble on the other woman's behalf.

'And it was someone from the church?' she asked, incredulously. 'The poor girl will never be able to look this Father Howells in the face again.'

'She won't have to, Mummy. He's leaving the parish.'

'Was he angry when you confronted him?'

'No, he told me he was glad. He *knew* it was wrong but he couldn't stop doing it – and he never realised that it was hurting Jenny. The upshot is that she's now decided to stay on as a policewoman and Gale Force thinks that I'm a genius.' They laughed. 'Right, you've heard enough about my triumph. Tell me about yours.'

'Well,' said Ellen, 'it was actually yesterday morning . . .'

Claude Chatfield needed a lot of persuasion before he agreed to send the two of them off to Kent. Before he'd left, Marmion had given him a detailed description of the murder suspect so that it could be passed on to reporters at the press conference. He and Keedy settled into the car that was to take them all the way to the Kentish village of Leeds.

'My worry,' said Keedy, 'is that Dufays and his wife may already have flown the coop.'

'I doubt it somehow. Civilians can't just roll up at the docks and expect to walk straight onto the nearest ship. Most of them are reserved for troops. They'll have to kick their heels.'

'Where will they be?'

'They could be in any of the Channel ports,' said Marmion, 'so it won't be easy to find them. But that description of Charlotte Browne may help. The papers will name her as a wanted person.'

'Thank goodness you remembered that address in Leeds.'

'It's standard police procedure – jot everything down. You never know when it might come in handy.'

'Do you really think this woman has a connection with Leeds?'

'Yes, I do, Joe. Criminals have got warped minds. They like to play games with us. I think that this woman might have been doing the same. Knowing that we'd check the hotel register, she gave us an address that would turn out to be false when we checked on it. But she couldn't resist teasing us,' said Marmion. 'Inside the false address was one that has some real meaning to her. Miss Browne was taunting us.'

'She's not the first person to do that.'

'The others lived to regret it. Let's hope she does the same.'

'Well,' said Keedy, 'even if we come back empty-handed, this trip will have served one useful purpose.'

'What is it, Joe?'

'It's saved us from having to listen to Chat boasting about how he tormented Buchanan before telling him – politely – that he was under arrest.'

When she put down the receiver, Griselda Fleetwood was glowing. She had just talked at length to the superintendent and heard about the latest developments. Buchanan had been routed and two people who'd helped him had been arrested and charged. She turned to Rex Chell who was standing beside her in his office.

'Superintendent Chatfield said that I should fight fire with fire,' she told him. 'Because Buchanan's handbills disparaged the Lotus, we should print some of our own, vindicating ourselves. They can be sent to everyone on our guest list. Be sure to point out that Buchanan was arrested – that's what he advised.' She chortled. 'Who's going to believe a jealous hotelier with a police record? The man is finished.'

She paused for a moment to consider that there was a time during her preparations for opening a hotel when she'd consulted Buchanan. He'd been so charming to her that she'd come perilously close to flirting with him. In retrospect, she saw how foolish she'd been. Now that the police had intervened in their feud, Buchanan was no longer a threat. Forgetting all about him, she could concentrate on rebuilding the trust of her clientele.

'I feel like celebrating, Mr Chell,' she announced.

He was cautious. 'Might it not be more sensible to wait until the killer has been caught, Mrs Fleetwood?'

'Of course it would be. Thank you for pointing it out.'

'There is one thing you might do, however,' he suggested. 'We may have lost Rogan, but we still have the person who gave us the information that led indirectly to his arrest.'

'You're talking about that girl, Millie Jenks, aren't you?'

'A pat on the back from you would not come amiss. She needs all the encouragement that she can get.'

'I'll go and find her this very minute,' said Griselda, heading for the door. 'She needs to know that she's appreciated.'

It was dark by the time that they reached Leeds Castle, so it was no more than a huge shape rising out of the gloom. The village itself was on a hillside above the River Len. It was dominated by a church with a massive tower. The headlights of the car caught examples of thatched roofs and Tudor half-timbering. Now that they'd finally got there, Marmion was having doubts about the value of the journey. The killer was an efficient, self-possessed woman with ice in her veins. Would she really shift a real address all the way up to Yorkshire to befuddle the police? It seemed unlikely. The clinical murder she'd committed pointed to someone who took no chances. As Marmion's hope began to dwindle, Keedy somehow became more optimistic.

'This is it,' he said, as they got out of the car. 'I like the feel of this place.'

'I can't say I like the smell of it,' said Marmion, reacting to the pungent agricultural odour. 'It's a bit too rich for me.'

'Let's find the house.'

'That should be easy enough in a village this small.'

It took them less than a minute to locate the address that had been in the hotel register at the Lotus. After walking through a well-tended front garden, Marmion knocked on the door. It was opened by a man in his sixties with a white beard and unusually large eyes. When he heard that they were from Scotland Yard, he invited them in at once. His name was Ernest Lunn. As the three of them sat down in the living room, he asked them a question with pride in his voice.

'Did you see our beautiful church?' he asked.

'It was too dark for that, sir.'

'St Nicholas has the second largest tower in England. We don't have many claims to fame but we're proud of that one. As it happens, I'm one of the churchwardens.'

His wife entered and offered the visitors refreshments but they declined. She left them alone with Lunn, who was intrigued by the arrival of two detectives. Marmion said very little about the case that had taken them there. His only interest was in the house itself.

'How long have you been here, Mr Lunn?' he asked.

'It's been over twenty years, Inspector.'

'In the course of our enquiries, this address popped up and we're not quite sure why. Who lived here before you?'

'It was owned by the Robbins family.'

'How many of them were there?'

'Oh, there were just the three of them – Archie Robbins, his wife and young Danny, of course. We lived in the next village but had always coveted this house.' He saw the disappointment on their faces. 'Have I said something wrong?'

'No, sir,' said Marmion. 'We were just hoping that someone of interest to us had a connection with this place. If you've been here over twenty years, she'd probably have been in her teens at the time.'

'If you're talking about Danny, that's exactly what she was.'

Keedy was confused. 'Danny was female?'

'Yes, Sergeant,' said the old man. 'Not that you'd know it, mind you. She was a real tomboy. Her real name was Danielle, but everyone called her Danny. She was a real bundle of energy. Most girls in her position wouldn't have shown the slightest interest in getting their hands dirty, but she loved to help out at Willow Farm.'

'You mentioned her position,' noted Marmion.

'Her father was an important man. Archie Robbins worked in the diplomatic service. He bought this house as a rural retreat and loved being here. As his daughter, Danny had an expensive private education and chances that none of the other children around here could even dream of. Yet she was happiest when she was feeding the animals or helping with the harvest.'

Keedy was doing the mathematics. If the girl had been a teenager when she left the house, she'd have become a woman in her mid thirties. Could Danielle Robbins have been posing as Charlotte Browne at a hotel in Chelsea? He was not convinced. The woman he'd interviewed at the Lotus was too refined to have a background in farming.

'Danny was a very intelligent girl,' resumed Lunn. 'She had a mind like a razor and loved to argue about anything under the sun. Danny just had to be the best at everything. She was also a talented pianist. There was even talk of her learning to play the church organ. Sadly, they had to leave the village before she had the chance.'

'Why was that?' asked Marmion.

'Her father died suddenly. So they sold the house and went off to live with her mother's family.'

'Where was that?'

'Somewhere not far from Chartres – Mrs Robbins was French.'

Alphonse Dufays finally had his wife back where he wanted her. By promising her cocaine – albeit in reduced doses – he had complete control over her. A lethal drug had got rid of the woman she'd loved, and an addictive drug had brought his wife back to him. All that he had to do was to remain in charge of her supply.

'Who is she?' asked Vesta.

'It doesn't matter.'

'Did she *have* to kill her?'

'Those were my orders,' he said. 'Since you refused all my entreaties, I was forced to take extreme measures. I did warn you, Vesta.'

'How did she find us?'

'She knows her trade and you left a lot of footprints. People in love can often be careless. You certainly were.'

'I *hate* you,' she hissed.

'That situation will improve in time.'

They were in their hotel room. After sleeping for hours, Vesta had woken up with the familiar craving. Her husband had allowed her only a measured dose of cocaine. Though it was less than her habitual amount, it nevertheless gave her that feeling of elation on which she'd come to rely. Unfortunately, it was over much sooner than usual and reality set in. She was locked once more into a marriage she'd come to loathe with a man who'd shown just how vengeful he could be.

'Why do we have to go back to France?' she asked, worriedly.

'It's where we belong, Vesta.'

'Think of the danger.'

'We'll be in our house near Bordeaux, a long way from the fighting. You can hear the guns booming more clearly here in Kent.'

'The police will be looking for us.'

'They haven't a clue where we are. We're perfectly safe. I took no risks. Because of the vague possibility that our names were discovered, I had false passports made for both of us. Because she's used to crossing borders, she has a handful of forged passports to choose from.'

Vesta was aghast. 'She's coming *with* us?'

'Of course – she lives in France. It was a stipulation in my contract with her. I had to guarantee her safe return across the Channel.'

'I don't want to be anywhere close to her.'

'You have no choice, my love.' They heard a loud knock on the door. 'Ah, with luck that will be her right now.'

Since it was only five miles away, it didn't take Marmion and Keedy long to reach the county town of Maidstone. They made their way to the headquarters of the Kent Constabulary. When they'd explained why they were there, they were taken to meet the chief constable. Martin Gleeson was well over six feet and powerfully built. There was a military air about his manner and his speech was clipped. He gave each of them a firm handshake then listened to their request.

'Are you sure that they're in Kent?' he asked, doubtfully.

'Dufays will be keen to get his wife back across the Channel,' said Marmion. 'They'd never feel safe here.'

'They'll hardly feel safer in Paris, Inspector. At the start of the war, the Germans got uncomfortably close to it.'

'They'll head for somewhere well away from there,' suggested Keedy. 'In their position, I certainly would.'

'What about the killer?' said Gleeson.

'I expect that she'll go with them, sir.'

'What was her name again?'

'We think that it's Danielle Robbins,' said Marmion, 'but she might be married and have taken her husband's name.'

The chief constable was sceptical. Too much guesswork was involved. While he admired their commitment, he saw no grounds at all for optimism.

'We don't have much to go on, do we?' he said, frowning. 'There are far too many unknowns. We can't even be sure if they're still in this country. Even if they are, we have no idea how they'll get back to France. It's quite difficult to secure a passage,' said Gleeson. 'They could hire a boat, I suppose – a fishing vessel, perhaps.'

'Oh, they'd want something more substantial than that, sir.'

'Then let's work on the theory that they're still here.' Going behind the desk, he opened the drawer and took out a file. 'I've got details of all ships sailing tomorrow. The trouble is that we don't have any idea from which port they'll embark.'

'All Channel ports have been alerted, sir.'

'Where will you and Sergeant Keedy be?'

'I'm not sure,' said Marmion. 'We'll obviously have to stay the night in Kent and then . . . rely on intuition.'

'It's no substitute for hard facts.'

'Perhaps not, sir, but it's got us this far.'

Vesta was incredulous. When the woman came into the room, she couldn't believe that it was the same person who'd committed a murder right in front of her. Late at night, the killer had been dressed entirely in black and had taken advantage of the fact that both women were too intoxicated to offer any resistance. Vesta was now staring at someone who looked quite innocuous, a handsome woman in her thirties, wearing a red dress and a smile of pure innocence.

'I'm sorry that we met under such difficult circumstances,' she said to Vesta, as if apologising for some minor social infringement. 'I hope you understand that, from my point of view, it was not a personal matter.'

'We needn't go into that now,' said Dufays.

'Is everything arranged for tomorrow?'

'We'll be on the first ship out of Folkestone.'

'What if we're challenged?'

'I paid a lot of money for the passports. They'll get us through. We'll be waved aboard without any trouble.'

'Who *are* you?' asked Vesta, glaring at the woman.

'I'm a private detective fulfilling a contract,' said the other, crisply.

'Do you have no remorse at all?'

'It's an emotion I despise.'

'You were so callous.'

'I had to be, I'm afraid.'

'Let's not talk about the past,' said Dufays, taking an envelope out of his pocket. 'We're into a new phase of our lives now – and that's down to you.'

'Thank you,' she said, taking the envelope from him and slipping it into her bag. 'So we're off tomorrow, are we?'

'Yes, I have the documentation that will help us get past police and customs officials.'

'What if I refuse to go?' said Vesta, defiantly.

'That would be a very foolish thing to do, my love.'

'You can't *make* me.'

'Consider this,' he said, quietly. 'There are two possibilities. You can either do as you're told and earn the reward you're craving for. Or you can join your friend in an early grave.'

'I wouldn't recommend the second option,' warned the other woman, voice steely. 'You saw how much pain was involved.'

Vesta was quaking as she looked into her eyes.

They were at the harbour well before dawn. Marmion and Keedy did their best to retain hope as they took up their positions.

'I wish that the chief constable was on our side,' said Keedy.

'He's provided extra police here and at Dover.'

'Yes, but he thinks we're just whistling in the wind. The chances are that he may be right. They could already have gone.'

'I disagree,' said Marmion. 'They're still on British soil. Don't ask me how I know because I don't have the answer.'

'But will they be sailing from Folkestone – and will it be today?'

'Only time will tell, Joe. The chief constable has increased security at the Channel ports and issued a warning that there will be three people to look out for – Dufays, his wife and the woman we only know as Danielle Robbins. We might not be able to pick out the first two,' Marmion went on, 'but you've *seen* the third person. You actually took a statement from her.'

'If she turns up today,' said Keedy, 'I'll take another statement from her – after an arrest.'

There was plenty of activity at the docks. Lorries were arriving at regular intervals and troops were being loaded onto the waiting vessel. A trickle of civilian passengers was guided through customs and taken to the gangplank where their passports were checked by an officer before they were allowed aboard. As he watched the soldiers going bravely onto a ship that might well be taking them to a gruesome death in the trenches, Marmion thought of his son, marching off cheerfully to war, then coming home with brutal memories that had warped his mind.

'How many of those lads will come back alive?' murmured Keedy.

'I daren't think, Joe.'

'This war just swallows them up and spits them out in pieces.'

'You don't need to remind me of that,' said Marmion.

'No – sorry I spoke, Harv.' His eyes roved everywhere. 'What do we do if they're not sailing on this one?'

'We wait for the next ship.'

'And if they're not on that one either?'

'We stay put,' said Marmion, determinedly. 'Sooner or later, they're going to come. I feel it in my bones. And if Chat doesn't like it,' he added with a grin, 'then he can bloody well lump it.'

London was a city that never slept and had to be policed morning, noon and night. Claude Chatfield had allowed himself only five hours' sleep before he left home to be driven back to Scotland Yard. He was not surprised to find the commissioner already there, stalking the corridors.

'Good morning, Sir Edward,' he said.

'I think I've actually beaten you for once, Superintendent.'

'I do try to maintain my reputation for being an early riser.'

'You also have a reputation for keeping your detectives' noses to the wheel. It yields results. Is there anything to report with regard to the murder case?'

'Yes,' replied Chatfield, uneasily. 'Marmion and Keedy are in Kent. They've picked up a lead.'

'Tell me more.'

'Well, it's rather complicated.'

Even when Marmion had explained it, the decision had not seemed very plausible to the superintendent. As he gave his own version of it to

311

the commissioner, he believed in it less and less. Inevitably, it aroused an amalgam of distrust and alarm.

'Did I hear you aright?' asked the commissioner, worriedly.

'I may have missed a few things out, Sir Edward.'

'You missed out any mention of real evidence.'

'It was in the hotel register.'

'That's possible,' said the older man, 'but I'm bound to say that it's a remote possibility. If the killer is still living in Kent, she would hardly provide a helpful signpost.'

'Inadvertently,' said Chatfield, 'she seems to have done that – or so the inspector believes. He has a name for me to mention at the next press conference. Marmion wouldn't do that unless he was utterly convinced.'

'I see.'

'All we can do is to watch and pray.'

'I've been doing that since the first shot was fired in the war.'

'We must put our trust in Marmion and Keedy – as well as in God.'

'That's asking a lot of me,' admitted the commissioner, 'but I'll make the effort. Where exactly are they at the moment?'

'They're in Folkestone, Sir Edward, and they plan to stay there until they're able to make some arrests.'

The commissioner remained ominously silent.


Two ferries had come and gone but there was no sign of the fugitives. As their long vigil took its toll on them, Marmion decided that they'd have to wait for another vessel. Three people then came around the corner of a building and walked towards them. Keedy was immediately on the alert. The older woman in the middle of the trio was being more or less supported by her companions, one of whom was an older man. Their luggage was being wheeled along on a trolley by a porter. When they got closer, Keedy could see enough of the younger woman to realise that he'd seen her before.

'It's them,' he declared.

'Are you sure?' asked Marmion.

'I'd bet my pension on it.'

'That's good enough for me, Joe.' Cupping his hands together, Marmion shouted out, 'Danielle!'

The effect was instant. After looking across at him, the younger of the two women took to her heels and showed a remarkable turn of foot as she headed for the dock gates. Keedy was after her like a shot. In his eagerness to catch her, he didn't forget that she was capable of murder. Such a woman wouldn't submit tamely to arrest. She'd fight for her life.

When he finally caught up with her, they'd run the best part of sixty yards and were both panting. Keedy grabbed her by the shoulder from behind and spun her round. As soon as she faced him, she pulled a knife out of her bag and brandished it. He stepped back out of reach.

'We've met before,' he said. 'I spoke to you at the Lotus Hotel.'

'That's a lie. I've never seen you before.'

'Well, you'll see a lot of me now, Danielle, because I'm going to have the pleasure of arresting you and of giving evidence against you at your trial.'

She was taken aback. 'How do you know my name?'

'We went to your old house in Leeds. You tried to be too clever and gave yourself away.' He extended a hand. 'Give me that knife before someone gets hurt.'

She lunged at him, forcing Keedy to jump back out of reach. When she looked around, policemen were coming towards her from every direction. There was no hope of escape.

'I may be heading for a death sentence,' she snarled, 'but at least I can have the satisfaction of taking you with me.'

Knife raised, she threw herself at him this time and tried to stab him in the chest. Keedy was too quick, grabbing her wrist and twisting it so hard that she was forced to drop the weapon. He kicked it out of reach. She was not finished yet. With a surge of strength, she pulled her hand free of his grip and began to belabour him with both fists. It was time to forget all about gentlemanly behaviour. Keedy threw a punch and caught her full on the chin, making her stagger backwards. Leaping nimbly forward, he caught her before she hit the ground.

The policemen cheered.

A day that had started with an interminable wait at the docks in a cold wind ended with a celebration. Marmion, Ellen, Alice and Keedy had the rare treat of a meal out together. Because of stringent food rationing, the restaurant wasn't able to offer an extensive menu but that didn't detract from the joy of the occasion. They were too exhilarated to notice any shortcomings. A murder case had been solved, the killer and the man who hired her were both behind bars and Vesta Lyle was being given medical treatment. Marmion and Keedy were basking in the glow of the praise they'd received from Chatfield and the commissioner. They'd also been thanked by Griselda Fleetwood, who'd apologised for any doubts she'd had and told them that they had just brought her hotel back to life.

Alice was shocked when she heard that Keedy had knocked a woman out but eventually accepted that it had been necessary. One thing still puzzled her.

'Why did Vesta Lyle stay at the hotel as Lady Brice-Cadmore?'

'I asked her that,' said her father. 'I'd assumed that she'd known him in her younger days and always yearned for the experience of being part of the English aristocracy, if only for a night.'

'So she wanted to revive a memory of Sir Godfrey, did she?'

'No, Alice. She wanted to do the exact opposite.'

'I don't understand,' said Ellen.

'Vesta Lyle knew quite well that the real Lady Brice-Cadmore had died years earlier. She wasn't trying to usurp the title. She did it to get her revenge. Yes,' Marmion continued, 'she *had* known Sir Godfrey in Paris when she was a young woman and she'd believed all the promises he gave her of marriage. But as soon as she told him that she was carrying his child, he disappeared out of her life without a word.'

'That must have shattered her,' said Alice.

'It was a wound that never healed. Dufays only agreed to marry her on condition that she had the baby adopted.'

'What a dreadful thing to make any mother do.'

'He needed a respectable wife, Alice, not someone who'd be seen as a slut. You can see why it was a fraught marriage.'

'It had its rules,' said Keedy, 'and she broke them when she fell in love with her model. Her name was Colette Fournier and we saw a painting in which she featured.'

'There's no need to go into detail, Joe,' said Marmion, interrupting quickly. 'The point is that the two women were drawn into a friendship that Dufays found intolerable. He was prepared to have his wife's lover killed, so he hired Danielle Robbins. She was not merely a resourceful detective. During her work for the French secret service, she'd become a skilled assassin.'

'Is this the woman you knocked out, Joe?' asked Alice.

'Yes,' he said, 'but only in self-defence. She was ready to fight like a wildcat. That knife of hers would have cut our wedding plans to ribbons, Alice. She'd have had no compunction about killing me.'

'We were wrong in thinking that Vesta Lyle was employed by the secret service,' confessed Marmion. 'In fact, it was Danielle Robbins who learnt her trade from the French. When you think of an assassin, you automatically imagine a man, but she was just as lethal and available for hire. Dufays was paying a small fortune to reclaim his wife.'

'He'll have to pay far more than he expected now,' said Keedy. 'Both of them will stand trial for murder. The verdict is foregone. When they're sent to the scaffold, they'll be dispatched by an unseen hand.'